ROUGH JUSTICE

Matt Hilton

This first world edition published 2019
in Great Britain and 2020 in the USA by
SEVERN HOUSE PUBLISHERS LTD of
Eardley House, 4 Uxbridge Street, London W8 7SY.
Trade paperback edition first published
in Great Britain and the USA 2020 by
SEVERN HOUSE PUBLISHERS LTD.

British Library Cataloguing in Publication Data
A CIP catalogue record for this title is available from the British Library.

ISBN-13: 978-0-7278-8978-2 (cased)
ISBN-13: 978-1-78029-673-9 (trade paper)
ISBN-13: 978-1-4483-0372-4 (e-book)

Typeset by Palimpsest Book Production Ltd.,
Falkirk, Stirlingshire, Scotland.

ONE

In the still of the Maine evening, the repeated sound was beyond unusual, enough so that it drew Jonathan Laird away from the campfire to stand peering towards the west. The sun was below the horizon, but still painted the heavens with broad brushstrokes of orange and yellow hues. There the Great North Woods were dense and Jonathan couldn't fathom the source of the noise.

It took him back to when he was a kid. He'd always lived in Maine, his home on a property surrounded by great fir and spruce not dissimilar to these. When he and his older brother, William, played baseball in their yard, it was inevitable that a home run would knock the ball among the trees – they'd lost count of the number of baseballs they'd sacrificed to the spirits of the woods – and the accompanying sound as the ball broke a path through the branches was stuck in his memory. *Tch-tch-tch-tch-tchhhh* . . .

Here the sound was so like that, only tenfold in volume and went on for longer than any ten-year-old could ever hit a ball. It ended with the dullest of thuds that Jonathan wasn't certain he'd actually heard; it was at the limit of his hearing, and could easily have been an audible creation of his own making. He could almost believe that something huge had hurled a boulder through the canopy, but there was nothing living in these parts either strong enough or with hands with which to pick up a rock that heavy. That was, of course, if he disregarded the local folklore that spoke of giant hairy hominids prowling the woods, and other supernatural creatures like the cannibalistic wendigo whose voice could be heard as a low dirge among the boughs, and who reputedly left bloody twenty-four-inch footprints in the snow. As an experienced field biologist, Jonathan gave no credibility to the local cryptozoological nonsense, but standing there facing the dense woodland he couldn't offer an alternative explanation for the sound. Truthfully, he was a little freaked out.

He sensed a presence at his left shoulder, and jerked aside, emitting a high yelp. Even as he squawked, his brain had already registered the whip-thin shape as his fellow field biologist Elsa Carmichael, and the yelp morphed into embarrassed laughter as he clutched at his chest.

'You heard that, right?' Elsa's eyes were huge in her otherwise narrow features, penciled on brows arching towards her puckered forehead. Though tiny in stature, Elsa usually exhibited a rare bravery that often shamed the men into activity, but right then she was as equally freaked out as Jonathan.

Heart beating out of his chest, Jonathan returned his attention to the near horizon. 'I've no clue what that was.'

A rustle announced that the third member of their team, Grant McNeill, was emerging from his tent, drawn by the recent clatter or the voices of his friends. He emerged, flashlight in hand, though it was not yet full dark. Grant, an undergraduate, and technical assistant to Jonathan and Elsa, acted as their unofficial cameraman, documenting their latest field trip, so he also aimed a digital video camera. He paced forward, using his camera to scan the woods, before he'd made any sense of what had drawn him outside.

'Did you hear an engine, Jon?' asked Elsa. From her expression she hadn't.

Jonathan shook his head, but the motion was barely discernible in the gloom. 'No,' he said, glancing once at Grant who'd aimed the camera lens at him. 'What about you, Grant?'

'Nope.' Grant turned the camera on himself, speaking into it. 'I only heard the back end of whatever went down in the woods. Sounded like branches breaking, one after the other.'

Without a doubt, Grant had put Jonathan's fear into words: something had gone down in the woods. His first thought – once he'd shaken off the ridiculous notion that some undiscovered north woods hominid was up to no good – was that an aircraft had crashed. The idea was firmly on Elsa's mind too, hence her question about hearing an engine, or the lack of.

'Do you think we should radio this in?' asked Elsa. There were upward of twenty-six million acres of the Great North Woods spread across the north easternmost states of the US and into Canada. Here, where they presently camped in Maine, the region included the unincorporated townships of Aroostook

County, but much of the area was uninhabited wilderness and there were no paved roads. It wasn't somewhere where you wanted to fall into trouble, or get injured, without a means of contacting the outside world. For that reason the biologists carried with them a satellite phone.

'And say what?' Jonathan wondered. 'For all we know that was just a rotten tree falling over. We shouldn't cause any alarm until we know for sure there's been an accident.'

Elsa gave him a doubtful squint. 'Are you kidding me? The sounds started towards the north and ended up petering out to the southwest; that'd be some huge tree, Jon.'

'Yeah, I hear you,' said Jonathan. 'But you know what I mean. The topography plays tricks on the acoustics. We've no idea what made those sounds, so we shouldn't jump to conclusions.'

'There could be people in need of assistance.'

'I'm not suggesting we don't go and check, I'd just rather we waited till we know for sure before calling it in. It's like you said, there was no engine noise, and we didn't hear an explosion and don't see any flames . . .'

'Shouldn't we get moving then and check?'

Team leader Jonathan nodded.

His team was in the woods conducting a study on the effects of sustained logging on the migratory passage of wildlife through the arboreal region, and their remit included the deployment of trap cameras through which they could study the various animals and conduct counts on certain species: already caribou and grey wolves had disappeared from northern Maine, and in latter years the number of moose was not as prevalent as before. Therefore, his team was experienced at woodcraft, and often their work was conducted at dawn and dusk, or in full dark. Trekking at night to the spot where something had possibly crashed in the woods didn't daunt them the way it might regular hikers.

They geared up with perfunctory ease, and Jonathan – with a nod towards Elsa's concern of possible casualties – grabbed the emergency medical kit. Within minutes of making the decision to search the possible crash site, they were en route. They wore head torches and carried brighter flashlights, and their tech savvy assistant, Grant, was also armed with his night-vision video camera and a handheld thermal scope. The

last nimbus of daylight was lost to them as they moved into
the thick woods.

Jonathan didn't believe they would have to travel far. The
topography had a deadening effect on sound, and it didn't carry.
He estimated that whatever had fallen through the trees had done
so within a half mile of their camp, and was probably much
closer if the volume was to go by. They'd beaten a trail part of
the way, when they had deployed trap cameras along an established game trail to the west of their camp, so the going was
good for the first two hundred yards. As they progressed, Grant
scoped ahead with the thermal scope, seeking hot spots against
the otherwise ambient temperature. He didn't alert them to a
hit, so Jonathan assumed he'd found nothing yet, so carried on.
Around them there was a hush over the woods, as if the fauna
cowered at the unusual sound and held its collective breath.

Elsa was small and slim, but she was sinew tough. She kayaked
and ran, and had twice hiked the Appalachian Trail for kicks, as
well as trekked throughout the Rockies and even climbed
Kilimanjaro in Africa. She could march for days through the
Maine woods without breaking a sweat or stopping for breath.
Jonathan was older and bigger, though fit enough, but he found
the going more demanding when at her pace. She was keen to
lope ahead, but he remained steady at the head of the small party,
dictating their progress through the trees. They soon passed
beyond the western game trail and found the land rising up in a
ridge that separated them from a tributary of the St John River.
They had a small selection of choices; follow the base of the
ridge in a southerly direction until they found passage; back track
around the northern tip of the ridge; or forge uphill where they
might find a vantage from where they could pinpoint the location
of the crash. Without debate they chose the latter, and began the
climb. Elsa could have gone up it with the agility of a white-tailed
deer, but the men were more encumbered, Jonathan with the
medical pack, Grant with his tech stuff. Again Jonathan set
the pace. They crested the ridge ten minutes later, and Jonathan
called a halt while he caught his breath. Grant scanned the valley
below with his thermal scope.

'Check it out,' he said.

Jonathan didn't really need the high-tech thermal scope to

spot the ribbon of shattered limbs below. Some of the trees had been shorn of their upper boughs and the exposed flesh of their broken branches glimmered in the starlight. There was a darker patch where whatever had hit the trees had plunged lower, and beyond that, about a hundred yards or so further on, something white was wedged between toppled trees.

Elsa stood with her hands fisted at her sides as she craned for a better view. Grant nudged her and handed her the scope. She checked out the swathe of destruction, following it to the white object beyond. 'We've got a thermal hit,' she announced, and for her companions' sakes she pointed, then backtracked the scope to the object jammed among the trees. 'Is that a plane's fuselage?'

Jonathan accepted the scope from her and studied the object. Through the thermal imagery it glowed white against the darker shades. The network of branches around it made it difficult to ascertain its exact shape, but in general it appeared tubular, narrower to one end. It could be the tail end of a light aircraft.

'Let's get down there and see.'

They descended in single file, taking an oblique route off the ridge. Immediately they lost sight of the wreckage, but they were on an approach to dissect the trail of destruction through the woods. On the western slope of the ridge the underbrush was denser, and the going slower, but they made it through and under the broken canopy. Here and there were smaller pieces of wreckage, and now there was no doubt that they'd heard a light aircraft go down. The lack of engine noise preceding the sounds of the crash didn't dissuade them; the engine had probably failed and the pilot forced to glide the plane in from a distance for an emergency landing.

They came across the fuselage hung up between the trees, and began to jog as they realized they were nearing where the cockpit had come down. There was no hint of wings or the tail but for small pieces of twisted wreckage; they'd have been among the first features to be torn off as the plane bulled a passage through the canopy and could be hundreds of yards behind them.

Jonathan was reasonably familiar with light aircraft, and recognized the almost intact shape that had bellied up against a mound of broken branches and fallen tree trunks as a Cessna

172 Skyhawk: to reach some remote research locations he'd
flown as a passenger in similar planes. It was a four-seat, single-
engine, fixed-wing aircraft, though it had taken a severe beating
on its crash landing. The high-wing configuration had taken the
brunt, and most of the wings had disintegrated. The propeller
was shattered, and the nose crumpled. The cockpit and passenger
compartment looked thankfully whole, but it would be miraculous if anyone had survived the plummet through the trees.
Smoke hung in the air, alongside a million motes of dust and
tiny fragments of forest debris, but there was no imminent hint
of a fire.

Jonathan took it in and considered all those details even as he
lurched towards the aircraft, with Elsa at his side. Grant, standing
a moment in situ, scanned the wreckage from front to back with
his camera before he moved to assist his colleagues The door on
the nearside was shut, beyond it shadowy forms were unnaturally
aligned in the pilot and copilot seats. Jonathan only realized he
was shouting, trying to get a response from the figures inside
when he heard Elsa doing the same. There was no getting around
the front where the broken propeller and crumpled nose was dug
into the mound of detritus. Instead he clambered over fallen
branches, intending getting to the far side where a door had been
torn open. Where the tail and fuselage had been broken off
the cabin was open to the air, but there was no clear way inside
because barring the way were passenger seats and a scattering
of luggage bags and other sundry items.

Forcing a path through twigs and larger broken branches,
Jonathan got to the open door. He called out again, reached for
the nearest man, the copilot, and shook him. The man's body
flopped, his head loosely bouncing, and he didn't rouse. Jonathan
pressed fingers to the pulse in his neck: there wasn't one.
Jonathan's guts clenched. He called out to the pilot, who was
hanging forward, contorted unnaturally in his seat. The windshield was shattered and some branches had invaded the cockpit,
spearing his chest and face. His skull had taken the brunt of the
collision, misshapen and bloody, and Jonathan knew without
checking that he was as dead as the copilot. Jonathan stepped
back, his hands going through his hair, and momentarily
knocking his head torch out of alignment. As he adjusted it, he

was aware of Elsa at his side. They exchanged equally shocked looks, and then with trembling fingers, Jonathan scratched for the satellite phone nestled in a belt pouch, now regretting that he hadn't called in the emergency services the instant they'd heard the plane go down.

A clatter from behind turned them around. A silhouette detached itself from alongside a tree trunk, and lifted an arm. As their lights painted the figure, they both saw a woman, and in her hand she held a pistol.

'Hold it,' she snapped, and aimed the gun at them.

'We . . . we're only trying to help,' Jonathan said.

She snorted. Blood was in her nostrils, and was exhaled as a shower of red droplets in the torchlight. 'I don't need your damn help. Now move aside, before somebody gets killed.'

TWO

'Back off, or things are gonna grow ugly.' The squat man aimed a thick stump of a finger at Nicolas 'Po' Villere, but his words at Tess Grey. 'An' don't rely on that long streak of cat piss to help ya.'

Po didn't react. He stood at the diner's entrance with his shoulders against the doorframe, arms folded across his chest. His turquoise eyes were lidded; as if so unmoved he was taking a brief nap. His languorous stance belied his readiness, and Tess for one knew how swiftly her partner could switch to a high state of precise and determined violence. She didn't want this job to end with blood but there was always the potential for it when Po got riled. All she had to do was serve the court papers to Charles Boswick, and they could leave with no further trouble. However, seated in the diner, a half-eaten breakfast before him, Boswick had spotted her coming, guessed at her intention, and refused to accept the legal document from her.

'Just take them and be done,' said Tess. 'There's no avoiding this.' She placed the folded papers alongside him on the counter. Boswick glanced at the papers, then swept them aside with his forearm. They fell at Tess's feet. She left them where they fell. Instead she said, 'I'm a court-appointed agent and have just served you a summons. Refusal to attend court at the given time and place could result in a warrant being issued for your arrest.'

'So I'll wait for the cops to come fetch me,' Boswick snarled. 'Now, get outta here and let me finish my breakfast in peace, or I'll show you the door with my foot in your ass.' In an act of further defiance he threw up a hand – perhaps hoping for Tess to flinch, which she didn't – summoning a server. 'Hey, girl! Hit me with another round of coffee.'

In effect the papers had been served, the terms laid out in them verbally related to Boswick, and if she need be persnickety, he had touched the official papers when knocking them to the floor. Tess could walk away, confident that she'd accomplished what she'd come to do at the Forest Avenue diner in the Back Cove area of Portland, Maine. She looked over at the server, a young girl who was equally intimidated by Tess's presence as she was by the brusque thug of a man seated at the counter. She stood holding the refill jug, and didn't approach. Tess felt for the kid, because she'd been caught in the middle of an incident that wasn't in her job description: Po owned a diner, and Tess wouldn't want any of his staff made to feel uncomfortable due to process servers entering the premises like this. Tess smiled support at the girl and then nodded at her to refill Boswick's cup. The sooner it was done the sooner the girl could put some space between them.

Boswick was looking to throw his weight around. 'You don't need no damn permission from her. Y'want yer damn tip, get over here and hit me again, like I said, girl.'

The server's face flushed red, and she almost tripped as she rushed to comply. Coffee sloshed in his cup, and also on the counter. Boswick threw up his arms as if it was the latest hitch to an already crappy morning. 'Whaddaya think you're doin'? Tryin' to freakin' scald me or somethin'?'

The girl immediately aimed to mop up the spill, but Boswick thrust her hands aside and told her to scram. The server backed away, unsure whether to apologize or be thankful of an excuse to get far away from him. At the same time Tess dragged the folded papers towards her with a foot, then stooped to pick them up. She slapped them down on the counter, and turned to leave. Boswick snatched the papers, crumpled them and swiped at the spilled coffee. Before Tess had taken more than three steps he hurled the wad of sopping papers at her head.

Tess halted as coffee dripped from her blond hair onto the shoulder of her suit jacket. She bit her bottom lip, aimed a shake of her head at Po who had straightened marginally, and again stepped off to leave.

'That's right, you'd better git before I come over there and ram this summons up yer tight ass.'

Boswick had stepped over a line.

Po shrugged off the doorframe, and walked towards him.

'Leave it, Po,' Tess warned.

'There ain't a man on Earth gonna talk to you like that in my presence,' said Po without missing a step.

Boswick rose from his stool and faced Po. He was not as tall as Po, but he was wider, built squat and powerful. His shaved head sat on his shoulders like a propane gas tank. He set his feet, curled his lip at Po.

Po scooped the wadded and coffee-stained papers off the floor and faced Boswick from about five feet. He bounced the wad on his palm as he met Boswick's challenge.

'Whaddaya think you're gonna do, streak?' Boswick sneered.

Po tossed the papers on the counter, and Boswick slapped down a callused palm over them. The noise was as loud as a gunshot in the sudden hush, as the other patrons tensed. He again shoved the wad through the spilled coffee. Suddenly a door banged open behind the counter and a heavyset man in white coat and checkered pants bustled out from the kitchens, flapping his hands: he was the chef and owner of the diner.

'Take your beef elsewhere, guys, we don't want no trouble here,' he commanded, his words for both men. He stumbled when he saw Po staring back. He knew Po for a fellow businessman, a competitor of sorts, but also for his reputation. 'Hey, Po,' he whined, 'this isn't on, man. You don't see me comin' into your place and kickin' up a fuss.'

'I'm happy to take this outside,' said Po, and ensured Boswick got the message. The thuggish man's face momentarily creased in thought as he played Po's name through his memory. He wagged a thick finger.

'So you're this Po'boy Villere I been hearin' about?' Boswick grunted in scorn, but suddenly he didn't look as keen to fight as before: however, he had to maintain face, or be made to look a coward in front of the diner's patrons and staff. 'To hear people tell it,' he sneered, 'you're some kinda bad ass who shits thunder and pisses lightning. A string bean like you? The way I see it, I don't think any of those fellas who got on the wrong side of your fists was worth their weight in chicken shit.'

'So let's take this outside.'

Boswick bunched his fists, but withered under Po's unflinching stare. Something in the turquoise eyes promised that any aggressive move Boswick made would be the wrong move.

'I'm finishing my breakfast.' As if nonplussed, Boswick turned his back on Po and forked egg into his mouth. He'd heard of Po's prowess, but also that he wasn't the type to cold cock a man from behind. Po stared at the thick neck, the bristling hairs poking out from the top of Boswick's shirt collar. He didn't move.

Boswick made a show of turning his head slowly. 'What?' A crumb of scrambled eggs was stuck in the corner of his lips. 'You still here?'

'You owe these women an apology, bra. You can start with your server, then my partner.'

'I don't owe any bitch a damn thing. This is supposed to be an age of enlightenment, right? Women want equality, so I'll damn well talk to them the way I would any other asshole.'

'A guy who uses the words "bitch" and "equality" in the same comment is one of two things. Either he's educated enough to realize he's a misogynist, or he's about as enlightened and as dumb as mud. Me, I'd say you were the latter.'

'I could give a shit for what you think of me.' Another crumb of egg spilled from his mouth.

'Your table manners are as crass as your potty mouth,' said Po. 'Here, let me get that for you.'

Po snatched up the wadded summons, and before Boswick could react, he smeared the sopping papers over Boswick's face. The would-be tough guy reared away, opening his mouth to bellow and Po rammed the papers between his teeth. As Boswick erupted from the stool, spitting out paper, Po merely stepped away to arm's length and said, 'Consider yourself served, bra.'

Despite being as dumb as mud Boswick understood the meaning of humiliation, and right then and there he was its epitome. He stood, swiping bits of damp paper from his mouth, shaking with rage, but knew better than launch at Po. He had been in enough street fights to know that Po was ready for any move he made, and it had come in a bright flash of inspiration to him that Po's reputation was to be respected: he wasn't the Cajun's match, and pursuing things would only end with his day getting crappier.

Boswick held up his palms in surrender.

Po was a man capable of sudden violence, but it was an aspect of his nature he could temper. 'Could've saved us all a lot of aggravation, bra,' he said, 'and just accepted the papers in the first place. It's done now. We're done. Are you done, Boswick, or do you want to take matters further?'

'All I wanna do is finish my breakfast,' whined Boswick, sheepish now. He blinked an apology first at the chef, then searched for the young server. He aimed a placating wave at her, then at other patrons whose breakfasts had been disturbed. He looked past Po for Tess, who was standing by the exit door, her fingers on the handle. 'I've acted like an idiot, ma'am,' he proclaimed. 'You're only doing your job and I was an ass. I'm sorry.'

Po nodded in acknowledgment and turned away.

Without checking, Po knew Boswick was returning to his stool. He walked towards Tess, who eyed him with her usual blend of mock scorn, ill-veiled pride and a hint of mild bemusement. 'Are *you* done?' she asked, echoing his questions of Boswick.

'Sure am.'

Beyond him, she could see Boswick attempting to smoothen out the damp papers on the countertop. She was confident he would attend court at the given time and place as instructed. 'Then our work here is done, Tonto,' she paraphrased.

She pulled open the door and held it for him.

'After you, *ke-mo sah-bee*,' he said, bracing the door open with his fingers.

Tess chuckled and had to duck under his arm. As they moved for where he'd left his vintage 1968 model Ford Mustang parked in the adjacent lot, Tess pawed through her hair, shedding the few clinging droplets of coffee. She was secretly relieved that it was only drips of coffee on her clothing, because there had been times when Po's tripwire nature had caused him to spatter droplets of a more vibrant color. Still, she thought, the day was early yet, and who knew what the rest of it would bring. Such was the nature of their work, she never could tell, but she was reasonably sure today's agenda would prove benign.

'Back to the ranch?' Po asked once they were seated in the muscle car. He was being literal: she'd recently moved into his ranch-style house near Presumpscot Falls north of the city.

'I need to check in with Emma first. Mind dropping me at her office and I'll grab a cab back home later?'

'Sure I can.'

Emma Clancy directed a specialist inquiry firm serving the Portland District Attorney's office, from where she often subcontracted tasks on a self-employed basis to Tess. Emma would one day become her sister-in-law – if ever Tess's brother Alex and she set an actual date for their wedding – but hiring Tess wasn't about nepotism. Time and again Tess and Po, by virtue of working closely alongside her, had proven their worth to Emma, who now purposefully threw jobs their way where her regular employees had struggled to get results.

As Po drove for Clancy's office a mountainous cloudbank pushed in from Casco Bay, obscuring the midmorning sun and casting a dark pall over the streets. The headlights switched on automatically – one of many modern features added to the vintage muscle car by Po – and a moment later the wipers flicked at the heavy droplets of rain spattering the windshield.

'You sure you don't want me to wait for you?' Po said with a nod at the encroaching rain showers. 'Getting a cab might not be easy if everyone's running for shelter.'

'A little rain never hurt anyone.' Tess gave a self-deprecating shove at her hair. 'It'll help wash the smell of coffee off me if nothing else. You get on back, I know you've stuff to do, and I'll see you in a couple of hours.'

'Sure thing,' he said without enthusiasm. He'd paperwork to organize before his tax return was due, and had been putting off the mundane task for long enough. That's what came of running successful businesses – an autoshop and a retro bar diner – a responsibility to ensure everything was in order and above board.

'I'll give you a hand when I get home,' she promised.

'I should hire an accountant to do this stuff for me.'

'That's your choice, Po, but I'm sure we can do it between us.'

'I know a guy I can trust,' he said.

Tess grimaced at the idea.

Po was in a position where certain aspects of his business dealings needed looking at with a skewed eye. Nothing about his businesses was criminal per se, but certain untruths existed. He owned Charley's Autoshop and Bar-Lesque, and had a stake in a number of other businesses in and around Portland, but his name rarely appeared on any of the deeds. Tess, an ex-cop, understood why Po, an ex-con, might want to keep his interests and assets private, but these days, especially while subcontracting to a firm directly connected to the DA, they must be impeachable. Before they'd made their partnership official it hadn't mattered as much, because back then he had simply been an employee of hers and Tess had the excuse of deniable plausibility when it came to his personal dealings. Now, as his fiancée, Tess's own employment status would come under IRS scrutiny during any investigation into Po, and she preferred to be beyond reproach. She didn't want a questionable accountant cooking his books, and placing them both in an untenable situation.

'We'll do it together when I get back,' she reiterated.

He shrugged, sanguine about it.

He dropped her in a no-stopping zone outside Clancy's office on Cumberland Street: ever the rebel. Tess leaned across for a kiss, then got out the muscle car. Po took off at speed, engine roaring, as if in a rush to get to those papers, and Tess smiled wryly because she knew he'd have nothing in order by the time she returned to the ranch. The Mustang's distant growl accompanied her long after it was out of sight, as she jogged through the rain, up the wide steps to the civic building where Emma's office had relocated after the last one had been targeted by arsonists.

Emma was taking a telephone call at her desk. Outside her office, Tess waited for her to finish, subconsciously rubbing at a scar on her wrist, a reminder of the injury that ended her career with the Cumberland County Sheriff's Department. Tess tried not to eavesdrop, but it was in an investigator's nature to listen, especially after she heard her name. Unfortunately there was little she could make out. As she was ending the call, Emma glanced towards the door and spotted Tess through the partly opened slats she only closed when full privacy was required. She waved Tess inside.

'Hey!' Emma said with no formality.

'Hi,' Tess replied. Emma might be the boss of the office, and had control of the purse strings that Tess's business benefited from, but more so they were friends, and almost family. Emma reserved her usual 'ice maiden' act for others, but couldn't hide her fondness for her future sister.

'I bet your ears are burning?' Emma said.

'Was that call about me?' Tess tried to look innocent and failed miserably.

'It depends,' said Emma. 'How do you feel about hiking in the woods?'

THREE

Mid-afternoon, a taxi dropped Tess home at Po's ranch-style property. Forest surrounded the single-story building and outbuildings, and the rain clattered through the leaves, competing with the nearby river to make most noise. Rain drummed on the peaked roof of the house and spilled from the gutters. Tess hurried through the downpour, and found the front door unlocked. Shaking off drips she stamped her feet on the welcome mat, before proceeding indoors. Po wasn't visible, but she could hear him talking from somewhere further inside. The conversation was one-sided, so they didn't have a visitor; Po was speaking on the phone.

She shed her jacket and handbag, and headed for the kitchen from where she could smell that Po had a pot of coffee brewing. She poured a large cup from the jug and added cream and too much sugar, and then stood there at the counter, drinking it while Po finished his call. Stacked on the kitchen table were bundles of printed invoices and receipts, but that was as far as her man had gotten in organizing them. She shook her head, as she'd expected as much. He ended his call and wandered through the house and into the kitchen.

'Hey,' he said.

'Hey.' Tess sipped her coffee, watching him through the steam. He'd briefly lightened at seeing her home, but his forehead creased into a frown.

'What's up?'

He thumbed towards the back of the house, as if their friend was physically back there. 'I just got off a call with Pinky.'

Just the mention of the flamboyant Jerome 'Pinky' Leclerc was enough to send a flush of affection through her. But Po's frown tempered her usual joy. 'Something wrong?'

'He's findin' goin' straight more difficult than when he was a bona fide rogue.'

'He's asking a lot of himself,' Tess said. 'But experience tells me that a roguish man can change his ways.'

He snorted in good humor.

Tess said, 'Pinky always was good at heart, just he made some bad decisions, and I'm sure once he puts them behind him he'll be happier that he did.'

'Pinky had those bad decisions foisted on him.' Black, gay, and with a medical condition, Pinky's choices were to be a victim of those circumstances or to rise above them. He chose to be the one in control, and not prey for the animals that'd otherwise have eaten him alive.

'Yeah,' she intoned. She knew well Pinky's story, of rising up from being an abused inmate at Louisiana State Penitentiary – where Po had become his protector – to one of the most successful criminals in Baton Rouge. Recently, directly through his close association with Tess and Po, he'd been struck by an epiphany that for years he'd been courting the wrong side and had vowed to give up his wicked ways. By turning his back on his criminal empire he'd ignited a turf war where his old allies and competitors alike now jostled for supremacy in the void he'd leave behind. 'He should just walk away and let them get on with it.'

'Therein lies the problem,' Po said.

Tess set down her coffee. 'How? He's been planning a move to Maine; he should do it. It's not as if he hasn't the resources to move here. If it's about having a home to come to he can use my place.' They were engaged to be married but despite moving into the ranch, she hadn't sold her apartment above an antiques and curios shop on Cumberland Avenue and would happily allow Pinky to use it until he found somewhere he could permanently settle down.

'He has heard rumors,' Po said and his frown deepened. His turquoise eyes were as hard as glass. 'You know people in his line of business are rarely allowed to walk away from it without repercussions. He knows too much about other peoples' illicit businesses, and they don't want his change of heart meanin' he'll turn fink on them. They're distrustful and paranoid: if he goes, they want him permanently gone . . . you get me?'

She got him. Pinky had a target on his back.

'More's the reason why he should get up here as soon as possible.'

'Sure is. An' I told him so. But you know Pinky. He doesn't want to bring his trouble to our door.'

'The foolish man! How many times has he helped us when we've needed *him*?'

Po held up his palms. 'You're preachin' to the converted here, Tess.'

'So get him back on the phone and tell him to get his ass here at once.'

'I did, but he declined. Said he wanted to sort things before he came up here.'

'Then play on his damn loyalty to us and tell him we need him here.'

'We do?'

'No, not really, and I'm not sure Pinky will be up for a trip to the Great Outdoors but . . .' she tailed off, realizing that not only hadn't she yet told her partner about Emma Clancy's request, but he might not be keen on a hiking trip either.

He searched her face for a hint. When she wasn't forthcoming, he said, 'The Great Outdoors? What you signed us up to, Tess?'

'I haven't signed *you* up to anything, Po, but I have agreed to assist Emma in quantifying rumors of a missing person. Do you remember that Cessna that crashed in the North Woods a few weeks ago?'

He didn't reply. But Po was good at saying a lot when verbalizing nothing at all.

'The pilots were killed on impact,' Tess went on, as if he required a reminder, 'but it has since come to light that there might've been a third person on-board, a survivor, but who hasn't been identified yet.'

'And they want you to mount a search party? Three weeks in those woods, if they ain't showed up yet, then they ain't showin' up at all. They're dead or they don't want to be found.'

'When they recovered the pilots' bodies the authorities conducted a search of the wreckage field, but at the time they weren't looking for a survivor. A team of field biologists initially called in the crash, and rendezvoused with the search team at the crash site. There was nothing about a passenger mentioned in the flight manifest, and no hint from them that anyone else had been onboard when the plane crashed.'

'So why the change in thinking now?'

'That's what needs checking out. One of the biologists, a guy called Grant McNeill, was allegedly overheard speaking about there being a woman at the scene, but when pressed by the crash investigators he denied it. Emma's asked that I go and speak with these biologists and push them for the truth.'

'Where'd the plane go down, Aroostook County, wasn't it? How'd this fall into Emma's lap?'

'The plane was out of Portland International, don't forget; and two out of three of the biologists are from Portland, while the third, Elsa Carmichael, lives within Cumberland County, so it is kind of in her jurisdiction.' Tess held up a finger. 'By the way, the job doesn't originate from Emma, she was only asked by an insurance company to recommend a local investigator – me – willing to go up and speak with Laird and the others at their field base, to see if I can get to the bottom of this mystery woman. Depending on what I can or can't ascertain, I'll be handing over the job to their loss adjustors.'

'So this is only about paying lip service?'

'I don't intend being out in the woods too long, only enough to speak with the biologists and then report back with my findings. Depending on who, what or why, it might end up nothing at all.'

Po grunted in laughter. 'You never could turn down a mystery, could ya? If there was a woman on that plane and she survived the crash, then who was she and what became of her? What're you thinking, Tess: she maybe had a bag full of stolen diamonds and the biologists killed her for it and buried her somewhere out in the woods?'

'Who knows?' She smiled at his ludicrous theory, but right then it was as good as any, and like he said, she never could resist a mystery to solve. The first hint of a crime, she must hand the case immediately to the police, but until then it was all hers to reason out. In her opinion it was more interesting work than serving summonses to the likes of Charles Boswick. 'You've got to admit, it does pique the interest, right?'

'F'sure, it does.' He nodded at the overflowing piles of invoices and receipts on the table. 'A walk in the woods defin-itely trumps growing calluses on my butt while I work through that stuff. I'm comin' with ya, Tess, an' if I have my way Pinky will be joinin' us.'

'Great,' she said, and was unable to hide a grin of victory.

'What? You thought I was gonna take some talkin' around?'

'I didn't think it'd be something you'd be up for,' she admitted. To conceal her satisfied grin, she picked up her mug and sipped her cooling coffee.

'You forget, Tess. First time we worked together you had me traipsing through the wilds up to our knees in mud. Whatever gave you the impression I wasn't an outdoorsman, did it look as if I was displeased?'

'Truth is, Po, once we came across that decapitated corpse, I don't recall much about your disposition. I was too busy trying not to puke.'

He pointed a finger. 'What're the chances of findin' another headless body this time?'

'You having second thoughts?'

'Nope.' He patted his gut, where he wore a scar as a permanent souvenir from their first job together. 'Just reminding myself not to let him get too close with his knife if we're up against a crazy butcher like Hector Suarez again.'

'Like I said, we're only going to question some scientists, and maybe make the most of the fresh air for a day or two.'

'So when do we leave?'

'Tomorrow.'

'What do we need?'

'I need you to phone Pinky. Make sure he gets on a flight here before the end of the day. Oh, and tell him to bring a weather-proof anorak and sensible footwear.'

'You do realize you're talking about Pinky Leclerc, right?'

FOUR

Pinky Leclerc never conducted business at his home – a reasonably sized property on the fringe of Harwich, Baton Rouge. If he stood on his front porch to take in the views, he had the greens of a golf course to one side, and the paddocks of an equestrian center further to the other. Directly ahead his view would sweep over reclaimed floodplains to the Mississippi River, where a constant stream of container vessels and pleasure cruisers plied the waters. Mostly he conducted face-to-face meetings in hotel suites, restaurants or in the less salubrious conditions of warehouses and freight yards near the riverside wharfs to the north of the city. As he took the call from Nicolas Villere on his cell, he'd been standing on the mezzanine floor in a crane supply depot alongside the ExxonMobil refinery, supervising a half dozen of his employees as they loaded crates of weapons disguised as machinery parts into a panel van. From the mezzanine he enjoyed a position of elevated power, reminiscent of a despotic Caesar deciding the fates of gladiators in the arena below. Currently though, he was wondering if, like Julius Caesar, it would be those closest to him who'd be the ones to drive knives into his back.

Those men loading the van had been loyal to him, one of them, DeAndre Freeman, being his personal driver, sometime bodyguard and confidant for years. He trusted that he was safe in their presence for now, but couldn't discount one or more of them being bought by a competitor, who'd rather watch Pinky sink to the bottom of the Mississippi than ride off into retirement. He couldn't allow himself to be sucked into a false state of security when one of his employees could try to claim the bounty on his head.

'*Et tu*, DeAndre?' he whispered under his breath, for he couldn't ignore that the one closest to him might be the one to end his life. For a long time Pinky had been the source of DeAndre's inflated income, buying him a lifestyle he couldn't have enjoyed from his meager salary as a Baton Rouge police officer, and Pinky knew his old friend was as dissatisfied as many that Pinky had announced his upcoming departure. DeAndre might think it necessary to curry favor, and secure a new paymaster, with one of those who planned on usurping Pinky's deserted empire.

He felt bad casting suspicion on his friend, but it was a necessary evil: an elevated level of paranoia could be the thing to keep him alive. He'd made provisions for DeAndre and his other employees, by way of hefty cash severances, but he couldn't depend on those golden handshakes to keep him safe. Criminals, in his experience, were greedy, and were happy to bite off the hand that once fed them if they believed it their final meal. He'd told Nicolas he wasn't yet ready to commit to a final move north, not until he'd gotten all his ducks in a row down here in Louisiana, but it was while being discretely eavesdropped upon by one of his men. He was for lighting out at the first opportunity; as soon as this delivery was overseen and he could make an excuse to slip away, he'd be off. If any of his men were planning on assassinating him, they'd think they had time on their hands, so he must take that opportunity away.

He'd prepared for this day.

He had a fast car and a seat on a faster jet on standby. He'd liquidated most of his assets and spread them about in various hidden caches. Certain physical belongings, not least his home in Harwich, a second apartment in Baton Rouge, and his fleet of luxury vehicles, would be casualties of his decision to abandon his past life, but better he sacrifice them than his own hide. He couldn't give a damn if his actions might be perceived as cowardice, because – for he was in a mood for quoting the bard that day – discretion was the better part of valor. This from a man who was once more apt to quote Daffy Duck when trading illegal arms to heist crews and gang bangers: 'It's not the principle, it's the money that counts!'

Pinky had suffered an awakening, a paradigm shift in his way of thinking, and his dearest friends Nicolas and Tess were responsible for him seeing the light. He joked that they were on the side of the angels, and by virtue he should be too. Therefore he could no longer countenance being associated with those who did the devil's work. It sickened him to think he could be responsible for putting guns in the hands of spree killers shooting kids in schoolyards, or in the hands of fanatics fueled by hatred who killed and maimed innocents for their misguided and often unfathomable reasons. He was done with gun-running, though not necessarily with bearing arms. The S&W Sigma 40 P single action pistol loaded with fifteen .40SW rounds in his shoulder rig stood testament to that; a man, after all, should be allowed to defend himself whatever his ethos; and besides, even Archangel Michael wielded a huge sword . . .

His cell rang again.

Nicolas.

'You're persistent, you,' Pinky said into the phone with a quick glance at the locations of his men: all were out of earshot. 'But that's good, Nicolas, 'cause now I don't have to give you another line of bullshit, me.'

Pinky's strange speech pattern was as much a part of his persona as his love for his friend, though he was occasionally guilty of exaggerating it for effect. It suited him, being a figure of exaggerated presence and mannerisms, a disarming trait that made him a subject of amusement and instantly likeable. Some people had learned to their peril that laughing along with his clownish antics was very different to laughing at him.

'Reading between the lines, that means you are comin' up here?' said Po.

'*Tout de suite*, my friend.'

'Things have grown that dangerous for you down there?'

'Put it this way, I'm not psychic, me, but I'm pickin' up a bad vibe right about now. Dudes that used to dote on me have been givin' me some funny looks, and whispering behind my back. I don't think they're planning on throwing me a surprise going away party, them.'

'I shoulda been down there with you, brother, to watch your back till you got your house in order.'

'You've got your own house and a little woman in it to protect first. Just don't let pretty Tess know I said as such, you; she'd have my guts for even suggesting she needs looking out for.'

'It's too late for that, bra. Tess is right beside me an' heard you loud and clear.'

'Uh-oh, maybe I should look for another bolthole far away from Maine.'

Tess cut in on the call. 'You'll do no such thing, Pinky, or I'll hunt you down and drag you here by your ears.'

Pinky chuckled at the threat. 'I believe you,' he said.

'You said you're coming right now?' Po said, back in charge of his cell phone.

'Well, I'm coming imminently, me. Got to get outta here without a tail, then I'll be on my way. All goes well, I'll be sharing a six pack of beer with you this evening, Nicolas.'

'Sounds like a plan. You need pickin' up from the airport, just let me know an' I'll be there.'

'I don't want to inconvenience either of you, me.'

'You ain't,' said Po. 'Listen,' he added, 'we've got a job on from tomorrow, but you want you can chill at my place, get your legs under the table and your head together.'

'There isn't room in your car so's I can come too?'

'There's room, it's just where we're goin'—'

'I'm adventurous, and like to experience new things.'

'How do you feel about sleepin' under canvas?'

'You're goin' camping, Nicolas? Hell, you'll have to shoehorn me into a tent, but it sounds like fun. Did I never tell you I always wanted to be an Eagle Scout when I was a kid?'

Po laughed in good humor at the idea, even as Pinky did, trying to picture himself robed in the khaki uniform and woggle of a Boy Scout. He sobered quickly, because he didn't want to be distracted from a possible imminent threat to his life, otherwise he could be soon wearing a pine box.

He promised that neither hell nor high water would keep him away from their planned trip, and hung up. In the cavernous space below, his men were done loading, and he watched as the van doors were closed. A couple of his helpers turned to regard him on his high perch, and he met their searching gazes, trying to read what was on their minds.

'All done, Pinky,' DeAndre called up to him.

Pinky acknowledged his friend with a raised hand. 'Go on ahead, you, I'll be right behind you.'

Two men were designated to travel with the van. Three in a Ford SUV parked alongside it, while DeAndre had initially arrived at the depot with Pinky in his Mercedes, which was parked more discretely outside at the rear of the warehouse. DeAndre gave him a questioning look: perhaps he could read the suspicion in his boss's demeanor.

Without another word to Pinky, DeAndre instructed the others to get moving. He himself didn't follow; he turned and began walking towards the steps leading to the mezzanine floor. Pinky owed him a goodbye at the very least, he only hoped he wouldn't have to place an absolute period at the end of it with a bullet. 'Hang on there, DeAndre,' he said, 'I'm coming down, me.'

DeAndre halted. His coffee-colored skin had a blue sheen to it under the artificial lights, and his eyes sank into the shadows, making him corpse-like. Pinky shuddered at the thought of slaying his driver, but if it came to it . . .

The van followed the SUV out under the roller shutter, and DeAndre paused momentarily to check they had the space to themselves. The watchman who'd been paid to turn a blind eye to their activities wasn't reneging on the deal. DeAndre returned his attention to his boss, as Pinky made his way down the steps. Pinky was a big guy, and due to a medical condition carried more weight on his lower half than the top: he should be ungainly, but his condition was no impediment to him, and in fact he could be light on his feet. He descended the stairs with very little noise.

'I meant you to go back with the others, you,' Pinky said as he alighted the bottom step.

DeAndre reached inside his jacket. Pinky knew he was packing, but didn't go for his own gun. DeAndre held up the keys to the Mercedes. 'Who'd take back the Merc, Pinky?'

Pinky's mouth pulled into a grimace of embarrassment.

'You're leaving,' said DeAndre, 'and it isn't in the same car as you arrived in, right?'

There was no need for Pinky to explain that he'd already parked another vehicle nearby, ready for his departure, because it was apparent to his driver already. Otherwise, why would he have instructed DeAndre to leave with the others without access to his Merc?

'I don't like goodbyes, DeAndre,' said Pinky.

His driver – no, his friend – looked hurt. It was not at Pinky's bending of the truth: he was affectionate and red-eyed whenever saying goodbye to those close to him. It was because he'd guessed Pinky had some other reason to be deceitful with him, and it didn't take much imagination to figure out why.

'You've been good to me, Pinky,' DeAndre said solemnly. 'I'd take a bullet for you, no question. Nothing's changed, man.'

'You think I'd've come down to you the way I did if I thought otherwise?'

'You have your suspicions. At least you didn't draw down on me first,' DeAndre said.

'Last thing I'd do, me,' said Pinky, 'without good reason.'

'I'm not goin' to give you a reason.' DeAndre again reached under his jacket, this time with his left hand, and he took his gun from its holster between thumb and index finger. He placed his pistol on the floor. He met Pinky's gaze. 'It saddens me you'd believe I'd turn against you, Pinky, but I understand your caution.'

Pinky aimed his chin at the open doorway, signifying the men who'd just driven away. 'It isn't you who concerns me, DeAndre.'

'I'd kill any of them that made a move on you.'

'I'd rather it didn't have to come to that. It's why I was going to slip quietly away, me, so's you weren't put in that position.'

DeAndre wasn't mollified, but he accepted Pinky's explanation with a nod and downcast eyes. 'So you're really goin' then? Never thought I'd see this day.'

'I'm leaving.'

'You know they won't ever let you come back.' The subtext of his meaning rang clearly.

'They'll forget about me within a month,' said Pinky, though he knew the lie even as it passed his lips. The almighty *they*, being the criminal underworld, didn't like loose ends. While Pinky was alive he remained a threat to either their liberty or their percentage in the business if he chose to return to his old ways.

'I'll do what I can to buy you some time,' said DeAndre.

'Appreciated,' said Pinky, and held out his hand.

DeAndre ignored the hand, moving in instead to hug his old friend. Pinky tensed for the briefest second, still not wholly convinced that DeAndre wouldn't plunge a concealed blade between his ribs. His reticence sickened him. This was a man who'd shown only complete devotion to him for a decade or more and who deserved much better from him. Pinky returned the hug.

As they parted, Pinky said, 'Pick up your gun.'

Now it was DeAndre who momentarily appeared suspicious, as if by reaching for his pistol he'd spring a trap of Pinky's making. Pinky squeezed DeAndre's shoulder. 'I deserve that look, me, but you deserve much better. I know you're loyal to the bones of you, DeAndre, but if you're still prepared to take a bullet for me I'm damned if I'm gonna take away your right to defend yourself first. C'mon, you can watch my ass one last time while you walk me to my car.'

FIVE

Alicia Coleman swallowed a handful of painkillers, chasing them down with neat vodka from the guesthouse's minibar. If the pills didn't help, then maybe the alcohol would dull the pain in her mouth. She'd cracked two teeth, and they hurt like a bitch, but she was thankful they were the worst of her troubles. She suffered aches and pains in almost every muscle and joint, and it was difficult to fully turn her head to the right without cringing, but those pains she could endure. The sharp and unexpected explosions of agony came from her teeth whenever she dropped her guard and made the most innocuous of mistakes in inhaling cool air sharply or drinking anything that wasn't at room temperature. She needed to see a dentist, but couldn't take the risk that she'd be recognized.

Earlier, using a false ID and cash, she'd booked a room for three nights at a hotel in Medway, a small community off the interstate, close to the banks of the Penobscot River. Having showered there, and then applied a disguise comprising a wig and tinted contact lenses, she'd abandoned her room without checking out and moved to a smaller, family-run guesthouse almost adjacent to the first. Again she'd used different false details and cash. From the window of her room, she could observe the comings and goings of vehicles to the first hotel. The hotel was situated to make the most of visitors leaving the I-95 en route to Baxter State Park, where Maine's tallest peak, Mount Katahdin, was a favorite of hikers, or to the wilderness areas around Debsconeag Lakes. Presently there was a single vehicle in the lot, a minivan, and it had arrived prior to her. Periodically she checked the lot, and also to either side of the hotel where somebody might have set up surveillance.

Only once since her arrival at the guesthouse had she had a reason for alarm. An electric blue state police cruiser had turned into the lot, and she worried that her ruse had been discovered and the cops called in to check out her sudden departure. She was being overly concerned, because there was no way the hotel staff could've reasoned she was on the run: even if her room had been discovered empty, for all they knew she had chosen to use the hotel as her base while she explored the nearby tourist attractions and would return later. The trooper hadn't even gone inside. He sat there for a while, and it became obvious to her – from the plumes of smoke from his open window – he was sneaking an illicit cigarette before continuing his patrol. Soon he'd chucked out his unfinished cigarette, and with the light bar flashing had peeled out, heading for the interstate.

She checked the contents of the minibar, this time for a soft drink. The anesthetic effect of alcohol was welcome but she must keep a sharp brain. She found a miniature can of 7Up and popped the tab. She tilted her head against the crick in her neck, dribbling the drink in the corner of her mouth, avoiding the cracked teeth at the opposite side. The act of swallowing, and the change of pressure in her mouth, caused a flash of pain. She groaned more in frustration and set the can aside while she searched for more Advil in her bag. She was out of meds, and weighed the risk of traveling to the next small town where she'd spotted a Family Dollar store where she could source more and decided it was worth it. She was miles from where the plane had crashed, and confident her disguise would work even if she'd been identified as a survivor and her face plastered over the news channels.

She grabbed her tote bag, and the padded jacket she'd purchased from a thrift store, which was overly large for her frame, but served dual purpose. It disguised her athletic build and was also roomy enough to conceal the Glock worn on her hip. Over the wig, she settled a beanie cap, and she thumbed on a pair of spectacles. The lenses were clear glass, the frames thick and black, and helped change the shape of her face. Before leaving her room, she checked there was nothing that'd identify her if it were searched while she was out. She took the empty vodka bottle, 7Up can – emptied of contents down the sink in the bathroom – and crinkled foil strip of Advil with her, and binned them in a trashcan in the lobby on her way out. As she left she was ignored by the owners who kept to a private room to the back of the guesthouse. She started her car, sourced for cash from a private owner in Bangor two days ago, and made the short trip into East Millinocket. In the Family Dollar she was perfunctory, shopping only for the meds, but was pleasant and polite with the teller so she'd only be recalled as one of many customers passing through that day – if at all. On exiting the store, she discretely checked the lot for suspicious vehicles and was happy there were none, before getting in her car and making her return to the guesthouse. Before turning in to the small private driveway, she scanned the lot of the hotel and saw that there were two newly arrived cars parked near the entrance: there were figures seated in both. Her pulse rate skyrocketed, but she tamped down the alarm, and ensured she made no erratic movements as she swung into the guesthouse drive. There she turned her car so it faced out, ready for a speedy departure if necessary.

Hunkered down in her car she observed the new arrivals. Each car held two occupants, but in one of them the driver's seat was empty: the driver had gotten out to enter the hotel. Were they chasing her, or were these people simply travelers seeking rest for the night? Hopefully the latter, but best she made certain. The cars were both similar model Fords, dark blue and anonymous, and even from across the highway she could read they had similar license plates: they were rentals from the same supplier. It wasn't unusual for a group of holidaymakers to hire a batch of vehicles from the same rental company, but usually when their party was larger. Given there were only five people in this group, all could have fit comfortably enough in one car, because there was no sign of luggage taking up the rear seats. Of the figures she could make out, they weren't dressed for hiking, but that meant nothing; there were plenty other attractions in Baxter State Park that didn't necessitate specialist attire. One of the four occupants was a red-haired woman, the remainder men, and she judged them as being in their late twenties to mid-thirties.

A second woman exited the hotel, and strode to where the cars waited: Alicia felt she looked mildly familiar. She too was in her thirties, and had the build of an endurance athlete. Her dark hair was pulled back in a short ponytail, and she wore a casual jacket over a T-shirt, jeans, and sneakers. She positioned herself between the two vehicles in order to speak to the occupants of both cars at once. Her hand gestures were sharp, and her otherwise attractive face twisted in a scowl. Alicia held her breath as the woman's head came up and stared directly at her. The look only held for a few seconds, and Alicia decided it wasn't her car, but the guesthouse the woman studied. Next the woman bent to the open window of the second car, leaning down to make her instructions clear to those inside. Her jacket swung open a hand's breadth, but it was enough for Alicia to spot the shape of a gun in a shoulder rig.

It still wasn't definite that the newcomers were hunting her: how could they have traced her to the hotel so quickly? Except Alicia was not about to ignore a potential threat. She felt for the Glock on her hip, bunching up her coat so she had access for a quick draw.

A man got out of the second car, and stood with the woman who directed the driver to move it to the exit ramp. She was obviously the leader of the group and had also been the driver of the first car. The woman seated in the back got out and transferred to the driving seat. She drove the car and parked alongside the minivan. The male passenger, thickset and square-headed, got out and peered into the minivan, seeking some kind of clue as to its owner. Done, he stood as if nonchalantly conversing with the female driver, but Alicia saw him adjust his jacket, freeing access to a weapon under his left armpit. At the exit ramp, the driver got out the Ford and stood so he could watch for anyone leaving the main door, or from any other egress on the far side of the building. Alicia deduced he'd be armed too. Once the others were in position, the female leader nodded at her companion, and together they moved for the front entrance.

Alicia had seen enough.

She waited a few seconds more until the couple was safely inside, and then pulled out of the guesthouse's drive. She was tempted to go right, towards the interstate, but she'd positioned herself in Medway so she could access the route past Baxter State Park and onwards towards the location where the plane had come down. She turned left, and forced herself to stare straight ahead as she drove past the hotel. In her peripheral vision she saw the man standing on the exit ramp look in her direction, and was happy when he didn't holler for his friends, jump in his car and give chase. Her disguise had worked, if indeed she was the object of their search. She drove on, showing no urgency. By now the crash investigators would have finished recovering the bodies and sifting through the wreckage for clues to the plane's catastrophic failure. After the plane crash she'd been in such pain and discomfort that she'd barely been able to drag herself from the woods into hiding. It should be safe to return to the site and dig up what she'd been forced to leave behind.

SIX

Taking scheduled flights from Baton Rouge to Portland International Jetport involved transferring to connecting carriers and could take from five hours upward traveling time. Pinky flew direct in a private Lear owned by a legitimate businesswoman he'd befriended and who extended him a seat on her jet without any pause, so his flight time was cut considerably. At Baton Rouge Metropolitan Airport he'd abandoned his car in the parking lot after locking his S&W Sigma and ammunition in the trunk. Inside the terminal he mailed an envelope containing the car keys to DeAndre Freeman with one final request of his loyal friend to collect the car and weapon and do with them as he thought best. Shedding his gun was both exhilarating and worrisome to Pinky. His days as a criminal were ending but he wasn't yet out of the woods. He chuckled at his clichéd phrase, because after he arrived in Portland he was setting off into another wood with Nicolas and Tess.

He had one carry-on bag, and didn't have to queue with other travelers taking scheduled flights. He passed through security without a hitch, having ensured there'd be no reason to attract any suspicion, dressing in a suit, shirt and tie so he looked exactly like a businessman en route to a meeting in the north. He had a short wait in a corporate lounge – plied there with alcohol and canapés – until he was escorted to the Lear by a personal attendant, and not long afterwards was in the air. He was fairly confident that the speed at which he'd made his escape would have thwarted any immediate attempt to pursue him, but he couldn't yet relax his guard.

Nicolas offered to come and collect him once he was wheels down at PIJ, but he'd been genuine when saying he didn't mean to inconvenience his friends: they were about to set out on a trip and probably needed the time to make arrangements. Therefore he joined the queue of other recent arrivals at the taxi stop. His wasn't the only brown face in the queue, but he was a head taller than everyone else and stood out like a careless cobbler's thumb, and felt vulnerable until he ducked into a cab and gave the driver Nicolas's address north of town.

The cabbie was a local, chirpy-natured, red-faced and broad shouldered, and Pinky guessed he'd recently traded a life at sea for navigating the streets of Portland. As they drove, the old salt pointed out local sites of interest, and Pinky didn't have the heart to tell him he wasn't a first timer to Portland, and chuckled along with the cabbie's anecdotal stories. He didn't notice the tall black-haired man that jogged to a green SUV idling at the curb and join a second younger man inside. Avoiding the tolls on the turnpike, the taxi driver took them over the Fore River to Congress Street towards Bradley's Corner and then cut north through the outlying neighborhoods, and staying a few cars back the SUV followed.

SEVEN

I t was a seven-hour, 330-mile drive from Portland to Brayton Lake, a village community in northwest Aroostook County, and for the last several of those miles Tess had felt every interminable minute in her aching back by the time Po pulled onto what she'd best describe as a wide place in the road next to the village's tiny post office. Allegedly there were upward of thirty campsites dotted around the immediate locale, but Tess saw no evidence of any of them, only the handful of small dwellings and businesses clustered around a patch of cleared forest next to the lake that gave the village its name. Supposedly this was the last outpost of civilization they'd find before plunging on into the true wilderness near the St John River where Jonathan Laird and his team had set up camp.

'Welcome to the middle of nowhere,' said Po as he eyed the tiny community.

Tess pointed northwest. 'According to Laird, the middle of nowhere's still fifteen miles that way as the crow flies.'

'Speaking of flying,' chimed in Pinky from the back, 'are my eyes deceiving me or does that signpost there say *Airstrip Road*? We coulda flown up here, us? Man, my butt has taken on the same shape and density as this excuse for a seat.'

Po laughed. 'If there's an airstrip hereabouts, I'm bettin' it's a field in the woods and can't accommodate a Lear jet. That's the thing about gettin' used to travelin' First Class, Pinky, it hurts when you havta come back down to earth with us normal folks.'

'Told you before, Nicolas, there's nothing normal about you. *Abnormal*, yes. We got time to stretch our legs, us?'

'I intend to.'

All three decamped the vehicle. Bringing Po's Mustang into the woods had never crossed his mind. Instead he'd borrowed a 4x4 Escalade from Charley's Autoshop, a vehicle equipped to handle this kind of terrain. It was a fifteen-year-old workhorse, but what it lacked in comfort it made up for in reliability. As

Tess knuckled her lower back, and Pinky waddled in an ungainly stride onto a pier to look over the brackish lake, Po pulled a pack of Marlboros from his shirt pocket and lit up. He smoked, while Tess checked the GPS coordinates on a unit they'd specifically brought for the job; it was unlikely that they'd get a signal on their cell phones once they left Brayton Lake, and though she trusted Po's wilderness skills, out there in the wild tracts of forest they could easily get turned around.

'We're a little early,' she said. 'Laird isn't due to meet us for another half hour.'

Po waved his cigarette for emphasis. 'I'm good for now.'

'I'm going to stretch my legs too,' she announced.

Po leaned his tall frame against the side of the Escalade and dragged in nicotine-laden smoke. 'Knock yourself out.'

She aimed for the pier, stretching out the kinks in her lower back as she walked. Her backside and thighs felt taut. Best she limber up for the coming hike through the woods. She'd dressed accordingly in sturdy boots, cargo pants, and a sweater, over which she'd a padded anorak in case the weather turned: she'd brought a hat and gloves, too, but they were in her tote bag. They'd left the rain behind south of Bangor, and the afternoon skies were eggshell blue and clear. Pinky wasn't exactly dressed for a downturn in the weather. He'd arrived at Po's ranch last night in a business suit and tie, and had little else with him. It was not his first visit to Maine, though, and over the last couple of years he'd built up a reserve of clothing stored at the ranch for him. He'd found a pair of Converse sneakers, jeans, a volu- minous football jersey, and a bullet-holed coat – worn last while scuffling in a life or death fight with Cal Hopewell, during their search for another missing woman, Jasmine Reed. Slope shoul- dered, Pinky stared off across the lake, and she wondered how far to the south his thoughts wandered.

She sidled up beside him at the end of the pier, and leaned into him. He gave her a wistful smile.

'Having second thoughts about leaving home, Pinky?'

'I'm only wondering why it took this long, me,' he said.

'I'm glad you're here; Po's glad you're here.'

He chuckled at his friend's nickname. 'I suppose I should give it a go, but I've always called him Nicolas, me. Now I'm gonna

be around a lot more often I'll probably get used to it . . .
but, man, *Po*? Sounds like he's some kinda kung-fu-fighting
panda, him.'

Tess laughed. That was exactly what she'd thought first
time they'd met, and he'd explained it was a shortened form of
Po'boy, a nickname given him by northerners in regard to his
Cajun heritage.

'Get me, laughing at any name when I go by Pinky!'

'It suits you to a tee,' Tess reassured him. 'I'd struggle to think
of you as Jerome, but if that's—'

'No, no, no,' Pinky cut in, flapping a hand. 'I'm Pinky, me,
and will have it no other way.'

'I wondered if, with your move to Maine, you'd try to shake off
your past with a name change: I guess that isn't going to happen?'

'No way, no how. I've some bad guys after me, but I've only
moved, I'm not running away from them. They want to, they'll
find me under any name. Big, bold and beautiful: it's not as
if I'm difficult to recognize, eh, pretty Tess?'

She stuck her finger in the bullet hole in the side of his jacket.
'Walking around like this is bound to draw attention.'

'Who's goin' see me around here? Is this place a ghost town?'

'I'm guessing the locals have better things to do than come
out for some random strangers cluttering up their pier.'

'They must see few new folks; I'd'a thought they'd put up the
bunting and throw us a parade, them. Then again, a face the color
of mine, and me dressed in these shabby threads, they're probably too busy hiding their kids in case I eat 'em.'

Tess again wiggled her finger in the bullet hole. 'Soon as
we're back in Portland, let's go shopping together, see if we can
find something more appropriate for someone so big, bold and
beautiful.'

'They have anything other than plaid shirts and dungarees
in Maine?' He took a lingering check over his shoulder at the
small community. 'Then again, maybe plaid shirts and dungarees
are *de rigueur* around here, eh? First pluck of a banjo string,
and we're outta here, us!'

Smiling at his joke, Tess surveyed the lake. It was surrounded
on three sides by never-ending forest. The location was remote
but undeniably beautiful. The blood was flowing to her extremities

once more, evidenced by a gentle tingle in the soles of her feet. She wiggled her toes inside her boots, and sighed in satisfaction. The soft grumble of an engine brought both their heads around. A green Ford GMC emerged from the woods to the east, following the same path into Brayton Lake they'd arrived by. Its driver momentarily slowed it, as if the sight of their Escalade was unexpected, but then carried on; it bypassed the gritty area where the narrow roads divided around the post office building, and went on along the main track. From where Po stood smoking a second cigarette, he observed the large 4x4 trundle past. Tess couldn't make out the driver or passenger because of a tint on the windows, but decided they weren't the biologists they'd come to meet, as they'd arrive from the opposite direction.

'Maybe it's not as dead around here as I first thought,' joked Pinky. 'All we need's another car turning up and the roads will be gridlocked.'

Tess snorted gently at the notion, but took a second look at the GMC before the forest swallowed it again: she also thought that Pinky eyed it suspiciously before shrugging off its presence. People lived hereabouts, after all, even further out at homesteads in the woods, and there were also the campsites she'd heard about; they'd attract visitors. A car passing through so soon after their arrival shouldn't be concerning. Subconsciously, her nerves had been thrummed like a harp string, and she was mildly perturbed. So too must Pinky have been, because without another word he struck out towards dry land, his head craning for another look at the GMC as it drove towards the west.

Po crushed his cigarette under a boot, then reached to retrieve it. He glanced around, seeking a trashcan but the nearest was outside the tiny post office. He loped over, flicked the end in the bin. Tess caught up with Pinky as they all reconvened around the Escalade. They'd purchased snacks at a gas station earlier, and dug into them now. Tess drank thirstily from a bottle of cola. Po and Pinky shared a humongous bottle of Morning Dew. While they sated their bodily needs, each had been thinking about the random passersby, and each had concluded it might not be so random.

'I'm sure I saw that GMC back at the gas station,' Po said, but without a flicker of concern.

'Stands to reason they'd stop at the same place as we did if they're traveling this direction,' Tess pointed out. They hadn't passed another petrol stop in the final hour of their journey. An instruction given by Jonathan Laird when Tess arranged their meeting was to refuel at that very stop, as it was the last commercially available gasoline within fifty miles. If those in the GMC had planned their route here, they too might have pegged the gas station as the place to stop. But she couldn't deny the trickle of suspicion she felt.

'You get a look at who was in it?' she asked.

Po shrugged. Ordinarily he was extremely counter-surveillance savvy, but only where it was necessary. He'd had no reason to suspect they were being followed, so hadn't given the GMC much thought until it turned up here.

'I don't like it,' said Tess.

'Once is chance, twice could be a coincidence, third time's the charm. If it shows up again, I'll check 'em out.'

'Man, and I thought I was the paranoid one,' said Pinky.

EIGHT

'We shoulda gotten things over and shot him at the pier, Frank,' said Carlo Lombardi. He was at the steering wheel of the green GMC. Seated next to him, his cousin Francesco Lombardi didn't immediately respond. He wasn't the most verbose of men at the best of times, and less so when in his younger cousin's company. His silence forced Carlo to think through his suggested course of action and see it for folly. 'OK. Maybe not my best idea,' he concurred.

'Why not?' Frank pursed thin lips as he stared across at Carlo.

'We'd havta shoot the others.'

'That's likely to happen. But why not back at the pier?'

Carlo thought about the pros and cons of the location. The tiny community adjacent to the lake had looked deserted, but probably wasn't: there was the potential for witnesses to the shooting. 'We'd havta shut up any witnesses?'

'You think we're on some kinda scorched earth mission, Carlo? You want to kill everybody in a village just to shut up witnesses cause of a dumb move you made? Whatcha gonna do, raise Brayton Lake to the ground cause you're impatient?'

Now Carlo didn't answer. Frank was exaggerating, but he was right. He thought some more as he drove the GMC slowly along Realty Road. 'If we were witnessed shooting him there, we'd have no clear escape route,' he finally decided. 'The only way back is the way we come in, and the cops would have it blocked.'

'Dunno about you, Carlo, but I don't wanna go back to prison.'

'So why take this job? There's always the risk of capture after any job . . .'

'Not if we're clever about it. We've been handed an opportunity on a plate here. Who knew Pinky Leclerc would end up all the way out here in the wilderness where we can put him in a hole where nobody will ever find him?'

'Gotta admit, Frank, when you asked me to be your wheelman, I didn't know I was agreein' to a drive into the ass-end of nowhere.'

'I had no clue either. I expected to get the job done at Villere's place, and have done. That didn't happen and now we're here, and we're all the better for it.'

Yesterday, when Frank Lombardi accepted the job to take Pinky Leclerc out of the picture, it had forced him to react quickly, as a source close to Pinky had claimed he was already airborne and en route to Portland Jetport. With no recourse but to call on Carlo as his back-up driver, they'd set up surveillance at the airport, and spotted Pinky towering over everyone else in the taxi queue. Following the cab through the city to its destination had gone without a hitch, but when Nicolas Villere greeted Pinky at the door of the ranch, it had given Frank pause. Frank knew of Villere by reputation, and his presence put a new spin on what should have been an otherwise simple enough task to put a couple of rounds in Pinky's head. As soon as Frank saw them together, it had become apparent that this job must be a two-for-one deal, because there was no way he could leave Villere alive – sooner or later Villere would discover the identity of Pinky's slayer and come for him. Best if it was on Frank's terms when they met than the alternative. It soon became apparent that if he launched an assault on the ranch, then it would be a three-for-one job, because Villere's woman was also home. Shooting a woman wasn't something Frank would shirk at – gender meant nothing to him when it related to that of a corpse – but aiming to kill all three in one go added a layer of risk he wasn't comfortable with. At one point, the stakes were lowered, because Villere left the house in his muscle car, leaving Pinky and the woman unguarded, and it was tempting to go in shooting. He resisted, because he'd be left with the same problem before of a vengeful Villere hunting and harrying him to his dying day. No, he decided, all three must be slain at the same time, but on a killing ground of Frank's choosing. When Villere arrived back at the ranch with the beaten-up Escalade and began loading it for a trip, Frank had decided to follow and see where fate took them.

Carlo and he took turns sleeping in the GMC, while the other staked out Villere's ranch from a safe distance. The trio was up early and on the road, and it was fortunate that they seemed distracted by each other's company because tailing them hadn't proved too difficult. During the drive up country, the Escalade had stopped twice, once for a toilet and smoke break, the second to refuel and stock up on supplies. At the latter stop, Frank had risked sticking close to them, because now they were off the interstate highway, there was the possibility of losing them if they allowed the trio any headway. Carlo had pumped gas into the GMC, and Frank had waited until an opportune moment to slip inside and pay. On his way out to join his cousin, he'd almost bumped into Pinky Leclerc but the man hadn't offered as much of a flicker of recognition: not that he should've, because before the previous day, neither of them had reason to know the other existed. They'd followed, this time with more distance between their vehicles, and it was sheer chance that they caught the back end of the maneuver as Villere took the Escalade onto Realty Road and across country. With no idea where the trio was headed, or when or where they might turn off, Carlo was forced to close down the distance between them, but the possibility of Villere spotting a tail was now very real. Other road users en route to camping grounds near Round Mountain offered some cover, but once they'd gotten beyond the Musquacook lakes they had only the undulating road and trees to be thankful of. Suddenly coming out of the woods and spotting Pinky and the woman standing on the pier jutting over the lake had startled Carlo, who'd made the mistake of braking. The shock was only momentary, and Frank's hiss of warning kept the younger driver going, but Frank was conscious that they'd raised a hair or two on the back of Nicolas Villere's neck. Stood there alone, smoking a cigarette, Villere's gaze had followed them with the intensity of a wolf appraising a flock of sheep for the weakest prey.

Since then, while trying to urge Carlo into thinking straight, he'd kept an eye on the mirrors, in slight expectation of the Escalade sneaking up behind them.

'Turn in there,' Frank instructed. Coming up on the right there was a dirt track. If the Escalade didn't pass soon, then it'd mean that Brayton Lake was the trio's final destination, and Frank and Carlo had overshot it.

'No. Reverse in,' Frank ordered when his cousin was about to nose onto the narrow track. 'We need to see them if they come past.' He didn't add that he'd prefer to face any oncoming danger if Villere spotted their GMC on the path and chose to investigate.

The track wasn't designed to accommodate a vehicle as big as theirs; it was more of a game trail that had been expanded upon by the passage of local homesteaders riding quad bikes. Carlo made reversing uphill into a task, grunting and cursing under his breath as branches scraped grooves in the GMC's paintwork. At a kink in the trail a hundred feet back from the main route, Frank called a halt. They were hidden in dappled shadows but had a clear view of any vehicle passing the road end. Frank loosened his gun from the harness under his jacket and laid it across his right thigh while he screwed on a sound suppressor. What the suppressor took away in precision he'd trade for silence: they were still too close to Brayton Lake to shoot without the aid of a silencer. Carlo's weapon didn't have a silencer, but he was under strict instructions to leave the shooting to Frank, unless things went to hell and Carlo had no other recourse. Frank lowered his window and told his cousin to kill the engine and stay quiet. The woods whispered and creaked under a mild breeze, birds distantly called and sang, but Frank tuned those sounds out. Within a minute he heard an engine. He opened his door and stepped out, standing alongside the trail; from the edge of the road, the sight of his form would be broken by the hanging branches and leaves. Carlo scooted down in his seat – a pointless exercise.

An SUV bypassed the end of the track, but it wasn't the one their targets traveled in: it was going towards Brayton Lake. This was dark blue, with a motif emblazoned on the driver's door. Frank couldn't read the wording surrounding a symbolic depiction of what might have been a deer or elk, and he guessed a wildlife ranger drove the SUV. The appearance of a ranger in these parts wasn't unusual, but the timing was more than co-incidental: he rightly surmised this time that a rendezvous had been arranged at lakeside, but for what reason he couldn't fathom. He thought about having Carlo drive them back to the village, but showing up again would definitely raise suspicion. He ducked into the car, said, 'Wait here, Carlo, and don't move. I'm gonna check things out.'

Carlo glanced around fearfully at the encroaching woodland, as if something frightening crouched in each shadow, and Frank was staking him out like a goat. 'Whaddaya want me to do if—'

'Don't do anything. Sit tight and watch for the Escalade. I can be back with you in minutes, wherever their next move takes 'em.'

Before his cousin could argue, Frank loped off down the track towards the main route. There he kept off the hardpack, staying tight to the tree line so he could duck out of sight if Pinky and the others approached. They were less than four hundred yards out of the village, but a bend in the track concealed both him and his targets from each other. He kept his pistol handy, but down by his thigh. At the final sweep of road before arriving at the village, he moved among the trees, stayed low and peered at the small gathering of people on the hardpack opposite the lake. He'd missed the initial meeting, and already the group appeared prepared to get moving again. He'd been wrong to assume the new arrival was a ranger: this burly guy was dressed not in a uniform but regular hiking gear. He waved a hand towards the west and all eyes turned towards Frank. He slowly crouched, making no sudden movements, but didn't think he was the object of their perusal. The new guy was giving brief directions. Villere's woman, tiny in comparison to her male companions, seemed to be their spokesperson, and it was she that shook hands with the new guy, then gestured at Pinky and Villere to get back in the Escalade. She joined the new guy in his SUV, and led the way. Before getting in the Escalade, Villere paused mid-step, turned, and Frank would swear that the Cajun dude stared directly at where he crouched in the shadows. Villere was still, eyes latched onto Frank's hiding place with laser intensity. Pinky broke the moment, calling in urgency, and Villere climbed in the Escalade and set it rolling.

The pair of vehicles drove towards Frank, and he stayed put, not moving his head to follow their progress for fear of alerting Villere, whom he was certain was making a second perusal of his hiding spot. Then the cars were past and their sounds receding down the road towards where he'd left Carlo. Only then did Frank realize he was holding his breath, and he exhaled in relief that he'd gone undiscovered. Villere, he decided, could prove problematic unless Frank was very cautious. The tiny convoy, heading west into the wilderness, was just out of sight when Frank broke from camouflage and jogged along the hardpack to where Carlo waited.

NINE

According to the route planner she'd brought up on her phone's browser, the travel time between Millinocket and the site of the plane crash was approximately four hours, and Alicia Coleman had planned on making the entire journey the day before. However, the arrival of her hunters at the hotel in Medway had spooked her more than she cared to admit, forcing her to run. Instead of following the most direct route to her destination, and risk being overtaken and captured, she'd chosen to zigzag her way to the west, following routes at times only loosely described as roads. Travel weary, and the pain from her cracked teeth leaching both her will and determination to travel onward, she pulled off the road at the remote Russell Pond and spent the evening sleeping in her car. She'd overslept, finally blinking awake surrounded by the impenetrable darkness of the wilderness. Panic flooded her as she experienced a sense of dislocation overwhelming her, and for a few seconds she slapped blindly at the steering wheel and doors before recalling where she was and why. Grasping the steering wheel with both hands she bent over it, wheezing as she tried to calm her breathing. Beyond the condensation on the windshield she could see nothing but blackness. Slowly her vision adapted to the night and from its depthless shade shapes began to coalesce into recognizable forms: trees.

She straightened in the driving seat. The simple act was enough to remind her how much abuse her body had sustained, afflicting her again with a deep pain in her neck courtesy of being thrown around by the colossal forces acting against the Cessna as it had plowed a furrow through the treetops. How she'd ever survived the crash was beyond her, but she'd paid a price since. In the days that had followed the crash she'd barely had time to rest and recuperate, so it was no big surprise that she'd slept longer than planned. Having given herself to sleep now, she craved more. She should get moving again, but the threat of falling asleep at the wheel and crashing the car was very real: in her current frailty she wouldn't survive another joust with the Grim Reaper.

Where she'd parked she was probably breaking the law, and was fortunate not to have drawn the curiosity of a passing patrol car. The fake identification she carried could fool a bored hotel receptionist but not a cop with a reason to be suspicious. She could try to conceal her true identity but sooner or later it would come out, and that would prove too dangerous for her daughters. The local police were not her enemies, but unfortunately she couldn't yet throw herself on the mercy of law enforcement, not until she'd recovered what was buried out there in the endless woods.

She stepped out of the car. Straightening fully was a chore, and she was a little ungainly as she took a few tentative steps. As she walked around her car she rolled her shoulders, furled and unfurled her fingers, and then shook out her arms. She stared into the darkness, suspicious of the slightest of sounds. From a distance, on the opposite side of the lake, she thought she could hear voices raised in good humor. There must be a camping ground out there somewhere. It was cool out, but the temptation to join campers around a fire never crossed her mind: she didn't require company, in fact the fewer people she crossed the better.

After fleeing Medway, she'd made a brief stop in Millinocket in order to plan her escape and to restock on essential supplies. She'd found a hunting and camping outlet and purchased a budget end tent and sleeping blanket, a folding shovel, a pack of cooking utensils and a gas stove. She had no intention of making an extended camping trip, but her return to the crash site might take more than one day. Everything she needed for a brief stay in the woods was packed in a backpack nestled in the trunk of the car. She'd added food and drink to her supplies at a convenience store, all of which was in a single box in the trunk. She should eat, and rehydrate, but the thought of putting anything in her mouth brought on more pulsating agony. She'd knock out her damn broken teeth with a rock if it would spare her from further suffering.

She considered – for no more than a couple of seconds – retrieving the tent, and pitching it further back, concealed by the trees that edged up to the lake. Instead, she groaned her way into the driver's seat, and reversed the car further off the shoulder of the road, down an old forestry workers' track. If it had been dark before, now it was absolute. For a passing patrol to spot her and decide to investigate they'd have to have the eyes of a nocturnal raptor. Realizing she was still wearing the wig and false spectacles, she dragged them off and shoved them on the passenger seat. She drew her Glock from the holster on her hip, and laid it across her thighs, and steepled her hands over it. Sleep took her in an instant, and she only roused when a staccato rap rocked the car on its chassis. She was stunned to find that the next morning had dawned, a couple of hours ago by the way the sunlight slanted through the treetops. She snapped her head up, and was again rewarded by deep, aching agony in her neck. The pain was the least of her worries. Standing close to the driver's window was a figure, large enough that she had no view of a face, only a wide chest clad in red-and-blue plaid. Her first thought was that her hunters had found her, and her reaction was to snatch up her Glock. None of those who'd traced her to the hotel yesterday had been wearing plaid, but this could be another one of their team she hadn't laid eyes on yet.

The figure – perhaps he saw the gun – lurched back, holding up both palms in surrender, and from her vantage Alicia saw an old man's weathered face, eyes wide and mouth writhing in dismay. She lowered the gun below the window, but kept it ready for anything. The man made a face of apology and again displayed the palms of his hands. Alicia cracked the window open a sliver.

'Ma'am,' the old man spluttered, 'my apologies, I'm sorry I startled you banging on your window like that, but I've been trying to waken you for a while.'

'What do you want?' She tried to sound authoritative but Alicia's voice sounded like a thin stream of melt water. She coughed a couple of times, tried to work some moisture into her mouth and was reminded how sore her teeth were.

'Um, er,' he said by way of apology. 'You're blocking the way down to the lake and I can't launch my boat. Would you mind, uh, moving so's I can get by?'

An old truck loomed almost at her front bumper. Beyond it was what she trusted was a boat on a trailer. The old man appeared to be exactly what she imagined a fisherman should look like in this neck of the woods.

'You'll have to back out first,' she told him.

He pointed behind her. 'It'd be a struggle for me, ma'am. If you just run your car back another length or two, I'll be able to get by you there were the track widens.'

She paused, weighing her options. Was he trying to get her further back from the main road so he could launch an attack on her? It was so isolated out here. He wasn't one of her hunters but who was to say he wasn't some crazy old man who'd found a lone woman at his mercy and hoped to do devilish things to her? *You're the one with the gun*, she reminded herself. She checked her rearview, and there was a wide spot in the trail she hadn't noticed in the dark. Immediately beyond it the surface of the lake scintillated under the morning sunlight, the sky overhead was cloudless and pale blue.

Slipping the Glock into its holster, it was her turn to offer apologies and raised palms. She started the car and reversed to the wide spot. The old guy didn't get into his truck, as he watched her make the maneuver. Alicia kept her face averted until she could get her glasses on again. He hadn't gotten a good look at her face yet, and she hoped if ever he'd a reason to describe her, the glasses would be the main feature he recalled. Sadly it'd more likely be the Glock she'd aimed at his chest. As he returned to his truck, she sought her beanie and tucked her hair under it. As he drove past, they'd almost be face to face. He stopped directly alongside her window. 'Ma'am, you okay?' he asked.

'I'm . . . I'm good,' she told him. 'Just got caught out by the dark and unfamiliar roads last night and had to pull over. I must've been more tired than I realized. Sorry if I caused you an inconvenience.'

'Oh, it's no matter. Those trout in the pond have avoided me catchin' them for years, so a few more minutes won't make a difference. Where you headed?'

'I'm meeting with a group of friends at Seboomook Lake.' The lie had come easily to her. She'd noted the name of said lake yesterday before her stop and knew it was ten miles or more south of them.

'Then it's a good thing you did pull over, 'cause you've come

the wrong direction,' he said, assuming she hadn't driven out
of the wilderness beyond this point. He directed her to go back
to the next intersection and take a right, and she thanked him
and assured him she would. She didn't. As soon as she reached
the main track she turned northwest and put many miles between
her and Seboomook Lake. Her misadventure in laying down a
false trail had added an entire day to her planned travel time,
so she didn't drive into the tiny village at Brayton Lake until
midafternoon of her second day on the road. By then she was
road weary again, her eyes gritty. As she drove past the vaguely
familiar village and took the bend in the road she thought it was
a deer or elk emerging from the woods and running ahead of
her, but this critter was on two feet. It was a tall, dark-haired
man, dressed in city clothes and shoes. Her internal alarms rang,
and she slowed the car to a stop without alerting him. In case
he looked over his shoulder, she quickly slipped the car into
reverse and crawled back around the bend in the road and paused
there at the edge of the village.

Who was that guy? What was he doing running out of the
forest in such a hurry? Nothing good, she decided, but hopefully
nothing to do with her planned return to the crash site either.
Her interest piqued, she allowed the car to roll forward once
more, only far enough so that she could see along the road, but
she herself was still obscured from view. Shortly a green GMC
SUV pulled out of a side trail and headed away at speed. Alicia
waited, considering her next course of action, but there could be
only one. She followed.

TEN

J onathan Laird kept his eyes forward for most of the drive out from Brayton Lake. When he did meet Tess's gaze it was with a brief sideways flick of his eyes and a reddening of his cheeks. His discomfort was not due to being in the proximity of an attractive woman, and fearful of being caught staring, he was concealing something and was ashamed by his lies. Before making the journey up to the North Woods, Tess had contacted Laird via his satellite phone – the number supplied to her by Emma Clancy – and she'd made no attempt at concealing what it was she wanted clarification on. Despite the findings of the crash investigation team, rumors had filtered out via one of Laird's team of biologists that a woman had survived the air crash. During her calls to him, Laird had denied this, but hadn't turned down her request to come and interview his team. To deny her request would have only added validation to the rumor, and that somehow his team was involved in the woman's disappearance. He'd resisted the idea of bringing his team back to a meeting with Tess, with the excuse that their field study was time sensitive and the crash and subsequent intrusion of investigators had already disrupted it enough. He'd also made it plain that she was a lowly private investigator, and none of his team was obligated to accept her request of an interview, so she was fortunate he'd extended an invite for her to join them at their camp. Possibly he'd hoped that the thought of a full day on the road, followed by a slog through the woods, would be enough to put her off, and the subject would be dropped.

He'd smiled, shook hands with them all, but had been more than disconcerted by the appearance of Tess and her colleagues at Brayton Lake. Possibly his plan was to lead them back to where they could leave their vehicles before trekking cross country, but Tess had interceded, more or less inviting herself to travel with him to the location while her male companions followed. It was an opportunity at getting the truth from him:

once back with his colleagues, they might close ranks and lips in solidarity, making the task of getting a truthful response more difficult.

Tess didn't directly broach the subject of an alleged survivor. She asked about the field study, what it entailed, and commented on her mixed feelings concerning the state's lottery approach to granting licenses to hunt moose, where only a selection of winners were allowed to take down game. She hated the idea of any of those magnificent creatures being gunned down for sport, or for food, but understood it was about conservation, and much better than the scattershot approach to hunting allowed elsewhere. Laird proved more sanguine than expected about the subject: if the population of moose wasn't thinned by selective hunting, then future culls might have to happen and that was a more disingenuous idea to him. 'Maybe if we hadn't eradicated the apex predators, the grey wolves, from the food chain there'd be no need for either,' he added.

Tess had no argument; in fact she was on the same page.

'Maine's moose population is getting healthier,' Laird went on, happy to avoid the subject of mystery plane crash survivors, for something he was passionate about. 'A few years ago we were losing one in four calves, and the population dropped by about fifteen thousand animals, but it's on the rise again.'

'Why'd we lose so many?'

'Parasites,' he explained. 'Winter ticks mostly. Would you believe that the drought a few years ago was the savior of our moose population because the ticks that fed on the moose died so there were fewer sick animals?'

'Amazing,' she said without any hint of mockery, because the way in which nature found balance was amazing to her. 'I'm so happy to hear that the numbers are recovering. It can only be a good thing.'

'It's particularly important to the tourism industry, and bringing in dollars. The moose is our state animal, it's our responsibility to protect them for the many people who want to come here and watch them.'

'What you and your team are doing is laudable,' she said. He shrugged and reddened again. Without looking at him, Tess added, 'The air crash must've negatively impacted on your workload.

Thanks for taking the time to meet with me, I'll try my hardest to keep our intrusion to a minimum.'

Laird flicked another of his brief glances at her. 'I don't know what more you hope to learn by coming here. It's as we already told the police, we heard the plane crash and went to investigate and found the crew dead and immediately called in the authorities. We can't add any more to that, so I think this will be a wasted trip for you.'

'How could being out here be a waste of anyone's time? It's beautiful here, and besides, I'm hoping to see one of your moose in the wild. We don't get to see many of them on the streets of Portland.'

He thumbed towards the Escalade following close behind. 'Those guys back there don't look like nature lovers.'

His comment was loaded with an unvoiced question.

She'd introduced Po and Pinky by name to him, but back at Brayton Lake hadn't fully explained their reason for accompanying her. 'Po's my fiancé, but he also works as an investigator with me. Pinky's a visiting friend.' Telling the biologist that Pinky was on the run from dangerous enemies might not be a good idea. 'His timing perhaps wasn't the best for his trip to Maine, coinciding with Po and I coming to speak with your team, but we couldn't leave him behind.'

Laird said nothing. Tess assumed he was trying not to be offensive, but she'd noted the way he'd studied Pinky's appearance, and had decided the effete southerner was out of his element.

'You needn't worry about Pinky. Looks can be deceiving. He'll manage a hike through the woods without a problem.'

By now they'd left the main trail and were wending their way across country on trails that were little more than ancient tire tracks in the dirt. Laird indicated a clearing in the woods ahead. Before reaching it Tess could see the ground had been churned up, and a wide expanse of grasses flattened underfoot.

'This is where the authorities had their staging area while they recovered the pilots' bodies. It's the closest we can get our vehicles to camp; from here on we're walking.'

Laird brought his SUV to a stop, straddling a hump of grass at the edge of the clearing. By the look of the adjacent stretch of muddy ground, the clearing must have been chaotic with the

number of vehicles and people arriving in the aftermath of the
plane crash. Here and there the ground was dotted by remnants
of trash left behind. Po drew the Escalade to a halt directly behind
Laird's car, and got out, already sparking a light to a cigarette.

Before getting out of his vehicle, Tess asked Laird, 'Why
would anybody say your guy, Grant McNeill, mentioned there'd
been a survivor if that wasn't the case?'

'Beats me,' he said, and his face grew beetroot this time. 'Grant's
just a kid; you know how kids BS with their friends. You ask
me he was only jerking someone's chain and he got carried away
with the prank.'

Nipping her bottom lip between her teeth, Tess stared at him,
forcing him to meet her gaze. His eyelashes flickered but he
managed not to look away. 'Jonathan,' she said, using his given
name, 'if I discover any hint of criminality, I'm obliged to report
it, or be found complicit. You do realize that if you or any of
your team are keeping anything from the authorities it could
come back to hurt you? If there's any truth at all in the rumors,
you should tell me now so that we can clear things up. Besides
that, if a woman did survive that crash, but has since failed to
materialize, then she could be in desperate need of medical
assistance. She's most likely injured, confused, maybe even
slowly perishing somewhere out there in the woods, or worse
still, dead . . . is that something you want on your conscience?'

He took a moment to answer, and in that void Tess knew she'd
fertilized a seed of worry he'd already planted himself. He opened
his mouth, but the words were trapped behind his tongue. He
shook his head, turned off the engine and reached for the door
handle. Tess placed her hand on his other forearm, stalling him.

'Are you and your friends in some kind of trouble, Jonathan?
Have you been threatened to stay quiet . . . what?'

'Threatened by who?' His previously red face lost all color,
the blood draining from his features and leaving his throat
blotchy. 'Why would *anyone* threaten *us*?'

Various scenarios had played through Tess's mind, some of
which might be deemed the fodder of conspiracy theorists. There
was more to the air crash than the catastrophic failure of its
engine suggested. To date nothing untoward about the tragedy
– other than that two men had sadly lost their lives – had hit the

media, and Tess thought it was because some kind of cover-up was underway to conceal the truth behind the flight. She'd been approached through Emma Clancy's firm to investigate the possibility that a survivor had fled the wreckage, allegedly by an insurance company determined to get to the bottom of the cause of the crash: if there was a survivor, then she was a valuable witness to be questioned. However, Tess wasn't stupid. Insurance companies had their own specialist investigators, and as far as she knew, rarely invited third parties to conduct investigations when their own claim adjustors would be looking for any angle from which they could save paying out. It was almost as if, she felt, the approach made to her was some kind of front, for an interested party more concerned in squashing the rumors than in determining the actual truth.

'As implausible as it might sound, I had to ask,' said Tess.

'We aren't being threatened,' said Laird, 'because we've nothing to hide. Now, daylight's burning and we've still got a way to go. I suggest we get moving, and if you've any other crazy ideas you can share them with me on the hike.'

Tess only raised her eyebrows in response. She'd gotten Laird fired up at last: in his anger he was more apt to say something he might not otherwise if given levelheaded consideration. He climbed out of the SUV, and she followed suit. Po and Pinky were standing alongside the Escalade, their backs to them. While Laird brought a backpack from his trunk, Tess went to usher her companions along.

Po squinted at her through an exhalation of cigarette smoke. 'D'you hear that just now?'

'Hear what?'

He returned his attention to scanning the dirt track they'd arrived on. 'Thought we heard another vehicle coming down the trail.'

Other than the ticking of cooling engines, Tess could hear nothing. She shrugged. Though they were about to enter an uninhabited tract of forest, there were homesteads between them and Brayton Lake – they'd passed one on the drive in – so the sound of another car wasn't unusual. 'What's your concern?'

Po and Pinky exchanged glances. Po said, 'Nothin'.'

'Let's get our butts in gear then,' she said, with a conspiratorial nod towards Laird. 'I might have rubbed him up the wrong way, so he's not in the best mood. Let's not give him another reason to decide against leading us to his camp.'

'Is it going to be muddy like this all the way?' Pinky gave a derisory squint at his sneakers. 'Maybe I should take these off and go barefoot, me.'

Po laughed at his idea. 'With you leavin' tracks all over the woods you'll have the Bigfoot fans goin' orgasmic over 'em.'

Pinky rolled rheumy eyes at the woods. 'You have bigfoots here?'

'Yup,' said Po with no hint of charade, 'an' the woods are also said to be haunted by blood-suckin' ghosts. Better watch out, Pinky, they love nothin' better than gettin' their teeth into a hot-blooded southerner.'

Pinky slapped a hand on his exposed neck, and drew it in front of his nose to inspect the tiny creature mashed on his palm. 'Do these ghosts, by chance, look anythin' like mosquitoes?'

Po popped the trunk of the Escalade, delved inside and came out with a can of DEET. 'Don't fret, Pinky, we've got ghost repellent. Can't say it'll do much to ward off bigfoots if one a them takes a shine to you.'

'Who says I want to ward 'em off, me?' He gave Po a sour grin and the stink eye. 'Tall, brutish and a little dumb; you know the kind of company I like to keep, you.'

Tess smiled at their juvenile banter, as she grabbed her own backpack and shrugged into it. She checked for Laird, and spotted the biologist kicking at clumps of dirt in his impatience to get moving. 'C'mon, guys,' she said, 'you'd better shake a leg.'

ELEVEN

'Arthur Jackman?' asked Virginia Locke, as she flashed an ID card at the old man standing beside a battered pickup truck. She approached him confidently, the card held out, but before he'd more than squinted at the official crest printed on the card and tried to line up the photo ID and her face, she was already slipping it away again. He nodded, because he'd no reason to think she was anything other than what she portrayed.

'You're the agent lady I was asked to meet,' he said, more a statement than a question and she inclined her head in acknowledgment.

'Thank you for coming out of your way, Mr Jackman, I appreciate it.'

They were standing in the tiny village of Rockwood, on a gritty expanse of dirt serving as a parking lot to pleasure-seekers visiting Moosehead Lake. From what Locke had learned from the Greenville Police Department to whom Jackman made his report, he had to drive a fifty-odd-mile roundtrip from his home to Rockwood.

'It's no problem, I havta pick up a few supplies anyways.' He shrugged; the miles probably meant nothing to him coming as he did from a remote homestead where you had to travel a distance to reach the most basic of amenities. Briefly he checked beyond her, to where she'd left her dark blue Ford parked on Village Road, before walking over to meet him. The windows were tinted, but it was apparent there were other agents in the car. 'Is that girl in some kinda trouble?'

'You thought so when you phoned the Greenville PD.' Locke phrased her words in a manner that placed the onus back on him to decide.

'I was concerned for her,' he admitted, 'but not because I thought she might be some kinda criminal.'

'That's still to be determined, Mr Jackman. You said she pointed a firearm at you?'

'It was understandable under the circumstances. I was a stranger coming up on her in a strange place, and had just roused her from sleep.'

'Did she threaten you with her weapon?'

'No. No, as soon as she saw I was no threat to her she put it away. Maybe I shouldn't've bothered anyone with this; I don't want to get anyone in any kinda trouble, not least a girl I mighta scared outta her wits.'

Locke raised her eyebrows, pursed her thin lips, and stared at him. Her acetic features could look attractive but right then she knew she'd the caste of a skull, as hers was a well-practiced expression. From her jacket pocket she took a cell phone, and she brought up a photograph on the screen. She held it out for him to peruse much longer than she had her ID. 'Is this the woman you spoke with?'

Jackman squinted, tilting his head back and forth. He grunted an apology and fished out a pair of glasses from his plaid shirt pocket and settled them on the bridge of his nose. He leaned in again. He nodded gently, but said nothing immediately. Locke didn't lower the phone.

He rocked his head. 'I didn't get a good look at her before she pulled on a hat and spectacles, but I'd say it's her.'

'Take another look,' she instructed, 'it's imperative you make a positive identification.'

'It's her,' he decided. 'Her hair's different and she had a bruise right here' – he touched the left edge of his mouth – 'but, yeah, I'm certain that's the same girl.'

'You said you came across her parked near some pond near here?'

'Yup. It was up at Russell Pond.' He waved distractedly, indicating north of their position. 'I'd turned out early to go fishing, but her car was blocking the track down to the boat launch. I had to rouse her; she was in a dead sleep. When she woke, she didn't look too well to me, and when she pulled on that hat it wasn't to cover her bed hair. Got me thinking . . .' He shrugged again, trying to convince himself he was making something out of nothing, but he couldn't deny his suspicions. 'She told me she was supposed to meet friends at Seboomook Lake and got caught out by the dark, but . . . I dunno, it didn't sound too plausible to me. The way she was parked off the road like that, I got to thinking she'd deliberately hidden, didn't wanna be spotted and the last she expected was to be disturbed. That gun of hers, well, I don't think it was intended to protect her from an ol' crock like me.'

'In your report to Greenville PD, you said you directed her back to Seboomook Lake?'

'That's right, but she didn't take heed. Not that I expected her to. My eyesight isn't great these days, but my hearing hasn't failed me. I listened to her drive north around the pond and up country.'

'Tell me about the car she was driving.'

'It was one of those Japanese imports, an older model Toyota Prius maybe? Metallic gray.'

'License number?'

Jackman only grunted.

'And you're positive she drove north?'

He took off his spectacles and fed them back into his pocket for safekeeping. 'Only two directions you can go and she didn't come south.'

'So she's headed back up into Aroostook County,' said Locke.

'It's that or she made a run for the Canadian border. Not much else out thataway.'

Locke momentarily stared northward, her face softening as she became lost in thought. Jackman watched her, wondering about her change in demeanor, until she grew aware of his perusal. She snapped her gaze back on him, causing him to flinch, then made a sharp nod of her head, while squeezing out a smile. 'You've been very helpful, Mr Jackman,' she said, and turned away before he could ask anything more.

She returned to her car, aware that she was under Jackman's scrutiny the entire way but didn't as much as glance back at him: he was wondering about her, and the mystery woman he'd come across, and trying to decide if he'd somehow betrayed the latter when his intention was to get her the help he believed she needed. Jackman had been helpful, but now Locke had no further use of him and didn't want to spare any time on soothing his conscience. She closed the car door as she settled behind the steering wheel, looking across at Billy James in the passenger seat. Another of her team, Lance Whyte, was seated in the back. 'I should've damn well known Coleman was returning to the crash site after we lost her at Medway,' she announced.

Yesterday they'd come within hours of catching Alicia Coleman at the hotel, traced there due to Locke's access to law enforcement databases – despite Coleman's usage of false details when checking in, it was still an ID she'd employed in the past, and was on a watch list. Locke had used her authority to check the hotel's security cameras, and had noted the blurry images of a grey Prius parked strategically in the lot, largely obscured from CCTV view by an old minivan. The woman that'd come and gone on screen wore a shapeless padded coat, hat, and glasses, and kept her face averted from the cameras. Disguised as she was, Locke was unable to positively identify her as Coleman, but was certain it was her, particularly after she'd covered her tracks by abandoning the first hotel and taking a guestroom in the house across the street. From there Coleman had spotted their arrival and given them the slip. As early as that Locke had considered that Coleman was trying to return to the crash site, but couldn't expend all her resources up there in case she was wrong. She'd sent Greta Peterson and Gabe Hubert north in the second Ford, while she, James, and Whyte searched the campsites and hotels around the tourist-heavy Debsconeag Lakes Wilderness Area, among whom Locke thought their prey had tried to lose herself. Pulling again on the law enforcement databases, she'd come across Jackman's report about disturbing an armed and desperate woman hiding at Russell Pond, and thought it couldn't be a coincidence. Lifting his number from the database, she'd telephoned the old fisherman directly, requesting the meeting. Concerned for the mystery woman's welfare, he'd aborted his fishing trip to return home to telephone the police, and he'd suggested they do so in Rockwood where he was due on an errand. The detour around Moosehead Lake, and the extra hours spent on bad roads, had proved worth it though.

Locke set off, driving north before updating the others about her discussion with the old man, instead instructing Billy James to plot the most direct route to Brayton Lake on the in-car satellite navigation system. To Lance Whyte, seated in the back, she said, 'Get Peterson and Hubert on the phone: tell them we're en route, and that Coleman might already be there. If they spot her they mustn't engage; I want to speak with her before the bitch dies.'

TWELVE

Overhead the branches gathered the night to them, enfolding the campsite in a shroud, and Tess was thankful for the lamps strategically strung around them, otherwise she wouldn't be able to see beyond the end of her nose. The field biologists had utilized the same location over a number of seasons, and they'd established certain features in the landscape. Three tents offered private sleeping arrangements, but there were other tents and a lean-to under which a workstation had been erected. A small portable generator powered the lamps, and also two laptop computers and several other electronic devices Tess was unfamiliar with. Plastic equipment boxes were stacked inside two of the extra tents, while a third mess tent contained a food preparation area and stoves, and a table the biologists could sit around to take their meals if the weather turned inclement. The mess tent was too small to seat six adults, so everyone had perched around a fire pit. Its yellow flames danced, and its glow painted their features in shifting patterns. They enjoyed, in varying degrees, a meal prepared for them by Elsa Carmichael in anticipation of their arrival, and coffee and also a bottle of bourbon was offered around. An air of conviviality had been extended to the visitors but it was strained. Grant McNeill, picking at his food, wouldn't meet anyone's gaze directly, and nervously hummed under his breath to avoid discussion.

Tess felt sorry for the guy; not only was he guarded about what he was prepared to say to her, his team must also blame his indiscretion for bringing Tess and her companions to the site.

Jonathan Laird hadn't made any concession for the least prepared of his visitors. He struck out, as he'd led them towards the camp, at a pace that Pinky shouldn't have been able to keep. But he didn't count on Pinky's ability to dispel perceptions of his disability: he looked cumbersome and obese, but he exhibited the nimble grace of a dancer as he negotiated the undulating terrain, always with a smile on his face and a story, or disparaging joke, for Po at his side. Po also made the trek without complaint, loping along with ease, puffing out blue smoke in his wake. If anyone struggled with the pace at first it was Tess, but she blamed her aches and pains on being cooped in the Escalade for most of the day, and she fell into a rhythm once she loosened up and forgot her discomfort.

Before they'd reached the camp evening was upon them, and Laird finally slowed to pull a flashlight from his equipment bag. Other than giving brief instructions en route, and cautioning them against the dangers posed by wildlife, he didn't give Tess a chance to engage in discussion until after they'd been invited by Elsa to sit and she began dishing out food and drinks. For the time being, Tess was happy to catch her breath, eat a little, and maybe have a slug of bourbon before getting down to business. Po had sat next to her on a cut log, Pinky next to him. Pinky's sneakers had defied expectation, surviving the trek, but he'd pulled them off to shake out an accumulation of fir needles and to wiggle his toes over the fire. Tess would've loved to yank off her own boots and bask her chilled feet in the warmth, but was too self-conscious in the company of strangers.

'After you're done eating, I'll show you where you can pitch your tents,' Laird offered. They'd already discussed staying over, as it would be too much to ask for Laird to do the return trek to where they'd left their cars again that evening, and besides, none of them wanted to stumble their way back in the dark.

'We might need a little help pitching them,' Tess owned up. 'It's years since any of us has gone camping. I'm pretty sure we brought those pop-up types, but if anything can go wrong it probably will.'

'We'll have you set up in no time and then can get this interview business out of the way,' Laird promised, then chewed his lips as if he'd confessed to something he'd prefer to avoid. Grant McNeill stared purposefully at the flames, his humming growing louder.

'I've to go through the process of interviewing each of you individually,' said Tess, 'but let's face it. I'm guessing you've already had your heads together and rehearsed what you're going to say. Let's be straight with each other from the get go: I know you're hiding something, and you know that I know it.'

Purposefully she aimed her words directly at McNeill. 'How's about you just come clean and tell me now, was there a survivor to the plane crash?'

McNeill searched Laird's face for an answer. The team leader was tight-lipped, and Elsa Carmichael made an excuse to return to the food preparation tent so she couldn't be dragged into a lie.

Tess held up both palms. 'I don't have a personal stake in this, certainly no agenda. As you know already I've only been asked to clear up a rumor on behalf of an insurance company, if there's something else that has no bearing on their case, it doesn't need to appear in my report. But Grant, they got wind that some of your friends were spreading a rumor on social media about you seeing a woman at the crash site. If that's the case, then she's a valuable witness to how and why the plane crashed, so needs to be traced. If there was a woman on that plane, why the big cover-up? Why not just say?'

'There was no woman,' Laird interjected.

Tess ignored him, restricting her attention to McNeill. The younger man – an undergraduate seconded to Laird's team, she mustn't forget – looked pained, under pressure to keep tight-lipped in his boss's presence. He only shook his head, electing not to speak because his voice would betray him. Laird stood sharply. The flickering light formed deep hollows under his eyes and cheekbones as he stared down, not at Tess, but in warning at his young charge. 'There wasn't a woman at the crash,' he said sternly, and again not solely for Tess's sake. 'Two men died, isn't that enough for everyone?'

'I'm trying to save us all some time and ill-feeling,' Tess said to the head biologist.

'The only ill feeling's because you're making us out as liars.'

'You're hiding something from me,' Tess stated, 'what am I meant to think?'

'You can think whatever you want, you don't have to be so damn open about it.'

'Would you rather I lied too?' Tess eyed him steadily, but he wouldn't be caught out so easily by wordplay.

'I'm beginning to regret bringing you here,' Laird snapped. 'It's not too late, I can soon show you back to your damn cars again.'

Po spoke up. 'OK, take it easy, fella. Tess has a job to do, and we ain't leavin' till it's done. We can all stay civil, right?'

Laird stared at him, and Po met his gaze. Po's expression was calm, but his message all the more powerful. Laird's head lowered, and he muttered something about the sooner things were done the better, and that was the end of it as far as Po was concerned. He stood and knuckled his lower back. 'Gonna step out for a minute and have a smoke,' he said.

'Sure,' said Laird, glad of the excuse to change the subject, 'but stay close to the lights. We have black bears that come around camp at night, and they might not take to strangers.'

Po asked, 'I thought it was the brown bears you had to be cautious of?'

'You've to be careful with black bears too. We haven't had a fatal black bear attack in Maine since the 1830s, but I'd prefer that tally didn't change. Just keep close, and if you do get approached, back up quietly into camp, and I'll handle it.'

'You don't have to worry about Nicolas, you,' said Pinky. 'One look at his ugly mug and the bear will run for the hills.'

Po showed his teeth in a grin, and they caught the firelight in a devilish caste.

'Jeez,' said Pinky. 'Keep that up and you'll scare the wildlife right outta Maine and across the Canadian border.'

More than one person in camp chuckled at Pinky's remark, and Tess was relieved he'd served to lower the tension. Po raised his eyebrows at her in silent question and she winked in return: everything was fine for him to step away. He dug his cigarettes from his pocket, and moved to the edge of the bubble of light. As instructed he stayed close, but with one shoulder against the bole of a fir, his back to the camp. Po enjoyed smoking, but he wasn't as much a slave to his habit as he made out. There was a reason for him making some space like this and she knew why; he needed to think because something troubled him. Po wasn't the type to share his concern until it was necessary.

Elsa began collecting empty plates. As she moved in on Tess's dish, she had her back to both her male colleagues. She met Tess's gaze, her eyelids pinching and her lips in a tight grimace. Her expression spoke of reproof, but not of Tess. She exhaled slowly through her nostrils, and it was as if she imported a message to Tess that all would be revealed, but not in Jonathan Laird's presence. Tess nodded surreptitiously, as she thanked the woman for the meal.

'Let's see about getting those tents up, shall we?' Laird announced.

Elsa jerked in response, almost dropping the plates she'd collected, and had to scramble to balance them again. She was flighty, but Tess had noted already that the woman was full of nervous energy; she was the type that half-ran everywhere, and completed the simplest tasks at a rush. Now though, she thought Elsa's jittery nature was down to poorly repressed fear. Not fear of Jonathan Laird per se, but afraid that by divulging their secret she'd disappoint a man she desperately wanted to please. Without looking at him, she headed for the mess tent at the clip of a wind-up toy.

Tess stood, brushing down the seat of her cargo pants. Pinky wallowed around, snorting in frustration as he struggled to shove his feet back into his sneakers, keen to help with the tent erecting. Tess looked for Po, and as if he had some finely tuned sixth sense, her partner glanced over a shoulder at her. She couldn't read in him what exactly he found troubling, but also understood it wasn't time to ask. He'd say when he'd concluded whatever was on his mind. If his concern was unfounded, she might never learn.

Grant McNeill also stood to assist, though he concealed any enthusiasm for the task by averting his gaze, and this time his humming found an accompaniment of randomly voiced words. Tess had no idea what tune he sung under his breath, but the melody reminded her of a funeral dirge. His singing was the equivalent of someone pretending everything was fine, but it lacked conviction. She hoped, as she did with Elsa, that he'd be more effusive once she separated him from the others.

Laird had collected Tess's backpack, but there was no need to bring Pinky's – he only had the barest of provisions in his bag. Tess grabbed Po's backpack from where he'd set it down on arrival in camp. Between them they'd brought two tents, one for Pinky, the other she'd share with her man. Laird indicated a spot on the opposite side of camp from their tents, where the ground was largely flat and safe from falling branches, and where a couple of extra lamps had been positioned. Tess moved towards it, lugging Po's bag.

An electronic alarm beeped repeatedly.

All in the camp looked towards the lean-to, Tess with her mouth open in silent question.

'Don't worry about it,' said Laird. 'Whenever one of our game cameras is activated we're sent an audible alarm. It's so we can check the footage live on the monitors. It's probably just one of those black bears I warned your friend about . . . uh, where did he go?'

Her attention had only been off Po for a few seconds but it was as if he'd dematerialized, all that was left to show he'd ever been standing by the tree was a fug of blue smoke hanging in the lamp light. She looked for Pinky, and he was as mystified by Po's disappearance.

In a mild state of alarm, Laird rushed to where Po had taken his cigarette. Perhaps he was worried that Maine's record on fatal black bear attacks had just risen, but Tess was under no such fear. Instead of searching the almost impenetrable darkness beyond the dome of artificial lights, she looked towards the lean-to, where McNeill had gone to hunch over one of the laptop computers. Was it Po who'd tripped the game camera and set off the alarm? Without knowing how distant the ring of surveillance was, she could only trust to McNeill's knowledge on the subject. She went to stand beside him as he brought up the appropriate camera. The infrared augmented view was sharply defined in varying tones of grey, and she could make out individual blades of grass near to the lens, and also the bases of fir trees either side of a game trail. A small branch bobbed as if recently disturbed, but otherwise there was no movement.

'Nothing,' Tess intoned.

McNeill gave her a sidelong glance, for the first time silent since she'd met him. He held up an index finger, begging patience, then tapped away at various keys on the laptop. The recording on screen began rolling backwards to the exact time when the camera was tripped. Too close to the camera to distinguish whom they belonged, a pair of legs crossed the trail. They weren't the legs of an animal, definitely those of a human being, but so close to the lens that the view was only from the knee up to mid-thigh.

In the invisible wash of infrared the material of the trousers glowed like phosphorous, and could have been Po's denims, or any other type of material. From past experience of scrutinizing CCTV imagery, Tess knew that under IR illumination, even black clothing could look white, or other shades of grey.

'Do you think that was Po?' she asked.

'He couldn't have got all the way out there in the last minute, not unless he's Superman and flew there. That camera's about two hundred yards to the north of us.' It was the first time she'd heard the young man speak, and his tone was surprisingly deep and melodious, more so than his singing voice.

'Do you get hunters out here?'

'No, this tract of land is protected. We do occasionally get poachers, however.' He looked for where the team leader had gotten, because Laird needed alerting to the possibility of armed poachers nearby. Laird and Pinky had their backs turned, both searching for any sign of Po in the woods.

Tess's mind played through the scenario of her partner stumbling across an illegal hunter in the dark and the potential danger he could be in, but something more pertinent held her attention. 'These cameras were running on the night of the plane crash, right?'

'Uh, yeah,' said McNeill, and he frowned so deeply his eyebrows almost brushed his cheeks.

'Any chance I could take a look at the recordings?'

'Uh, ehm, I'll have to check with Jonathan first.'

'You're in charge of the tech, right?'

'I am, but Jonathan's in charge of me. I'm not sure he'll—'

'It's OK, I'll ask him,' Tess cut him off.

McNeill was obviously uncomfortable about allowing her to see the recordings, and she suspected why. She'd no authorization to requisition the recordings, or even to demand to see them, and if she pressed him McNeill might take the extreme action of scrubbing the images to hide the truth. Tess would be surprised if he hadn't already done so. She quickly changed the subject back to the mystery figure caught on camera minutes ago.

'You guys aren't expected to confront poachers are you?'

'No. But we're passionate about wildlife conservation. Jonathan contacts Inland Fisheries and Wildlife on the sat phone and reports them. They'll usually dispatch a game warden to check things out.'

'Wasn't it the Department of Inland Fisheries and Wildlife who organized the search and recovery operation after the plane crash?' Tess asked, and before McNeill could confirm or deny, she went on, 'I'm surprised that they didn't seize your camera evidence.'

'Why would they? Our trap cams aren't positioned near the crash site, and besides, they're trained on game trails, not the sky. We *are* studying the migration routes of terrestrial cervidae, not eagles.'

He was right, she concurred, though she'd no idea what a *cervidae* was. Plus, the authorities had no reason to suspect a survivor might have wandered away from the wreckage, so why would they want to see the cameras?

A second alarm bleeped. McNeill was on it in an instant, tapping keys and replacing one camera feed with another on the laptop. Again a human figure passed too close to the camera to distinguish who it was, but Tess could tell simply by the gait that the slim figure wasn't Po. Before either of them could comment, a second figure moved through the woods, striding past the lens and out of sight. Tess and McNeill exchanged glances.

'Was that a gun he was holding?' Tess asked.

'One thing I do know, poachers carry rifles; they don't usually hunt big game with an automatic pistol.'

Depends on the type of prey they're hunting, Tess thought, and was suddenly more concerned about the reason behind Po's sudden departure.

THIRTEEN

There was a spark of suspicion inside Po that he couldn't extinguish. The manner in which the driver of the green GMC had almost braked to a halt at the sight of their Escalade in Brayton Lake didn't tally. As the vehicle drove by him, he could barely make out the figures seated in the front, but enough to tell it was two adult males. They'd kept their eyes forward, studiously avoiding eye contact, which, to Po, was the behavior of people with something to hide. The biologists in the camp similarly averted their gazes, but their secrets were for Tess to tease out. He was more concerned with the strangers in the car. He'd told Tess it could be a coincidence that they'd previously seen the GMC at the gas station, but he wasn't a man that believed in coincidence. Tess had reasoned they'd all refilled at the same gas pumps as it was the only fuel available within fifty or so miles, and she could be right, but Po didn't buy it.

Po knew about cars – he still got his hands mired in oil at Charley's Autoshop on occasion – and had a finely tuned ear to engine performance. Once they'd parked at the biologists' staging ground, both he and Pinky had heard the sound of an engine as they continued on foot. Po was certain it was the GMC. He had to consider that those in the GMC were dogging their trail and it could be for no good reason. He and Tess had their enemies, but Pinky had fled Baton Rouge with a price on his head. He had taken a fast car and faster jet to Portland, but neither was faster than an instruction over a telephone.

There was also that moment back there at lakeside when Po had got the prickling sense of unseen eyes watching them from the woods. Having spent fourteen years behind bars, in one of the country's most notorious and violent penitentiaries, he had quickly learned to trust his senses. More than one attempt had been made on his life and he hadn't survived through inattention.

He'd promised himself that should the GMC turn up a third

time he'd check it out, and he was a man of his word, to which Pinky had made the crack about him supposedly being the paranoid one. Once you dip a toe into paranoia, it is rarely satisfied until you wade in and Po would rather satisfy his curiosity than face the alternative and end up buried in a shallow grave out here in the wilderness. Since hiking in, he'd acted cool and untroubled, smoking vigorously to cover his real purpose: keeping track of the path behind them. While they'd trekked overland, he'd kept one ear cocked to the path behind, and more than once had heard the crack of a twig underfoot, the dull thud of something tripping and going to a knee, the faint grumble of annoyance afterwards: those black bears Laird just warned him about were more surefooted and certainly didn't swear in anger.

As he'd smoked, shoulder to the tree, he'd filtered out the sounds from camp, listening instead to the ambient noise of the forest. As a child he'd spent countless hours at play in the swamplands around his family home; it was a different environment, but one in which he'd learned to read the signs of possible danger, and in that the North Woods of Maine were much the same. As he listened he heard birds startled from their roosts, taking to noisy flight, and it was because something or somebody had alarmed them. Before the squawking and clattering of wings through branches had faded, he also heard the crackle of breaking twigs as a path was forced through the underbrush. He doubted those birds would have taken flight because a bear was rooting around for berries below them; rather they feared something capable of reaching them in the highest branches.

Behind him an alarm beeped, a motion detector had been tripped, and his mind had been made up. While everyone else in camp turned towards the lean-to, he slipped out into the woods, and was instantly enveloped in darkness.

By putting his back to the camp's lights he had allowed his vision to adjust to the night: it was still dark, but he could make out the form and shape of the landscape. He moved confidently through the woods, aware of rocks, branches, and undergrowth that'd snag his clothes or trip him, on a tangent from where the birds had taken to the sky. Once he was fifty yards out he adjusted his path so that he'd parallel whoever was sneaking in on the camp. Once he'd put some distance in, he crouched, keeping his back to a tree to help disguise his silhouette, and rested his right hand on the hilt of a knife protruding from its sheath in his high-topped boot. He gently closed his eyes, opened his mouth, and listened.

He turned his head fractionally, ever so slowly, and stopped. There his eyelids slid open once more and he peered into the gloom to where he'd pinpointed another crackle of breaking twigs. To his left, the dimmest of glimmers cut through the woods, the lights from camp the interlopers were using to guide them in. He didn't rise, didn't draw his knife, only observed.

Two figures, blacker than the blackness around them, moved through the woods on the same track Laird had earlier guided Tess's party in by. One figure was marginally taller than the second, and led the way with his right arm cocked at the elbow, fist held a few inches before his chin. In his hand an elongated tubular object projected higher than his forehead. The second figure was a few yards to the rear, and he too carried something, but down alongside his thigh. Po surmised they were idiots, because carrying handguns like that over this uneven terrain was an invitation to stumble and shoot themselves in the face or foot. No, not idiots, he decided a moment later, only prepared for action as they moved in closer to their target: perhaps they were more disciplined than he first thought and they had their safety's locked and their fingers out of the trigger guard, situations that could be rectified in a heartbeat. He drew his blade, and reversed his grip so the six inches of bared steel was concealed behind his forearm.

He allowed the two skulking figures to move adjacent to him, and then beyond, observing them all the while. Only an occasional glance was cast backwards, and usually by the man at the front, checking his partner was still with him. They were so intent on approaching the camp they never once checked that they were being stalked in turn. Once they'd gone another twenty yards, Po rose up, and he slunk after them, ensuring he always had a tree or bush between them so that he was never in their line of sight if they did grow more surveillance conscious. He took extra care to move softly, placing his feet only when he was sure of not stepping on the twigs or branches littering the ground, choosing instead the exposed stones where he could. Making some noise was inevitable, but he ensured it was less than the pair of gunmen made, their own soft clattering offering cover. All the while Po watched his back. It would be a crappy end to his day if he neglected to check behind and ended up mauled by a bear.

The front gunman halted about ten yards outside the perimeter of the camp, waving the second man to crouch. The leader craned, using the bole of a tree for cover, and spied into the camp. From where he'd also paused, Po couldn't see Tess, Carmichael or McNeill, only Pinky and Laird standing close to where he'd taken his cigarette minutes ago. Pinky was an open target, and the gunman was staring directly at him. Po was prepared to yell a warning to Pinky, but bit down on his bottom lip. The gunman had slunk back, talking at too low a whisper with his partner to hear. Po assumed they were contemplating their odds, aware that to make a clean escape they'd likely have to slay everyone in camp, and debating if they were prepared to do it. As they considered their next move, he crept forward. He was tempted to rush them, but armed only with a knife, he'd be shot dead before he could reach either.

Thankfully Pinky and Laird responded to a summons to the lean-to, turning together and walking through the camp. From Po's vantage he could no longer see them, and that could be the same for the gunmen. He kept moving, closing down the gap on the men step by cautious step. They had their heads together, whispering, the leader gesturing with his left hand to enforce his point. The shorter man's shoulders drooped, as if he was unhappy with his instructions, but he then duck-walked away to the left. The second man went right. They were repositioning in order to overlap their arcs of fire. Po couldn't stop both men from shooting, but he must try. He made a snap decision not to shout in warning to the camp, instead creeping right on a converging tangent with the leader.

FOURTEEN

H e had eyes on Pinky Leclerc, an open target in the glare from the camp behind him. Frank Lombardi could drop the fat man with a close grouping of rounds placed at the center of his chest, then rush in and put another into his skull for good measure, but not without complications. He'd also have to shoot the dude he earlier thought was a game warden. He wasn't confident that he could kill Pinky, then the other without the second man alerting everyone in camp. He'd no idea if anyone was armed, but at the very least thought that a loaded gun would be in reaching distance to ward off dangerous wildlife. He could do without a gunfight – but wasn't averse to one either when he had the advantage of darkness and surprise on his side. More concerning was that somebody in camp could get out an emergency call on a sat phone or radio, and their escape route shut down when the inevitable police cordon was thrown around the area. None of those people in the camp meant a damn thing to him, and he'd slay them all if necessary to ensure his liberty, but he had to be certain that if he killed one then he'd killed all, especially Po'boy Villere. He didn't want that sumbitch hunting him for the rest of his days.

Carlo was crapping his pants. Frank had first instructed his cousin to stay put with their car, but Carlo argued against the idea, and swore to Frank he was ready to step up. Originally he'd called on his inexperienced cousin to be a wheelman and no more, but the kid had a point. When'd he ever learn if he wasn't given a chance to prove he was capable? Coming through the woods, a terrain alien to both of them, had Carlo jumping at shadows, and Frank knew he was regretting ever leaving the comfort and safety of the GMC. If Frank had to be honest, he wasn't totally comfortable either, as they followed the small group to their camp, wondering if they in turn were being stalked by a pack of ravenous coyotes or a mountain lion. In order that they didn't get lost, he'd ensured they kept within earshot of the quartet, though it was risking discovery. At one point Carlo had blundered into a bush, slipped and gone down hard on his knee: the idiot had cursed in pain before Frank managed to clamp a hand over his mouth to hush him. Fearing they'd been overheard, Frank had called a momentary halt, and had slipped his gun from its rig and screwed on the suppressor: alongside him, Carlo had also taken out a gun, a .38 revolver which Frank would ordinarily frown at as a hitman's weapon of choice. Out here, though, miles from anybody in all directions, the sound of the revolver wouldn't be heard by anyone but those being shot at.

In the distance, Frank had heard the low babble of voices and a faint beeping sound. He'd urged Carlo to follow, and led the way towards a dim glimmer through the trees. They made it within ten yards of the perimeter of camp when he crouched down, Carlo at his side, to observe, and that was when he'd spotted Leclerc and the other guy peering out into the woods and his mind had whirred on overdrive, computing the outcome of shooting down the fat man at this first given opportunity.

Now Leclerc had retreated to some kind of lean-to, where another younger guy and Villere's woman were hunched over a laptop. The older guide and a skinny, dark-haired woman moved to join them. Frank had guessed already that the camp belonged to some kind of research team, and was relieved there was no more than a trio of scientists to deal with. None of them would prove too much trouble. He could march into camp, and shoot every last one of them as they clustered around the work-station, but for one important fact: where the hell was Villere? The Cajun must be inside one of the tents, or maybe he'd stepped outside the camp to take a leak or something. Frank couldn't leave him alive, no way, no how. They must wait until Villere showed his face, and then he'd be killed alongside the others.

At a whisper he explained this to Carlo, then instructed his cousin to sneak to the opposite side of camp, and enter from that side, gun drawn and ready to shoot the instant Frank moved on them.

Carlo checked out Frank's suppressed pistol. 'How will I know you've made your move?'

''Cause you'll hear the fuckers dyin',' Frank said in that long-suffering tone he often used with Carlo. 'Your job's to stop anyone trying to get away from me. No fuckin' around; no mercy; man or woman, it doesn't matter, you just bust a cap in 'em. You get me?'

Carlo grimaced, showing no enthusiasm for the task ahead, but he'd asked for a chance to step up and here it was. He nodded.

'You'll do fine,' Frank said, and waved the kid towards the left side of camp. He'd watched him as he moved away – his ass puckering no doubt, but following instruction – and Frank thought that maybe he could make a half-decent triggerman out of his stupid cousin yet. Once he was happy Carlo was almost in position, Frank crept the other direction, curving around the western edge of the camp, intent on entering from the darkness untouched by the fire's glow once he had Villere in his sights: he'd do Villere first, then Leclerc, and then let the others fall in the order they did.

He took a knee next to the base of a tree that offered cover. In among the underbrush, he was only one of countless dim shapes, and would escape detection by anyone in camp whose eyesight was affected by the lamps' glow. He could see between two tents, to where the group was still huddled in the lean-to. They were focused in whatever was on the youngest scientist's laptop screen, but also seemed to have differing opinions on what action was required. It didn't occur to Frank that he and Carlo were the objects of interest, because he'd no idea they'd tripped the motion sensors on infrared cameras. Leclerc and Villere's woman looked more alert than the scientists did, but they were peering towards the head of the camp, where Frank and his cousin had originally approached, and neither glanced his way. He had them in a clump, where he'd only have to move his gun barrel in increments to gun them all down. Frank itched to move in, but again he wondered where Villere was.

Something cold pricked the skin below his right earlobe, and Frank froze. A trickle of blood welled out and slid down his neck.

'Oh, there you are, Po'boy,' he wheezed regretfully.

FIFTEEN

'Hands above your head,' Po whispered into the gunman's ear, 'or I'll stick you like a hog and roast you over that fire pit.'

He'd no intention of cooking the guy, but his threat to stab him held validity, and it must have gotten across because the guy raised both hands skyward, his suppressed pistol dangling loosely.

'Pass the gun into your left hand, take it by the barrel.'

The guy did as commanded. He had no option with the tip of Po's blade nestled in the hollow under his ear.

'Good,' Po said, as he reached and grasped the gun by its stock. Very briefly the gunman held onto the barrel, the suppressor jutting from the side of his hand, as if contemplating swinging around and using it as a club to batter Po. He relented when the knife broke his skin a second time.

'OK, take it easy, man.' The guy released the gun and Po transferred its barrel to the nape of his neck. The knife was withdrawn and slipped back into its sheath.

'You know who I am,' said Po. The guy had used the nickname given to him when first he'd left Louisiana and come north to Maine. Originally it was meant sarcastically, disrespecting his Deep South heritage, but had soon gained an element of admiration, then healthy fear from his would-be dissenters, as Po proved he was nobody's boy.

'This isn't about you,' the guy said, as if that would win him mercy.

'You came here to kill Pinky.'

The guy said nothing; he didn't have to.

'Pinky would be the first to admit he's fair game, but you were also gonna kill the others.'

'No, no, man, I'm only here for Leclerc.'

'Don't bullshit me. Only one reason you sent that kid over there. Between the two of ya, everyone in that tent was gonna get cut down.' Po tapped the suppressor against the man's skull. 'But I stopped you, bra.'

Again the gunman didn't reply.

'Pinky's like my brother. Tess is the girl I love. Those biologists are innocents. D'you think anybody would complain if I put a bullet in your skull right now?'

'The cops would. It'd still be murder.'

'How'd the cops ever know? I can drop you, then drag you out in the woods and leave you for the critters. I hear the bears are mighty hungry just now.'

'You ain't goin' to shoot me in cold blood.'

'My reputation precedes me. You're right, I won't murder you. That isn't to say I won't kill your ass if you as much as twitch the wrong way. See, you're a threat to all those good people over there, and I'll happily shoot you given the alternative.' Po waited a beat. 'Do you hear what I'm sayin'?'

'I hear you.'

'Good. What's your name?'

'Frank.'

'More,' said Po.

'Lombardi.'

'The infamous Francesco Lombardi? I've heard of you.'

Frank grunted, and he echoed Po's earlier words. 'My reputation precedes me.'

'Only as a punk who'd shoot his mother for the price of a two-bit whore. Whoever sent you after Pinky musta been hard placed for finding a decent shooter in time.'

Frank exhaled sharply through his nostrils.

'So what now, Po'boy?'

'For starters you quit the po'boy shit. My friends call me Po . . . you can call me Villere. Now stand up, nice and easy, and keep shtum. We're gonna take a walk back around camp to where your friend is.'

Frank stood, but stayed facing away, hands high. 'He's just a dumb kid.'

'He'll be a dead kid, unless you do exactly what I tell you. Those bears are hungry enough for the two of you.'

'He's my baby cousin. He's no killer, go easy on him, will ya?'

'He's armed and now I am. It's up to you how this plays out.'

'Whaddaya want me to do?'

'Get moving.' Po grabbed him, turning him away from the camp and prodded the gun between Frank's shoulder blades. 'Keep your hands where I can see 'em and step easy. Y'don't want that baby gettin' twitchy and puttin' a bullet in your chest, do you?'

Po took Frank in a semicircle, deep enough into the woods so that none of his friends in camp could have a clue how close they'd been to being ambushed. The last he wanted was for any of them to grow alarmed, inviting a panicked response from Frank's young cousin. As they neared where the younger shooter hid in the undergrowth, Po grasped the collar of Frank's jacket, keeping the man between him and the cousin, and he braced the suppressor alongside Frank's right ear.

'Drop your hands, and lace your fingers at your lower back. Good. Now call out to him,' he whispered, 'but not too loud that the others hear.'

'Please don't shoot him, my uncle will have my balls.'

'I'll send your balls to your uncle in a pickle jar if you don't do as I say.'

A shiver went through Frank, and Po braced for the guy going for broke and turning on him, but the shiver was in response to what was on the cards for him if he didn't obey.

'Carlo,' he stage whispered.

Carlo jerked around, his revolver shaking wildly as he aimed it at Frank.

'Whoa, steady on, kid. It's me, Frank.'

'Frank? What you doin'? I thought you were—'

'Forget what I told you before, Carlo. The plan's changed. I need you to drop your gun.'

'Uh, what?' Carlo glanced at his revolver, realized it was still trained on his cousin, and immediately lowered it. He squinted, probably trying to make sense of why his cousin had aborted their plan and crept up on him like this instead. And why Frank was standing so strangely, arms behind him, with his neck bent and face craning to one side.

'You need to drop the gun,' Frank repeated, his whisper strained.

Carlo didn't drop it; he brought the gun back up, as he rose from concealment. He thrust the gun out with both hands, arms extended and trembling.

'What you gonna do, son?' Po asked over Frank's shoulder. 'Try to shoot me through Frank? Go ahead. I'll kill you and you'll have done me a favor by killin' this sack of crap.'

Carlo searched Frank's face for help, but in the dark he couldn't have made out more than the whites of his cousin's wide eyes.

'Carlo. Drop the gun, goddamnit.' Frank kept his voice pitched low, but deliberate so even a dumb kid would understand the importance of what he was saying.

Carlo spread his arms, the revolver hanging by its trigger guard from his index finger, and he bent so that he could toss the gun down near Frank's feet.

'Drag it back to me with your foot,' Po instructed the older man, while never taking his aim off Carlo.

Frank reached with a heel, hooked the revolver and dragged it back through the forest litter. Po placed his left hand flat against Frank's laced fingers, braced his arm as he crouched low enough to scoop it up. He shoved Frank towards his cousin, and before the man had stopped staggering he had the revolver in his left hand and both guns aimed unerringly at individual targets. Carlo raised his hands in surrender, but fearing Po might misconstrue his action, Frank didn't loosen his hands from behind his back as he turned to face him. His tongue danced over his lips, trying to moisten his dry mouth.

'No more talking,' Po ordered. 'Now, come on, walk this way. Frank, make sure Carlo behaves. I'd hate to have to shoot him in the leg to get my point across. If that happens you'll be the one carryin' him.'

Exchanging glances, neither man offered trouble as Po ushered them through the woods back to the trailhead at the entrance to camp. There he made them halt while he once more reminded them of their situation. With both of his captives cowed, he called out. 'Hello, camp. It's Po, and I've brought uninvited guests.'

SIXTEEN

Tess asked, 'Have you any weapons in camp?'

'We've my rifle,' Laird said. He'd carried it with him while leading them through the woods, a deterrent – and last-ditch defense – against aggressive bears. Since arriving at camp the rifle had stood within easy reach at the entrance to Laird's tent.

'Go get it,' Tess instructed.

'What for?'

'Trust me, I think we might need it.'

'I should call the wardens.'

'Then what? How long will it take for them to arrive? Hours I'd bet. Whoever's out there in the woods, they aren't your normal poachers, they're here for something else.'

'How can you possibly say that?'

Tess exchanged a glance with Pinky, who looked ashamed that he'd brought trouble here with him. 'I can't be certain,' she admitted to Laird, 'but I've a feeling they're following us and I'd rather we're prepared for them when they show up.'

Laird pointed at her. 'This is to do with *you guys*? How? What's going on and who's out there?'

'I honestly don't know who they are, but you're right, if there's trouble it'll be due to us.'

'More specifically to do with me,' Pinky injected, deciding that honesty on this occasion was the best policy. 'There's dishonest stuff in my past I'm not proud of, me. There's a possibility some of that crap's come back to haunt me . . . in the worst possible way.'

Laird stood open-mouthed. 'Who exactly are you, man?'

'I'm Pinky, me. I've made some dangerous enemies. You don't need to know any more than that, you.'

Laird made a double-take study of Tess and Pinky, before again gesturing at her. 'You're supposed to be here on behalf of an insurance company. Are you telling me that your friend's some kind of criminal, and you're protecting him?'

Grant McNeill snapped up his head from viewing the camera feeds. His mouth fell open in a mixture of awe and dismay as he studied Pinky anew. Elsa Carmichael also regarded him, rocking on the balls of her feet as if about to take flight.

'Pinky's my friend,' Tess said, in a tone that said he wasn't to be judged as anything else. 'Despite what you might think of criminals, he's a good person. We haven't time to explain further, just do as I ask and go fetch your rifle.'

Laird dithered. It was as if by arming himself he'd be personally inviting trouble he wanted no part of.

'Forget it, you,' said Pinky, 'I'll get it.'

'No, wait!' Laird shot a worried look at Elsa and McNeill, and it was apparent neither of them wanted a gun in the hands of an alleged criminal either. 'I'll get it.'

'Fetch any spare ammo you have for it too,' Pinky commanded.

Tess addressed the others. 'That's it for weapons in camp, only the rifle?'

'We've hatchets and knives,' Elsa said, 'but they're tools for—'

'You might want to grab something,' Tess cut in. Her suggestion went some way towards reassuring the biologists that it was not Pinky they should be fearful of but who might show up next. But arming themselves was different. She doubted any of them had ever had to defend themselves with a weapon. Elsa grabbed an axe, though Tess suspected she'd never use it. McNeill drew a sheath knife, but didn't know what to do with it in his hand, so placed it down before him on the table. Tess beckoned him up.

'Those lamps,' she said, indicating the lights hanging around the camp. 'They put us under a spotlight. Can you switch off the ones nearest us, but leave on the ones on the other side of the fire?'

McNeill shook his head, making a stab of a finger towards the softly rumbling generator. 'They all run off the same circuit, if we cut one, we cut them all.'

'OK,' said Tess. It was better that they had light to see their enemies by than none at all. At least they'd get a warning if anyone approached from the trail, where the fire lay between them. She wondered where Po was, though now she had a fair idea why he'd slipped out of camp without warning, and what had been on his mind. Since spotting that green GMC, and the driver's odd reaction to seeing them in Brayton Lake, she'd sensed Po's wariness, bolstered when recalling seeing the same vehicle at their last fuel stop. After they'd decamped their vehicles he'd mentioned again hearing a car nearby. It'd since come together in her mind that he'd suspected that they were being followed and there was only one reason why, and his senses were pricked enough that he chose to go check things out . . . as he'd promised he would.

She could tell that Pinky had been giving Po's disappearance some thought, and had concluded the same. When she met his gaze, he offered her a grimace, and a shrug of his wide, sloping shoulders. He'd be regretful that he'd dragged trouble after them, but there was nothing for it now, and it was probably best that Po was out there somewhere in the darkness looking out for them. Tess was licensed to carry a firearm, but on an agreeable trip into the woods, who'd think she'd ever need one? Her grandfather's service revolver was locked in its strongbox, tucked in behind the linen in a closet at Po's ranch.

Pinky frowned at Laird. The team leader had returned, lugging a belt sowed with rifle cartridges. He also held his rifle, but it was clear he'd no stomach for using it on another human being. Elsa looked ready to chop kindling, and McNeill's knife was uselessly discarded on the table. Pinky flapped a hand at the trio. 'Come on, y'all. I think the best thing's you get outta sight and leave this to us. Laird, gimme that rifle.'

Laird shook his head.

Pinky emitted a high-pitched whistle of exasperation, and he strode forward and took the ammunition belt and rifle from the biologist's hands. Laird jerked back, raising his palms, and earned himself another of those strange noises. 'Go on. Take the others inside one of those tents, you, and keep your heads down till you get the all clear.'

'Wait up! I'm in charge here,' Laird reminded him. 'You've no right ordering us around like this, not when this is *your trouble* in the first place.'

'Don't be a dick, Laird. If you want us to save your goddamn asses, you'll do as I ask. Yes, those guys out there probably mean to kill *me*; d'you think they'll want to leave live witnesses behind? Now go. Get down on the ground and don't make a peep.'

Laird still floundered. Tess understood the man's indecision: he was caught up in a situation out of his experience, with the responsibility for Elsa and McNeill's safety to think about. His go-to response was to call on the law, but Tess's words had rung loud and clear to him. *What then?* Even if the authorities flew in by helicopter, it'd take them an age to arrive – he only had to recall how long it had taken a rescue team to be mounted following the plane crash – and they all could be shot to death by then. He probably felt he should be the one offering guidance to his team, whereas he was being commanded against his better judgment by a stranger, and a criminal to boot!

'Pinky's right,' she said gently, as she herded Laird towards the tents. 'Hopefully we've misread the situation and there's nothing to worry about, but it's better being safe than sorry. Let's just get you safely out of the way until we see what happens next.'

'I should call the cops.' Laird halted, and his tone indicated he equally meant that they should be told about she and Pinky.

'That's up to you,' she replied, 'but you'll end up looking dumb if those guys out there are just a couple of locals hunting their dinner.'

He frowned, but nodded in acquiescence, then turned to wave Elsa and McNeill to join him. Before any of them moved to join him under canvas, Po's voice rang out from the woods: 'Hello, camp. It's Po, and I've brought uninvited guests.'

His announcement wasn't specific enough to Tess for her to lower her guard. For all she knew Po was being forced to make the announcement at gunpoint. She slashed a hand at the biologists, indicating they take cover, while she and Pinky hustled forward, Pinky with the rifle stock braced to his shoulder.

'Stand down, Pinky,' Po called out, 'all's good, bra.'

Into the wash of firelight stumbled two men, one taller and older than the other, their faces rigid with fear. Immediately behind them came Po, with an appropriated gun in each hand, one of them sporting a tubular silencer. The presence of a suppressed pistol spoke volumes to Tess; these men definitely weren't innocent turkey hunters. Pinky was also instantly aware, and his face darkened with anger. Despite Po's assurance, he wasn't putting down the rifle.

'Found these two boys out there in the woods,' Po explained, 'and it has come to my notice they had bad intentions for y'all.' He told the two captives to drop to their knees, and they complied. 'Hands behind your backs,' he added.

Pinky went around one side of the fire pit, Tess the other. Behind them, Laird and Elsa disobeyed Tess's warning to stay out of sight, but it was a largely moot point now. She could hear them chattering, but not what was said. She'd enough questions of her own to be getting on with. Pinky beat her to the punch.

'You came up here for the price on my head, you? Who sent you?'

The younger man kept his eyes on the ground, looking suitably nervous as he gnawed a lip. The second man raised his head, squinting up at Pinky through a fringe of wavy black hair. He sucked air through his teeth.

Po knocked the end of the suppressor off the side of the kneeling man's jaw. 'My friend asked you a question.'

'What can I say?' said Pinky's would-be slayer. 'It was just the voice of a middleman on a phone. You know the way these things work.'

'Can't say as I do,' Pinky responded. 'I'm not in the habit of hiring shit-for-brains killers, me.'

'Maybe so, but you move in circles with people that do.'

'*Moved*,' Pinky corrected him. 'I'm out of the business now.'

The guy eyed the rifle with a sour twist to his mouth. 'Really?'

Pinky unashamedly adjusted the end of the barrel so it loomed close to the captive's forehead. 'Really,' he stated. 'But that doesn't mean I've grown soft, me.'

Tess knew Pinky too well to believe he'd shoot in cold blood, despite what the gunman had come here to do. She checked out the younger man and saw tears tracking down his cheeks: he believed Pinky, and thought he might die. His tears didn't move her to pity. Had Po not captured them, both men could have murdered everyone in camp, then disappeared a long time before their remains were ever discovered. With a job well done on their resume, their services would be in demand; they could continue taking jobs from nameless middlemen directing them to slay other innocents. It was fortunate they'd been stopped: who knew how many future victims had also been saved?

The older gunman squinted across at his companion. 'Quit yer sniveling, Carlo, they ain't gonna execute us.'

'You're confident of that, you?' Pinky demanded.

The gunman made a gentle nod in Po's direction. 'Villere had the opportunity to do us quietly, out there in the woods; you ain't gonna do it here in front of these witnesses.'

Pinky lowered the rifle so that it was centered on the man's chest. 'D'you think they care what happens to you? From what I've learned of our friends here, they know how to keep their mouths shut, them.' Pinky gave Tess a wry smile and wink before returning his attention to the captives. 'I'm in a bit of a quandary, me. I want to kill you; it's what you deserve after what you came here to do, but I've got a point to prove to myself, and to these other good folks here. Hmmm, gonna have to do some deep thinking, me.'

Relief washed over Tess, happy she hadn't been required to intervene. She'd worried there for a moment that Pinky might lash out, not that he'd shoot, but he might use the gun to physically beat the two men in punishment. It was good to note that he was trying hard to embrace his new direction in life. Po wore a sanguine expression, but that wasn't unusual. She looked back to where Laird and Elsa had crept closer: they observed from a safe distance at the edge of the fire pit. 'What have you got in camp we can use to restrain these prisoners?' she asked.

There was a proliferation of ropes and straps and electric cables, but Elsa fished out something more to Tess and her male companions' liking: plastic zip ties. While Po and Pinky secured the gunmen, their backs to a pair of trees at the edge of camp in full view of the tents, but distant enough that they couldn't eavesdrop any discussion regarding their fates, she tried to reassure the biologists there was nothing further to fear from them. In the morning, she promised, once their business was conducted, the men would be taken with them to be handed over to the police at first opportunity. It was a false promise, because at that moment Tess had no real idea how the situation would be resolved: how could she explain to the police Pinky's role in this without throwing a heap of stinking trouble on his shoulders that he'd specifically come here to avoid? It was mainly for this reason she argued against Laird calling in the authorities on the sat phone, but there was also the issue of the mystery woman to solve. She wouldn't get to the bottom of it if everyone here were questioned about this thwarted attempt on their lives. 'Don't forget, Laird,' she added as a none-too-subtle warning, 'the cops will also want to know my purpose for being here, and they might press for answers about this alleged survivor in ways you won't like.'

'I could only tell them what I've told you, there was no woman.'

'Yeah, you could say that. But then you'd be lying to the officials and when the truth comes out you'll be in real trouble.'

Laird's features grew blotchy, and he turned away, brushing at imaginary cobwebs caught on his hair. He slunk away, determined to avoid Tess and everyone else while he thought through his quandary. Elsa turned to follow, but Tess observed a shiver pass through her and wasn't surprised when she suddenly spun on a heel and returned. Bending over, so that the movement of her mouth couldn't be observed by anyone else in camp but Tess, she whispered, 'It'd be best if you leave things well and good alone. Jonathan's a good man and being obstructive is twisting him up inside. There's a reason we can't say anything about a survivor; if we do, she won't be a survivor for long. And hers isn't the only life in danger.'

Tess was struck dumb for a moment as she tried to make sense of what she'd heard. She opened her mouth to speak, but was cut off before the question could form on her tongue. Elsa's gaze bore into her hers as she asked, 'Do you want the deaths of two small girls on your conscience, Tess? No? Well, then, I beg you . . . please don't push.'

Before Tess could respond, the woman was away again, legs scissoring as she rushed across camp to the refuge of the mess tent. Tess paused for only a beat, before she was compelled to follow. A voice halted her in her tracks. Grant McNeill waved to her from behind his array of equipment. 'Miss Grey,' he croaked, 'I've got to show you something.'

Elsa had busied herself with the chore of washing up their supper plates in a basin, her head down as she scrubbed furiously at the pots, studiously avoiding any further eye contact with Tess. For another second Tess considered doing the exact opposite to what the woman had begged, press her for more, but now she had confirmation that there was a survivor, she could probably get more out of the youngest member of the team. She angled towards the lean-to. 'What is it, Grant?'

'Something's wrong,' he said, his head darting as he checked all around. 'Come see.'

She joined him at the laptop screen. He tapped a finger on a camera feed, eliciting a frown from her. She looked across camp to where Po and Pinky crowded their captives, getting another look at the faces of the restrained gunmen. Neither man's was the same as the face that McNeill had brought up on the screen.

'I thought there was something odd about where those two were captured,' McNeill said *sotto voce*, 'because they were nowhere near where the cameras were first tripped. While everyone was busy with them, I kept a listen out and got another alarm. This camera here, it was tripped after Mr Villere brought those guys in at gunpoint.'

'Shit, no,' Tess wheezed.

'Shit, yeah,' McNeill unnecessarily clarified for her, 'there are at least another two gunmen out there, and they're closing in on us.'

SEVENTEEN

Greta Peterson wiped dirt off her palms on the bark of a tree, scowling more at her clumsiness than at the mess she'd gotten in. The knees and backside of her pants were also filthy with dirt, and she could feel something wriggling around in her thick red hair. Angry at her stupidity, she dug for whatever bug was trying to build a nest next to her scalp and crushed it between her fingernails. She spied back up the incline. Seconds ago she'd been at the top, before the earth gave out beneath her boots and she skidded halfway down on her butt, hitting a rocky protuberance that had spun her over and she'd rolled the rest of the way. She bit down on voicing an actual curse; luck might actually have been in her favor. If the cliff had been taller than the fifteen feet she'd tumbled she might have more to worry about than a bit of dirt and scraped palms.

She should give herself a break, she decided. She was a city girl, a product of an urban sprawl, not this type of untamed environment. Moving through it without alerting everyone within a ten-mile radius was difficult. Everything crunched underfoot, branches crackled, twigs got caught up in her hair, once she'd almost been blinded when following too close behind Gabe Hubert, and he'd let a springy bough whip her face. After that she'd allowed a safe distance between them as he plotted a path through the woods, following a wrist-mounted GPS device towards where the plane went down. Earlier, they'd almost stumbled across two guys creeping through the woods, and with no idea who they were, they couldn't discount them as a threat, so had drawn their weapons. And now she'd dropped hers.

She'd been in the woods long enough for her vision to adapt to her gloomy surroundings, but a quick scan around showed no sign of her firearm. Out here her cell phone was largely useless, but she took it from her pocket, and used the flashlight app to illuminate the area around her. There was no possible way anyone from the nearby research camp would spot the meager glow, not when she was at the bottom of a gully. She scuffed through the forest litter, pushed aside a scraggly bush, and spotted her weapon. She retrieved it, checked it over, and blew some fir needles out the muzzle, in time before Hubert had backtracked far enough to find his missing colleague.

'Enjoy your trip?' Hubert's figure was a matte silhouette against the mottled canopy above, but Greta could imagine the shit-eating grin he aimed down at her.

'You're hysterical,' she growled. 'Idiot.'

'It isn't me standing at the bottom of a hole with crap all over my face. What are you doing down there?' His Canadian accent made him sound more concerned than she knew he was.

'What do you think? I'm waiting for a gentleman to come rescue me. Sadly there's few of those around here.'

Hubert laughed at the disparaging remark – he couldn't argue with the truth. 'That path you're on slopes up to the rim over there. Meet you there, Greta.'

She paused to wipe at her face, but found none of the crap Hubert had alluded to.

'Got you!' He moved away, chuckling at her displeasure.

Greta grumbled under her breath at his childish antics, but she lacked animosity towards Hubert. He was an insufferable asshole at times, but he was better company than most of the other dour-faced sons-of-bitches she had to work with. Hubert poked fun at her, but it was with affection mostly, while Billy James and Lance Whyte made no attempt at hiding their displeasure of working with a woman: they thought it demeaning. Of course, they didn't extend similar disliking towards Virginia Locke, not in earshot anyway, because Locke wouldn't put up with their macho BS for an instant. One show of disrespect and she'd remind them who was the boss: there was a rumor that Locke once shot a man in the face for calling her a *lezzie bitch*, and Greta believed it. The woman was reptilian in her coldness, and Greta would bet she hadn't even blinked when she wiped the misogynist's brains off her clothes.

Nope, Locke wasn't one to cross; neither did she suffer tardiness or negligence. She'd instructed Greta and Hubert to recce the crash site for any sign that Alicia Coleman had returned, and as yet they couldn't faithfully say they'd carried out her order.

She hurried forward, feeling the ground rise as Hubert promised, and within another thirty seconds was at the end of the gully, standing alongside her companion. He checked her over for injury, though nothing but a seriously misaligned limb would have been visible in the dimness. 'You OK, Greta?'

'Good to go,' she reassured him.

He showed her the GPS unit's screen, a blinking cursor on it. 'The crash site's just over that next ridge.'

'D'you really think Coleman's come back to this godforsaken place?'

He shrugged. 'She could be anywhere. Here's as good as any and more likely than most. The thing is, Greta, Locke wants us here. Are you going to be the one to tell her we could be wasting our time?'

'I happen to value my attractive features.'

'Yeah,' said Hubert. 'Me, too. Ha! Don't worry, Greta, by that I mean I value *my* attractive features. I wasn't coming on to you.'

'Noted,' said Greta. 'You are quite attractive, Gabe. Y'know, the way a baboon's ass is attractive to other monkeys.'

He snuffled out a laugh once more, and was about to set out towards the ridge ahead. He halted and looked back, Greta too had paused to check the lay of the land to the east.

'What's up?' Hubert asked.

'All these strangers in the woods . . . I don't like it.'

Hubert had also been mulling over the sudden explosion in the local population. Besides the two dudes they'd narrowly avoided in the forest, they'd also observed another party trudging towards the camp of field biologists that were first to report the downed plane. Leading a trio of oddball characters – a curvaceous blond woman, a gaunt-faced fella in leather and denims, and a humongous black guy dressed in mismatched clothing who was more camp than the cluster of tents they headed towards – was the head biologist Jonathan Laird, whose face they knew from the intel supplied to them by Virginia Locke. Counting the other two scientists reportedly in camp, that made eight people where it'd be best there were none while they conducted their deadly business with Coleman. Eight people were eight too many possible witnesses, and knowing Locke, she'd be displeased.

'You think they're also here 'cause of Coleman?' Hubert asked.

'We're only here because some kid swears one of those biologists let slip he saw Coleman alive after the crash,' Greta reminded him unnecessarily. 'Could be these newcomers have a similar interest in discovering her whereabouts, or maybe it's because they're here that Coleman's also on her way back. Who knows?'

'You think maybe we should confirm it, before Locke arrives?'

'I think we'd better do exactly what she said; get to the crash site, watch for Coleman and don't engage until she's here.'

'Maybe you're right,' he said. 'But I'm tempted to go on over, take those biologists by their throats and squeeze the truth out of them. Who knows, maybe Coleman's already in that camp and she's been hiding there all this time.'

'Locke's certain that was a positive ID the old fisherman made of Coleman this morning, and she's equally certain she headed this way. If she didn't beat us here, she's not far behind.'

Hubert gestured in the general direction of the camp. 'Maybe she'll call in on her pals on the way to the crash site first. Think about it, Greta: if she's there, we can guide the others in and surround the place. There'd be no chance of Coleman escaping us again.'

'Why would she go there? Nobody's her pal there.'

'Aren't they? If it's true those biologists saw her, it's equally true they're covering up the fact. Maybe she somehow bought their silence, maybe she did something to earn it.'

'Or maybe the guy that slipped up and told his friend about her was drunk and talking bullshit,' said Greta.

'So who'd the old guy see this morning, who was it that gave us the slip back at Medway? Who has Locke got us out here watching for?'

'You win,' said Greta. 'Let's go take a peek at the camp, and we can at least rule it out that she's there before Locke arrives. If she isn't, though, you're going to be standing in front of me when we tell Locke how we wasted time.'

Hubert grunted in dark humor. 'Fair enough, just don't stand directly behind me; if she puts a bullet in my face, it'll come out the back of my skull and hit yours too.'

'Yeah,' she agreed, and gently knocked a knuckle on his forehead, 'there ain't that much grey matter up there to slow a bullet down, is there?'

He gently shoved her, and she resisted, rubbing her shoulder against his chest. He reached and plucked a small twig from her hair, his fingertips lingered. Their eyes met and she recognized a twinkle in his that must have been mirrored in her own. Hubert's wasn't bad company to be in at all, she reaffirmed.

'Come on,' she said, pulling her thoughts together, 'we'd best get serious again. We get to the camp, check things out, then if it's a none starter we head for the crash site.'

'This way.' Hubert set off, walking toe-to-heel with a tightrope walker's balance, gauging direction through the GPS unit strapped to his forearm. In his other hand, he held his pistol. As an afterthought, Greta took out her sidearm again and followed.

EIGHTEEN

Virginia Locke scowled at the vehicles parked on the muddy staging area. It wasn't surprising to see the 4x4. In a prior visit to the crash scene while searching for Coleman's missing corpse and the evidence she'd taken, she'd identified it as belonging to the biologists who'd reported the plane crash, and it was apparent they regularly left the car there while they were in the field. The presence of the Escalade was more troubling. A quick check of the DMV database gave current ownership details as Charley's Autos, a repair shop in Portland, Maine. Charley Banks, said owner of the vehicle, was an eighty-three-year-old grease monkey and an unlikely visitor to the North Woods: she had to assume he'd loaned the vehicle to whomever had brought it all the way up here into the wilderness of Aroostook County. With more time and inclination she could probably discover who the actual driver was through the interrogation of the law enforcement systems she had access to, but there was no point in wasting time and resources at this stage.

More concerning than those parked in plain sight was the third car they'd discovered hidden at the side of the track leading here. At first she'd entertained the notion that Alicia Coleman had ditched the motor bought in Bangor in favor of the rugged GMC, but the DMV had thrown up ownership details as those of Carlo Lombardi, a twenty-two-year-old male from West Brook, a suburb of Portland. Carlo's record was unremarkable – a couple of misdemeanors, a drunken assault, possession of cannabis resin – but his name had been flagged as a person of interest due to his direct familial connection to Guido Lombardi, the suspected head of a local criminal family. What interest did the son of a wannabe *Cosa Nostra* don have way out here in the woods? Didn't he realize he was poking his nose into the business of an authentic organized crime syndicate who'd eradicate his entire family from the face of the earth? There was a remote chance that Lombardi's presence was coincidental, but she didn't accept a mundane explanation when the opposite was probably true. Perhaps Guido Lombardi had learned the value of what Alicia Coleman had been traveling with and hoped to profit from its retrieval, and had dispatched his son here. Perhaps the boy was a more adept criminal than his rap sheet gave credit for; maybe he simply hadn't been convicted of any serious crimes because he was careful, and therefore dangerous to her and her team. It must be taken into consideration that he had brought along more accomplished triggermen to watch his back while conducting his own hunt. On that note she instructed Lance Whyte and Billy James to gear up.

When they decamped their Ford, it was with Whyte toting an M110 semi-automatic sniper system, while James had added to their firepower with a Remington R5 RGP – a military grade assault rifle. Locke favored her sidearm but added to their armament with a compact SIG MPX-K submachine gun clipped to her shoulder harness. All three wore flip-up head-mounted N-15 Gen 3 night-vision goggles that turned the night to green-tinged day, and tactical anti-ballistic vests. It looked as if they were going to war, and their equipment might be deemed over-kill, but Locke was of the adage that you hoped for the best but prepared for the worst.

Unhindered by the darkness, they entered the woods, following the coordinates – as their comrades already on the ground did – on a wrist-mounted GPS unit, which James periodically checked. Cell phone reception out here was nil, but it didn't thwart their ability to communicate. All of the team, Hubert and Peterson included, possessed walkie-talkies and, as a backup to reach the wider world, satellite phones. Locke had relied on the latter while her team was separated by many miles, but now they were closing in on the crash site, she keyed her radio and spoke a single command. 'Switch channels.'

'Roger that.' The swift reply came from Gabe Hubert.

Locke's instruction had been prearranged. She and the other four members of her team switched to an encrypted channel. This close to Canada, the Border Patrol conducted surveillance, alert to smugglers, human traffickers and felons fleeing justice. As well as patrols on the ground, they also used manned aircraft and drones fitted with FLIR heat-seeking technology and listening devices. Ergo, their radio communications could be monitored: Locke was confident that their transmissions couldn't be cracked in real time, but she enforced a strict radio protocol so that if later deciphered their conversations were ambiguous and unlikely to raise an alarm.

To Hubert she asked, 'Any sighting of that white tail?'

'Negative. We've got eyes on a herd of does and bucks.'

'On the range?' She referred to the crash site.

'Negative. They're in the glade.' The glade was their pre-arranged code meaning the research camp.

'Why aren't you on the range?'

'With nothing scoped there, we thought the white tail maybe sought safety with the rest of the herd.'

'And has it?'

'No positive sighting yet, but this herd's interesting. Eight in total, six bucks, two does; two of the bucks are hobbled and sitting targets.'

Locke mused over what she'd just learned. She keyed her mike again. 'As interesting as it sounds, we're only licensed to take down a white tail. Have your partner return to the range, you stay on the glade.'

'Understood,' Hubert replied. 'Thought maybe those hobbled bucks have been staked out to attract our trophy.'

'Stand by,' she said.

Locke raised a fist, and Whyte and James halted. Listening into the radios through their earpieces they'd heard Hubert's suggestion too. They waited for Locke's next command, on high alert while scanning the environment through their night vision goggles.

She was mildly pissed that Hubert and Peterson had gone off mission, but understood why. The presence of Guido Lombardi's son continued to trouble her. From what Hubert had told her, there were two men in camp being held captive, and it was reasonable to assume that they were being used as bait to attract Alicia Coleman. She surmised that the wannabe gangsters had invaded the camp and taken hostages: perhaps they hoped to force the truth from Grant McNeill, the source of the rumor concerning Coleman's survival. Locke had previously considered torturing the truth out of McNeill herself, but to what end? She

was 99.9 percent convinced that Coleman was alive, so didn't
need him to confirm it. The same conviction might not be said
of Guido Lombardi, so he'd sent his kid and some triggermen
up here to terrorize the truth out of McNeill and his fellow
biologists.

She should assume nothing. Assumptions could lead to false
responses, and false responses could lead to mistakes that could
lead to certain death. She had to see what was going on with
her own eyes.

She keyed in Hubert. 'What strength does the herd show?'

'One long, two short.'

He meant they were armed with a rifle and two handguns.

'Ping your coordinates,' she instructed, 'and hold position
while we flank the glade.'

'Understood.'

Locke waved her companions forward, with James taking
point, leading them on an approach path that'd take them to the
east of the camp, opposite from where Hubert's location had just
appeared as a static red dot on the GPS unit's screen: Peterson
was returning to the crash site as instructed.

They were still a good distance from the camp, but with so
many newcomers in the area, they couldn't chance lowering their
guard while moving in. Also, Coleman was still in the wind; for
all they knew, she could be very close by. They advanced carefully, their weapons primed and ready for anything. Locke, and
no doubt her companions, was thinking through this latest turn
of events and what they might mean to their mission. Whyte was
close enough to Locke that he could speak at a whisper and still
be heard clearly. He said, 'If this is some other outfit trying to
move in on us, they're going to have to be taught a lesson.'

'Yes.' Locke imbued that one word with a lot of meaning.
Her mission was to find Coleman, and retrieve from her the
information that could bring down the criminal network she
moonlighted for, but Locke also had other responsibilities
equally as important. One was protecting said organization
from outside threat – for instance, halting any subtle or aggressive incursion into their business by other criminals – while also
concealing her own ties to federal law enforcement.

She was fortunate that Lombardi had chosen to send his son

out here to the ass end of nowhere and that their meeting ground hadn't been in one of the cities where Coleman must have taken shelter recently. Here Carlo and his triggermen could be dealt with without the worry of intervention from the cops: they could simply be made to disappear without a trace. However, there was the complication of the scientists and whoever had joined them from the Escalade. If a bunch of hoods went missing, there'd be grumbling at street level, and perhaps a lot of chest pounding and gnashing of teeth from Guido Lombardi, but the old man couldn't do much about avenging his son when he'd have no idea who'd taken his life. Silencing the scientists and their guests would be a different story . . . but that depended on the situation. She'd need to manipulate the scene so it appeared some kind of deal had gone bad between the opposing parties, and not a living person could escape the scene. Taking eight lives in order to conceal her activities was quite a toll, and couldn't be approached lightly, but neither was it something she'd shy away from.

She could walk away entirely, leave whatever was going down in the camp to come to its natural conclusion, and concentrate on her hunt for Alicia Coleman. However, that allowed the threat of Lombardi to creep up on them and jeopardize their mission to catch Coleman, because after he'd concluded business with his hostages he'd surely move his operation to the crash site. She couldn't, and wouldn't, allow that. There was only one course of action, she decided: all threats must be neutralized.

NINETEEN

'How many of your damn buddies you got out there, Frank?' Po loomed over his captives, the suppressed pistol tapping his thigh being his only hint of unease.

'I swear to you, man, whoever's out there, they ain't with us.' Frank was perched on the bones of his rump and his heels, arms stretched torturously around the bole of a tree. His wavy black hair had fallen in his eyes again, and he had to throw his head around to convey the sincerity in his features.

Tess winced as Po jammed the suppressor to Frank's left knee. 'Try again, punk. Who's out there and how many?'

If he could have he would've spread his hands wide for emphasis, but Frank had to make do with sending his eyebrows arching into the stratosphere. 'C'mon, Villere! I'm tellin' the truth, and you know it, man!'

Tess laid her hand on Po's wrist, gently guiding the gun away from Frank's knee: there was no way on earth that he'd purposefully maim his prisoner, but she didn't want any accidents.

Pinky also loomed, his normally jovial features set in granite. He had Laird's rifle in both hands, ready to snap up and take a shot. The younger captive – Carlo Lombardi, they'd learned – sobbed between his feet, tears dripping from the end of his nose. The guy wasn't only out of his depth, he was almost drowning in his own snot. Pinky gave his foot a jab with the toe of his Converse sneakers. 'Yo! What you got to say for yourself, you?'

Carlo only mewled and Frank jumped in in his defense. 'I told ya already; the kid's only my driver, man, and he ain't too good at that. He doesn't know right from left mosta the time . . . Jeez, he couldn't find his ass with both hands unless you drew him a diagram.'

'He's not so dumb you trusted him with a hawgleg, him,' Pinky snapped.

'The revolver was for his personal protection, just in case things went south between you and me.'

'Things sure went south for ya,' Po put in. 'Those other shooters out there, are *they* your backup, Frank?'

'How many times, man? They ain't with us. You said you spotted us at the gas station, and again back in Brayton Lake. What? D'you think we had another bunch of our guys hidden under a tarp in the back?'

'They coulda been following you at a safe distance,' Po said, 'and you guided them in.'

'How? With fuckin' smoke signals? You tried your cell out here, Villere? It don't work for shit!'

'All right, less of your lip, Frank,' Po warned.

Frank had a point though. Their captives had been searched and their phones taken off them, even if they were useless without a signal. Tess went to where the cell phones had been dumped on the ground and powered up the screens. They weren't password protected. No calls or messages had been sent or received on either since the evening Pinky flew in from Baton Rouge.

'They didn't guide anyone in,' she confirmed.

Frank set his mouth in an 'I told you so' smirk for Po's sake.

'So it's somebody else,' Po said unnecessarily.

Tess thought of the face she'd viewed on the laptop: it was that of a man in his thirties, square-faced, shorthaired, beyond those few details she couldn't add much more except that from the earlier alerts from the trap cameras he traveled with a companion and both were armed with automatic pistols. Was it beyond belief that more than one hitman had been hired by Pinky's enemies and was working independently of Frank Lombardi? Pinky had already told her that he didn't possess enough fingers to count everyone who'd like to see him dead.

Po pushed the silenced pistol into his jeans. His brow was lowered, and Tess knew exactly what was going through his mind. He'd stalked and captured the Lombardi cousins, there was nothing stopping him doing the same with the other gunmen, particularly now that he was better armed. Catching his attention, she shook her head. Frank and Carlo had proven inept; the same might not be said of this new threat. 'We have to think about the safety of Laird and the others,' she told him.

'What do you suggest, we walk 'em outta here? What about these two?' He nodded down at the captives. It'd be one thing guarding themselves from attack, let alone protecting the three biologists; they could do neither efficiently if they also had to march out Pinky's would-be executioners.

'We could always shoot 'em in the feet and let 'em loose to find their own way back,' Po said with a wry gleam in his eyes. 'Bears might get 'em, but hey, at least they'll get a chance.'

His suggestion didn't deserve a serious reply from Tess. The Lombardi cousins were a definite problem for them but she wouldn't countenance doing them harm now they were no longer a threat – and neither would Po. She was still trying to come up with a convincing lie that didn't involve Pinky for when the cousins were handed over to the police. Nothing she'd thought of would work without the Lombardis cooperation and they weren't about to admit to attempted murder. Momentarily lost for what to do next she shoved the revolver in her belt, and then her hands in her hair, and she peered back towards the tents. There was nothing for it: with three innocent victims and two hostile captives to care for, she must call in reinforcements. Where were Laird and his satellite phone?

The elder biologist was nowhere in sight, but Grant McNeill had left the lean-to to crouch at the edge of camp. He held some sort of device that threw a cold blue light on his youthful features. She moved towards him and laid a hand on his shoulder, squeezing gently. McNeill started in surprise, but immediately returned his attention to the device as soon as he registered Tess standing over him. She checked what he found so interesting. She was familiar enough with the technology to recognize the thermal scope he aimed at the forest, one which he'd hard-wired to a tablet so he wasn't limited to the tiny view through the eyepiece. He was searching for the heat signatures of those who'd tripped his game cameras earlier.

'Anything?' she asked, intrigued by the imagery on the screen.

McNeill shook his head. He adjusted the scope so that it scanned the nearest trees. 'Up close, a person would stand out like a firework, further back, not so much. The ambient temperature of all those trees is working against me, it's washing out the thermal signatures of everything else.'

'So they could be nearby?'

The young man shrugged, but continued to scope their surroundings.

'Come on further back into camp,' Tess cautioned.

'I can see more out here,' he replied, meaning the camp's lights didn't interfere with his view of the screen.

'You're too vulnerable out here. I need you to stay with your friends so we can protect you. Where are Laird and Elsa?'

Briefly McNeill glanced away from the screen, a quick look over his opposite shoulder. 'They were here a minute ago.'

Tess squeezed his shoulder a second time. 'Any hint of those others on your device, you move back and come get me, OK?'

He nodded, began aiming the scope to the extreme left of camp. Tess backed away, staring out into the impenetrable wall of blackness beyond the lamplight. She'd no hope of seeing anyone the scope couldn't pick up. Furious whispers filtered through canvas to her. She ignored the mess tent, heading instead directly for Jonathan Laird's tent. Within, Laird and Elsa were in heated disagreement.

'But we swore we'd stay quiet about her, Elsa!' Laird hissed.

Elsa's voice was equally sibilant. 'I know, but that was then, Jon! We kept her secret, but where has it got us? *They* know she survived: why else do you think they're here?'

Tess paused. Their words confirmed what she'd traveled here to find out, but the stress in Elsa's voice told her she wasn't referring to Tess and her friends. Inside the tent, Laird and Elsa fell silent. The atmosphere was pregnant with anticipation, and then the tent flap was thrown back and Laird poked out his head. He gave Tess a stern look of disgust as if she was a pervert caught spying on an intimate act. His reproof didn't faze her. Tess leaned towards him, fixing him in place.

'I think it's time to come clean about this woman, don't you?' she said, and then with a swipe of her hand towards the woods. 'Who's out there? They're after the survivor too, right?'

Laird clammed up, but he was shoved aside, and Elsa appeared. Her features were pulled so tightly that she resembled a skull. Laird tried to grab her, to haul her back in the tent, but she elbowed past him, saying, 'No, Jon! We have to tell Tess!'

'We swore we wouldn't!'

'Our promise doesn't matter now. Don't you see, they're coming, the ones Alicia warned us about!'

'Shhh! Don't say her name—' Laird grabbed Elsa's wrist again, but she wrenched it away.

Tess reached to assist her as Laird made another grab to restrain Elsa, and the small woman was caught in a tug-o'-war. Laird realized too late that he was overstepping a mark, and withdrew his grasp with a grandiose show of contrition, hands thrown overhead. Elsa staggered against Tess, and the two women jostled for balance.

Laird shook his head, turned as if to go back inside the tent, then halted, swaying back and forth in indecision: hiding like the proverbial ostrich with its head in the sand wouldn't help. He'd made a promise not to speak about her, but Elsa was about to spill all about the survivor. It was best, he must have decided, that he ensure that Tess understood their reason for staying quiet. He blurted: 'You've got to understand! We were asked to keep her secret because she has children who might be endangered if her true identity is discovered.'

'OK. Keep your voice down,' Tess cautioned him as she scanned among the benighted trees for hint of an eavesdropper. She gestured Elsa and Laird to follow, and led them towards the center of the camp. They followed, Laird still reluctant and heavy of foot, and with Elsa wringing her hands in nervous anticipation. They whispered loudly to each other, weighing their decision to come clean. Tess indicated them to sit down on the log she'd earlier used. When they did as asked, their shoulders touching, she said, 'We've established that there was a survivor, and you agreed to keep her a secret so that her family isn't endangered. The important thing I need to know is – right now! – who she's hiding from, because I'm certain those people are on the way here and they mean business.'

The biologists exchanged glances, and Laird's face reddened, but he finally grimaced, tilted down his head and nodded for Elsa to take the reins. Before speaking, she took his hand in hers and gave it a gentle squeeze. 'She wasn't specific, Tess. She only said that her enemies were ruthless and would stop at nothing to silence her.'

'Her enemies are criminals?'

Elsa snorted at the description. 'Not all; not at face value anyway. Some of them are legitimate industry leaders and politicians, but according to Alicia, it's a masquerade. Despite their public personas, she said they're conducting the dirtiest of businesses, and they'll do anything to hide their involvement.'

'So she's some kind of whistleblower? She's found dirt on these people?'

'She didn't say . . . she said it was too dangerous for us to know. All she kept stressing was that if they knew she was still alive, they'd come for her, and for anyone who could lead them to her or who they could use to get to her. D'you see why we had to stay quiet, Tess? We aren't bad people; we're not only trying to protect Alicia and her children, we're also trying to protect ourselves!'

Tess understood, and she sympathized with them. 'How on earth did Grant slip up and tell his friend about her?'

'He swears he didn't,' Laird said, joining in now that the truth was out, 'but you know what guys are like when they're trying to impress their pals. I'm pretty sure that he let slip while the pilots were being recovered from the plane. We'd returned home to Portland for a few days while the FAA had the area under quarantine. He was out drinking with some buddies, and must've gotten a bit loose lipped. It was one of his buddies that began spreading the rumor of a survivor on Twitter, stating he was close to the source. Grant's a good kid, he wouldn't have put any of us at risk on purpose.' Laird halted. Purposefully or not, McNeill's indiscretion had placed them in danger, and it was coming for them. 'Alicia warned that informing the cops about her would make us targets, and at first I didn't understand how. She said there'd be no way of stopping her true identity getting out, and if that happened anyone associated with her could become targets. Her enemies would suspect we knew more than we were letting on and wouldn't stop at hurting us to find her.'

They'd promised not to call the cops, but now that Alicia's enemies were en route the promise had become redundant. Tess would prefer no law enforcement involvement until she could figure out how to protect Pinky, but weighed against the alternative . . . well. She wouldn't be protecting anyone if they all got shot to death in the next few minutes. She said, 'Where's your sat phone?'

Laird reached for his belt, but his hand fell on an empty pouch. 'Ah,' he grunted, 'I took it to my tent . . .'

'Go get it,' Tess instructed, 'and call the police. Tell them we need urgent assistance, that there are an undetermined number of gunmen threatening us.'

'You warned me against calling them earlier, saying I'd look a damn fool if those people out there are only hunting their dinners.'

'I was wrong about their motive that time, wasn't I?' For emphasis she nodded over at where the Lombardi cousins were under guard of Po and Pinky. 'This time I'm under no illusion.'

TWENTY

E ven cloaked in darkness, the crash site was easily discernible. Alicia Coleman stood on a ribbon of scarred earth, flanked on two sides by the stumps of felled trees. During the recovery of the pilots from the Cessna, a clear path had been chain-sawed through the woods to allow access to the workers on the ground. The bodies had been removed by helicopter, taken up in slings, and later some of the wreckage had also been recovered, winched out to a staging area east of the site where it had been loaded onto flatbed trucks for transportation to an FAA facility. Smaller portions of the doomed aircraft had been left behind, some trodden into the earth, some still caught up in the branches over the couple of hundred yards where the plane had skidded across the canopy before crashing to its final rest. From what she'd learned of the investigation so far, foul play was not a consideration, the consensus being that the plane had suffered engine failure, and – through pilot error – had been brought down in the forest, where they could have glided it towards Brayton Lake and the airstrip there for an emergency landing. Alicia suspected if anything happened to her the truth would never be known: there were powerful people involved who could influence the findings of the investigation, be that through reward and collusion, or threat and coercion.

For the first few days after the crash she'd suffered too much from her injuries to care about the initial news reports, but after that had made a point of interrogating the media and news channels for any suggestion of what had happened aboard the aircraft. The presence of bullet holes should have sent up a red flag, except most of those shots had been fired at her in the passenger compartment, and most of that had been torn to ribbons during the crash. Portions of the fuselage had survived, but the rear of the passenger compartment had been shredded to tiny nuggets of twisted aluminum when first the wings and then the fuselage had been obliterated. She wondered if any of those small ribbons hanging further back in the trees held bullet holes: if so, they'd likely never be studied.

Recalling the devastation wrought on the plane she couldn't begin to understand how she'd survived, but she'd avoided impalement on the branches she smashed during her plunge to the earth, only to hit a down-sloping embankment that took the brunt out of the impact. If she was a woman of faith, she might accept that some divine power had been watching out for her that day, but she wasn't. Besides, what kind of benign force would place her in such an untenable position in the first place that they need step in at the last second to waft her down to earth on a cloud? No, her survival had nothing to do with godly intervention, and more to do with pure luck.

Neither luck nor godly favor had played any part in her survival, only pure circumstance, and it was a continuation of circumstances that had brought her back to the crash site now. After being roused from sleep by the old fisherman, and lying to him about how she'd ended up sleeping there by the pond, she'd driven a winding path north, approaching the site from a different direction than the one she'd originally used to flee the scene. Coming in via Brayton Lake, she'd been surprised when the dark-haired guy broke from cover to run to a green GMC and speed off away from her: she'd concluded his presence had nothing to do with her, but she preferred not to take any chances. Her return had to be clandestine; she couldn't chance being witnessed here again as she'd been the last time. To those field biologists she'd finally spilled some truth in order to gain their trust and their silence, but one of them must've cracked their vow of silence for those hunters to turn up at Medway. Whether or not they'd been pressed into betraying her she didn't know, but now that her hunters had gotten a sniff of her scent, they would be a source of information to be mined. Perhaps they'd already been forcefully interrogated and now lived in terror of her hunters' return. She couldn't approach them again; they were probably instructed to inform her hunters the instant she showed up. Sadly, Alicia could trust no one.

She'd trekked through the forest, and as daylight waned had set up camp in the depths of a ravine to the south of the site, where she'd sat in her tent without lights or fire, with her handgun in her lap, dozing sporadically before the creak of a branch or distant animal call woke her, startled and expecting the worst. Finally, knowing that restful sleep would continue to elude her, she'd picked up the folding entrenchment tool purchased at the camping outlet in Millinocket, tucked her pistol in her belt, and settled into her backpack once more. Under darkness, she'd navigated the woods, as stealthily as possible and alert to danger behind every tree and bush. She'd made formidable enemies, and those sent after her had access to resources beyond her dreams. She'd already concluded that the team chasing her were professionals, and probably had access to mercenary-grade tech and armament. Every step she took could be in the crosshairs of a riflescope augmented by night-vision technology.

She made it to the crash site alive: either her hunters hadn't caught up yet or they were watching, waiting for her next move. There was only one reason why she'd come back to this desolate spot, and that was to recover what she'd buried. Maybe they were simply biding their time until it was dug up and then they'd shoot, saving them the time and effort of another search. She wouldn't hear the bullet destined to kill her, but neither could she live in fear of it.

Finding the crash site in darkness was one thing, pinpointing her cache another. The terrain had been dramatically altered since last she was here, the felling of the trees where the plane had come to rest being the greatest change: she'd originally used some of them as landmarks to direct her to where she'd buried the cache. Hewn logs had been piled at the margins of the cleared area, a tangled barrier to be negotiated. In the dark, they formed what looked like an insurmountable obstacle and she'd few options except scale them or retrace a path through the woods and find another approach on the far side. The sensible move was the latter, but before she could do either she must get a handle on her current location in relation to where her cache was. There was nothing for it, she put aside her shovel and dug out a flashlight she'd avoided using. Cupping her left hand over the top of the lens, she aimed the flashlight at the ground and switched it on: she couldn't help tensing, expecting a bullet to instantly slam between her shoulders. When she was still alive a few beats later, she relaxed and – with the light still blocked from above – aimed the beam at the jumble of logs in her path. It wasn't such a challenging barricade as it first appeared, there were ways between the stacked logs, though it'd be a squeeze. She directed the partially obscured light higher, seeking anything recognizable.

It took a minute or two to adjust her position, triangulating one scarred fir tree with a boulder that had gone undisturbed by the rescue team, before she had her first coordinate set in her mind. She moved forward, entrenchment shovel now unfolded so it could be used as an axe to clear her way, and she struck a path through the brush between the stacks of logs. She shone her light again at the scarred fir, then darted it to the boulder: still on track, she moved forward, counting her steps as if she were a pirate seeking hidden treasure. Reaching twenty paces, she halted. Directly to her left was a gnarly old tree that wouldn't look out of place in a fairy tale, and she nodded in recollection of the branch that resembled a witch's pointing finger. She followed its direction, again counting out her paces until she was thirty deep into the forest. There she again flicked on the flashlight and inspected the ground. This far out from the crash the ground had gone undisturbed by the recovery team, but she was unsure if she was on the exact spot. She kicked around through the leaf litter and twigs and found a patch where the earth had recently been turned. When last she was here it was without a shovel, and she had been concussed and hurting from crashing to earth, and she hadn't labored too long at digging the hole with nothing but her hands and a bit of twisted aluminum as a shovel. She'd barely scraped the surface before dragging forest litter over her cache.

She scraped back the uppermost layer of camouflage, forcing down the excruciating pain in her broken teeth. Her fingers brushed against heavy canvas. She found her cache. She sat down heavily in relief, taking a moment to gather her strength. Her pain was such that beads of sweat broke along her hairline and trickled down her forehead into her eyes. She blinked, groaned at her discomfort, and then batted the sweat off her skin with the back of a wrist. From her jacket pocket she withdrew a strip of painkillers and dry-swallowed four pills. She dragged a canvas holdall into her lap, knocking off the dirt stuck in the zipper. She knew exactly what was inside but couldn't resist the instinct to double check. She tugged the zip open and using her cupped flashlight again she scanned the dozens of sets of plastic wallets inside. Each was a pastel shade, semi-opaque, but she could still make out the headings on the uppermost sheets of paper within. She exhaled through her nostrils, nodded in relief, and then carefully zipped up the holdall. Now wasn't the time to sort the important papers from the hundreds of others they were hidden among: at least this time she was fit enough to carry the holdall and its contents out of the woods. She shrugged out of her backpack, and stuffed the weighty holdall inside, securing the flap with an adjustable drawstring and toggle. Standing, she kicked the earth back into the shallow depression then arranged some broken twigs and leaves over the turned soil. Collecting her shovel she straightened, listening intently. She hadn't been shot . . . yet. Now was the most dangerous point during her return to the site: steeling herself, she took a step, and when she survived it, she took another. One footfall followed the next and she was soon back at the gnarly tree and still breathing. Things, she decided, were going better than anticipated, and the thought proved anathema. The harsh bark of a rifle split the quietude.

TWENTY-ONE

The entire purpose of their trip out to the woods had changed and not for the best. Sure, Tess could now confirm that there had indeed been a survivor of the plane crash, but the how and why of 'Alicia's' situation would have to wait. Right now there were greater concerns. If Frank and Carlo Lombardi were the greatest of evils she had to contend with she might actually feel relieved, but from what Laird and Elsa had just intimated, the people they'd been warned against were dangerous criminals and of a different caliber to the two snakes in the grass that Po had easily defanged.

Po was stalking back and forward, growling under his breath like a panther prowling its cage in a zoo, while Pinky's attention was shared equally between his prisoners and the surrounding forest. Po would prefer to take the battle back to their enemies, but how could he do anything when his priority lay in protecting those in the camp? If he were alone his response would be very different but then and there he was torn: there was Tess's safety to think about, and Pinky's, but he also felt responsible for protecting the trio of biologists, and even the Lombardi cousins. She understood. Tess loved him equally, and her feelings for Pinky more than bordered on platonic love too. She'd fight tooth and nail to defend them, and by virtue she'd extend that protection to the biologists. The revolver liberated from Carlo Lombardi was a heavy weight at her waistband: she took it out and checked the load. Six rounds. She approached Po, aiming a nod towards the prisoners.

'They didn't have extra ammunition when you searched them?'

'Nope.' He tapped the silenced pistol tucked in his jeans, while aiming the stink-eye at the elder cousin. 'This has an extended mag, seventeen rounds. Frank was probably confident he could drop everyone here with plenty bullets to spare.'

'This isn't good.' She wasn't referring to their ammunition

reserves but the situation they'd fallen into the middle of. 'I've asked Laird to fetch his sat phone and call the cops.'

Po inclined his chin, his mouth a straight line, but didn't argue against her course of action. He wasn't afraid of a fight, and neither was he one to walk away from one, but he wasn't a fool. They could be outgunned, outnumbered and those weren't odds anyone could like. He squinted out at the forest. 'What we up against, Tess?'

'There *was* a woman on the plane,' she began.

'Yeah, I figured. So what's her story?'

'They said she called herself Alicia. Apparently she's hiding from some dangerous criminals and swore these guys to secrecy . . . to protect her identity and her children.'

'You think she was spinning them a lie?'

'Couldn't say. Whatever's the truth, she warned that if they spoke about her they'd attract her enemies and they wouldn't stop at hurting them to find her.'

'The shooters out in the woods, you're confident they're the ones searching for Alicia?'

'Unless it's another team after Pinky . . .'

'Doubtful,' he said.

'From the game camera footage we know they're armed with automatic pistols.'

'Numbers still the same?'

'Yeah, still only two. But we have to assume there are more.'

'We need to move those punks.' He meant the Lombardi cousins. They were sitting ducks at the edge of camp. He thumbed towards the nearest lamps. 'We need those shut down; we're lit up like a Christmas tree and I can't see for shit for them.'

Tess checked on McNeill. He was still crouching at the edge of camp, scanning the woods with his thermal gizmo. 'I'll get Grant to douse the lights, can you and Pinky shift those two?'

He winked, and approached the captives, making a single dip to his boot and coming out with his knife. Tess watched Carlo's eyes widen in horror and again felt mildly sorry for the young man. Po said something to Pinky she couldn't hear, and Pinky straightened up, the rifle going to his shoulder again. Po dipped behind Carlo, snicking through the zip ties on his wrists and the

young man flopped forward, groaning, and rubbing his hands
as the circulation returned to his fingers. His relief didn't last
long: Po slotted fresh zip ties over his wrists, this time at the
front. Tess turned her back on them and began to cross camp
to hail McNeill, but was distracted as Laird and Elsa appeared
from Laird's tent. The man was fiddling with a bulky sat phone.
These days technology had advanced to a point that sat phones
were comparable in size to regular smartphones, but apparently
Laird's budget hadn't allowed for a recent upgrade. He adjusted
a thick antenna on top as he tapped buttons, and read off instructions on a display screen. Elsa huddled at his side, offering
advice. The last time he'd used the phone, Tess assumed, was
when he'd reported the plane crash, and wondered if he'd
dithered as much that time too. He again adjusted the aerial,
checked the display screen, and finally looked at Tess before
opening his mouth to speak.

There was an explosion of parts, and the phone spun out
of his raised hand. Laird emitted a shriek, and he spun too,
clutching his hand under his opposite armpit, while Elsa stumbled
in surprise and sat down heavily on her backside. For the briefest
time Tess thought the phone had somehow malfunctioned and
blown apart. But that was not it, and in the next instant she
shouted wordlessly, charging to tackle Laird down to earth even
as beyond the fire Pinky's rifle barked in response to the sound
of gunfire only now rolling into camp.

Laird's mouth was a wet oval of dismay as Tess tumbled
with him, their faces only inches apart. He attempted to pull out
of her grasp, to kneel, to inspect his damaged hand, but Tess
forced him down and he hadn't the strength to resist. She pushed
him so he was lying on his side behind the log she'd sat on
at supper. He checked his hand, squawking in disbelief at
the horrific trauma he'd sustained. In the flickering glow of the
campfire she could tell he was missing fingers.

'Stay down!' Tess's command was almost as sharp as the recent
gun retorts. Laird was too distraught at his injury to obey; he
again tried to rise, so he could inspect the magnitude of trauma
to his hand. Tess forced him back. 'Do you want the next bullet
in your head?'

She avoided looking at the ruined mess of his hand, instead searching for Po and Pinky, but the fire was between them. Where was Elsa?

The woman was still sitting in the dirt.

It was only seconds since the bullet had destroyed both Laird's hand and the phone in it, and shock could have frozen Elsa in place. She needed to move, because limned by the fire's glow she was an open target.

'Elsa!' Tess hissed. 'Quickly! Get over here.'

The field biologist didn't answer. She did nothing. She sat as she'd sat down moments ago, legs splayed and hands cupped in her lap, chin resting on her chest.

The blood roared in Tess's skull.

'Elsa?'

The woman's head came up, juddering at the effort as if every inch gained was hard fought. In the fire's glow her eyes were wet, and her mouth twisted as though struck by palsy. Her upper chest was awash with blood, pumping from a hole that'd been punched through the side of her neck. She didn't look at Tess, but at Laird. She croaked, but he didn't hear, too wrapped up in his own misery to notice she'd been hurt worse. Elsa worked her tongue, swallowing expansively as she tried to gather the strength to call to him and more blood gushed from her wound. 'Jon . . . Jon . . . Jo—'

There was finality to her last utterance, and then Elsa keeled over to one side, her shoulder thumping the dirt. Tess had witnessed death before, and in more horrific circumstances, but this hit her like a punch to the gut. Her instinct was to rush to the woman's aid, to drag her to cover, except placing herself in the gunman's sights was a reckless exercise when Elsa was beyond help. Minutes ago, she'd thought things had turned bad, but that had been nothing compared to what had happened since, and events could only get worse.

TWENTY-TWO

Virginia Locke had ordered one round down the range from Whyte's M110 sniper rifle, his instruction to stop Jonathan Laird from calling the police on his satellite phone. At less than fifty yards the shot was an easy one for him, and she was sure he was being cocky when shooting the actual phone out of Laird's hand. The biologist's fingers were collateral damage; that the bullet had gone right through the device, his hand and then his female colleague's neck could be deemed an economical use of a single round, but it hadn't been Whyte's intention. The bullet had destroyed the phone and Laird's hand, but its trajectory was also altered so that it ricocheted through Elsa Carmichael standing beside the target. The woman's death was a surprise, but Locke felt no regret. She'd already decided that all in the camp must die to protect her dual mission, and with one bullet Whyte had both taken out one target and neutralized their ability to contact the outside world. She was confident that her team would finish the others with equal ease.

However, an obese black man snapped up his rifle, returning fire at Whyte almost as if he was laser tagged. The bullet struck the fallen tree Whyte had stabilized his M110 on, throwing up splinters of bark, and the ricocheting bullet cut a streak of flesh out of Whyte's shoulder and nicked his cheek. Cursing, Whyte flinched, dropping low for cover, and missed an opportunity to take out the black guy who immediately ducked and charged towards the center of the camp.

A second man, tall, broad shouldered, and tough-faced, shooed his pair of captives after the black man, while he retreated, a silenced pistol raised. He didn't waste a shot, for he could have no idea where his targets were. Locke was tempted to empty a magazine, cut the gunman to ribbons, but at fifty yards proximity the accuracy of her SIG MPX-K was woeful on fully automatic fire. Her submachine gun was designed for close combat scenarios, and from here she'd only waste bullets shearing foliage at best. She let it swing on its harness, drawing instead her sidearm. Ten yards to her left Billy James's Remington assault rifle blared, throwing down tight clusters of three rounds with each squeeze of the trigger. The tall gunman tackled his prisoners, taking both men to the ground as James's shots cut the air over their heads. There was a scramble in the camp to find shelter, except there was little to choose from beyond a few logs set around the fire and the tents erected at its southern perimeter. Laird, cradling his damaged hand, and staring in abstract horror at his downed colleague, was dragged down again and again by a blond woman who'd yanked a revolver out of her belt.

Lance Whyte was up again. To take his initial shot he'd doffed his night vision goggles. In Locke's augmented vision the smear of blood on his cheek looked silver. He batted at it with his left wrist as he jostled his sniper rifle into position. With every target now on the ground, or hunkering behind the flimsiest of obstacles, Locke could leave the shooting to him. He could pick off everyone in the camp, one by one, and his bullets would cut through them and whatever they hid behind with the same ease they'd passed through Laird's hand and phone.

Again, the black man thwarted her expectations.

Belly down, his rifle resting over a backpack he'd pushed into position, he fired again, targeting where he'd sent his counter shot a moment before. This time the bullet didn't trouble Whyte, snapping ineffectively through the branches above his head, but it slowed him from picking his target long enough for the tall man to pop up from concealment and return fire at Billy James. James's assault rifle chattered once more, and the tall man darted away, almost as if he could outrun bullets. The woodland behind him was chewed by James's fire. When Locke next checked, the black man had rolled aside, and found shelter in a natural dip in the ground. The prisoners were currently unguarded: one of them jumped up, swung to and fro in indecision, then hurtled off towards the tree line. James plugged him with a tight bunching of three bullets to the torso and the man went chest down on the earth, kicking up a cloud of dirt that hung in Locke's night vision like twinkling fairy dust. The second prisoner roared in denial, but he'd the sense to keep his head down.

The assault rifle's muzzle flashes made James a target. The

tall man appeared fearless as he stood at the edge of the clearing, arms extended, the butt of his pistol resting in his cupped palm for stability as he deliberately chose his shots. He squeezed the trigger twice in rapid succession, and the silenced rounds were barely discernible at Locke's distance, but she heard the corresponding grunts of pain from James: he was hit twice but not yet dead, his vest absorbing the bullets. He returned fire, and the tall man was forced to lunge for concealment, but again he centered on the muzzle flash and returned fire. The assault rifle fell silent. Locke also fell still in surprise. Things were not going the way she'd imagined less than two minutes ago. She snapped out of her funk, raised her sidearm with the intention of putting three bullets in the tall man, but already he'd melted into the woodland and her N-15 Gen 3 goggles didn't help locate him because somebody dumped fuel on the camp fire and it roared, casting glaring light deep into her optic nerves. Cursing, Locke tore off her goggles as she tried to blink away the swarming shapes burned into her retina.

The camp was bright from artificial illumination as it were, and she found she could see more detail without the goggles, except for when she checked on Lance Whyte: her colleague was a dim blur in the darkness to her right. James had fallen, and there was no sign of him or his possible killer. From the camp bullets rained, the rifleman shooting with skill and determination, and pinning down Whyte. 'Hubert,' she snapped into her radio mike, forgoing the protocol she'd demanded earlier, 'if you've a shot, take it. I want that black fucker dead!'

'Aye-firmative,' replied the Canadian.

From the western side of camp a handgun cracked thrice in quick succession, and she was satisfied when the rifle fell silent.

'You get him, Hubert?'

'Negative. Sent him to ground.'

Making the black guy seek cover wasn't good enough. She needed him dead, and the blond woman too. And where had the tall fella in denims gotten?

'James, you hear me?' she demanded. 'Sit-rep?'

Billy James didn't answer. He was injured too badly to respond to her demand for a situation report or he was dead. She felt the loss of an asset as a hard wedge in her throat, if not the loss of another human being. To her and her employers every man and woman among them was expendable, but each that fell was one more gun she had to do without. Taking out a bunch of civilians should have proven child's play to her team, and two to one odds were too high a price she liked to pay. This must be ended quickly, and without any further losses to her team.

'Hubert, move in,' she commanded. 'I'll flank from the east. Whyte, you see any movement in that camp, put them down.'

'Aye-firmative,' said Hubert.

'Copy that,' said Whyte.

Locke sloped off to the left, her sidearm ready as she slalomed between the boles of trees.

The fire was burning down again, whatever accelerant was dumped on it was now exhausted, but the lamps in the trees still cast the illusion of day over the camp. There were few places to hide inside, and once Hubert moved in adjacent to her, everyone alive in the camp would be caught between them, and anyone attempting to fight back would be captured in Whyte's scope and dead a split-second after. For the first time since arriving at the campsite she allowed her mouth to form the facsimile of a smile.

The lamps went out, and as night folded around the camp, Locke's smile dissolved.

She'd dumped her head-mounted goggles when the sudden flare had temporarily blinded her, and they lay where they'd fallen. The lights she'd since been forced to look at had impaired her natural night vision, and with their cessation she was engulfed in impenetrable blackness. She forced herself to stand still, to wait while her pupils expanded and made the most of the ambient starlight. Trusting Hubert would do the same, she counted off ten seconds, then began a slow advance, gun ready. Opposite her the woods lit up in a brief strobe as a handgun spat twice. She followed Hubert's attack, moving out from the perimeter of the camp, into its interior. Near the fire she spotted the corpse of the female biologist, and she tracked right, and there was Jonathan Laird, huddled down behind the cut logs. He had his hand tucked under his opposite armpit, head down, softly mewling at the loss of his fingers, or the loss of his colleague, perhaps both. His misery didn't matter to her: Locke aimed her pistol at the biologist's head.

In the woods Hubert's gun spat fire again. Oddly, he made a harsh grunt after each shot, the sounds carrying to her, and it was the oddity of his vocalizations that momentarily stayed her finger from pulling the trigger. Her attention drifted from the sitting target of Laird, to where she fully expected Hubert to emerge from the woods, but part of her knew he wouldn't be coming.

'Shit,' she exhaled under her breath, and began a rapid retreat.

'Hold it!' The blond woman emerged from the other side of the fire, and in the place she stood she must be an open target for Whyte's sniper rifle. The woman aimed the revolver, and judging by her stance she was familiar with her weapon. Locke halted. She was side-on to the blond, her gun on the far side. If she twisted quickly enough, she could kill Blondie with no problem at all: too slow though and it'd be she who'd die.

'That's it,' the woman ordered, 'show me your gun. Easy now. You've just killed two innocent people, harmed another, and I've no qualms about shooting you dead.'

Why the fuck hadn't Whyte taken a shot yet? Perhaps he was waiting, letting Locke squirm a little first. Locke, though, squirmed for no fucking man, and certainly not for a prissy bitch either! She met the blond's gaze, and the corner of her mouth rose in a sneer. 'Careful there, princess,' she warned, 'we don't want that gun going off by mistake.'

'Trust me, when I pull this trigger it won't be a mistake. Now do as I said and show me your gun.'

Locke weighed her options. She still favored her chances.

'Aren't you listenin', you?' a voice asked from deeper in camp, and Locke was forced to crane her head to see where the black man kneeled with the rifle stock braced to his shoulder. In the dimness she hadn't noticed him kneeling there, but now she could see the starlight reflected off his sclera, his teeth, and the luminous highlights on his sneakers. Her chances had diminished drastically.

Locke held her sidearm out, allowing it to dangle with her index finger through the trigger guard.

'Good,' said the blond. 'Now let it drop.'

Locke dropped the pistol.

'Now get down on your knees and link your fingers behind your head.'

'OK,' Locke said, 'you've got me.'

She began lowering to her left knee.

Finally, Whyte fired.

With no idea who he'd shot at, Locke didn't waste time figuring it out. The sound of the shot would force a reaction from both the blond and the black guy, and seeing as a bullet didn't instantly hole her, she concurred they had flinched in response to the shot or witnessing the other taken out in bloody fashion. She dropped to her knee, even as she pivoted, and snatched at where her SIG hung on its sling. She primed it for action with swift professionalism, and was firing even before it had risen from the vertical. The submachine gun blared, muzzle flash lighting the scene like a firework display. She shot at the blond, who flung herself bodily to the ground on the far side of the fire, then continued pivoting and bullets slashed towards the black man. In the face of raining hell he fired back, but his bullet missed her by a mile, though it did throw off her aim. In the next second, Locke was up and she charged for the safety of the woods, shooting wildly behind her as she ran.

Bullets chased her, but she was between the tree trunks in seconds, and darting deeper into the foliage. She could only hope that now Whyte had gotten his act together and drop those shooting at her while they were lit up by their muzzle flashes.

TWENTY-THREE

The distant crack of the rifle halted Alicia Coleman in her tracks. Immediately another gunshot followed it, and soon there was a crackle of competing gunfire. The terrain had an effect of dampening sound, and for confusing the direction of its source, but she was under no illusion: there was a battle underway beyond the nearest ridge, at the field biologists' campground. She'd sworn the trio to secrecy about her, pulling them deep into her trouble, and this was where helping her had gotten them. They were under assault, but if the sounds of return fire were anything to go by they were putting up an admirable defense. However, it couldn't last; up against such dangerous foes there was only one way the battle could go.

Run away. Run away and leave them to their fate. While her hunters were engaged in assaulting the camp they were not nipping at her tail. She could leave, and be miles away and free of them while they took control of the camp. What more could any of the biologists tell them about her? They'd obviously concluded that she'd survived the plane crash, so attacking the biologists – why? To force some sort of confirmation from them? – seemed extreme. Perhaps the assumption was that she'd divulged to the biologists her reason for being on the plane, and they'd been deemed too dangerous to be allowed to speak about it. Had her hunters' mission changed to a cleanup of all possible threats to their employers?

'Just keep running,' she whispered under her breath. In her backpack the holdall and its contents were a heavy weight to bear. The sooner she could lighten her burden the better, but could it be any heavier than the weight of the three innocent souls she'd have to carry for the rest of her life?

'Keep running, Alicia,' she told herself, this time a little louder. Her mission was more important. If she were captured now, with the evidence she'd retrieved, everything would have been for nothing. *Keep running, get back to the car and drive away.* Once the evidence was in the right hands, those murderous bastards would be brought down with all the others. They'd be made to pay.

It was good advice, but nothing she could obey. With each thought she took another step, but it was towards the gunfight. How could she run away and leave innocent people to suffer the consequences of stumbling into her radius when there was a chance she could help them?

With each step she also picked up pace. Within a half dozen steps she was jogging, and then running, swiping a path through the brush with the entrenchment spade. It could be employed as a bladed weapon, but it grew too unwieldy so she cast it aside. She dug instead for her pistol, because only a fool took a blade to a gunfight. As she ran, following a trail cut out by the retrieval crew as they were led to the crash site by the biologists, she made better progress than if she plowed directly through the forest, but she found it didn't lead directly to the camp. Soon she was over the ridge, but there she cut into the woods, listening as the sounds of gunfire intensified. What the hell was going on ahead? It sounded as if all-out war was being waged – the chatter of an assault rifle had joined the racket, and she heard the cry of somebody mortally wounded, the howls of another torn between pain and grief.

A dim glow leaked between the trees. Sparks and flashes of light lit the canopy. Alicia slowed out of caution, moving more tentatively as she slipped between tree trunks. A fireball turned night to day and she had to look away to avoid being temporarily blinded. The assault rifle had fallen silent, but another rifle continued to add a staccato beat to the fight: it was the gun of a defender she assumed. Nearby she caught movement. It was the figure of a man, bulky and square-headed, and if not for the roaring campfire she wouldn't have noticed him at all. She turned towards him, bringing her pistol to bear, trying to decide if he was friend or foe. Out there in the darkness she believed him the latter, but she must be certain. Muzzle flare lit the man in a sequence of super bright flashes, and they were enough to recognize him by. He was the hunter who'd gotten out of the Ford driven by the redhead to check out the minivan parked outside the hotel at Medway. Immediately he crouched once more, and could barely be differentiated from the stump he sheltered behind. His raspy voice was lowered as he communicated with somebody else through a radio mike, but she zoned in on it, treading softly, never lowering her gun. Here she was in danger of the camp's lights painting her as a target.

Without warning the woods around her were plunged into darkness. There was still the glow of the fire, but it was diminishing now, and its touch didn't extend to her. From the camp she could hear only pained sobbing; the rifle had been silenced. Was she too late to help anybody, and should she listen to good sense and move back into the woods, disappear while she still had the opportunity? The decision was taken from her. Twenty feet away the man stood, as if he were invincible now that the cover of darkness was to his advantage. She remained still, and he'd no idea how close death loomed, she was just another dark figure cloaked by the night. He moved forward stealthily, but something must have caught his attention because he jerked to a halt, sighted down his barrel, fired twice in quick succession. He immediately followed his shots by stalking forward, and was almost between the trees at the edge of the camp. It was now or never if Alicia intended changing the tide of battle. Without further thought she lined up the man and fired. Her target side-on she aimed for his torso, beneath his extended arms and her bullets punched through his ribs, eliciting a harsh grunt with each impact. He didn't die instantly, but he'd no fight in him as he turned and faced her with a desperate expression briefly painted on his face by the next flash of her gun. This time he slumped down dead in the underbrush.

Her hand shook and nausea overwhelmed her, but Alicia fought down the urge to throw aside her weapon. Taking the life of another human being should never be taken lightly. It was the first time that she'd been forced to kill, and Alicia suspected that – if she survived – she'd spend many nights reliving her victim's intense look of sadness on her victim's face in troubled dreams, but for now she must put aside any regret. The man she'd shot had been in the act of terrorizing innocent victims, and given the opportunity could have gone on to slay them; she must tell herself that under the terrible situation his execution was justified. Plus, she must be prepared to kill again to save the lives of other innocents. She turned towards the camp, but the sounds of voices halted her. She took a knee, again feeling the weight of the backpack on her shoulders, and peered towards the only illumination in camp.

Beside the fire a tableau played out. She recognized the dark-haired woman as the leader of her hunters . . . and was again struck by her familiarity. She was hemmed in on two sides by a prettier blond, who held her revolver with an air of experience, and a kneeling black man whose clothing appeared to have been gleaned from a thrift store: the rifle he braced to his shoulder was the one she guessed had laid down defensive fire earlier. Almost at the blond woman's feet huddled a man in outdoorsy clothing, who Alicia thought was the head biologist, Jonathan Laird, sobbing in agony. Nearby, lying slumped on one side was the little bird-like woman Alicia recalled from the crash site, Elsa Carmichael, and it saddened her that she'd arrived too late to save her. Without doubt Elsa was dead. Further across camp, the dark-haired man she'd seen emerge from the woods near Brayton Lake tried to make himself small behind some fallen equipment, and near him another man was sprawled in the dirt, unmoving. There was no sign of the third biologist, the young undergraduate, Grant McNeill, who'd filmed her at the crash site, and who'd reluctantly given up his camera's memory card when she'd aimed her pistol at his head before she could reason their silence from them.

She'd no idea who any of the strangers were, but it took only seconds to work out the dynamic. The blond and black guy had fought to protect the others from Alicia's hunters, and that made them the lesser threat to her. For all she knew though they could be other hunters, dispatched by her enemies and in conflict with the first team. No, she decided, she could read goodness in them that didn't exist in the first team. They were here for another reason entirely and it wasn't to recover Alicia or the evidence she now carried. On that note, she hoped one or the other would put a bullet between the dark woman's flinty eyes and end things. Unfortunately, they were more intent on having the bitch lay down her weapon.

From somewhere at the front of camp a weapon fired, and as the sharp crack reverberated from the surrounding trees it caused a hellish reaction in camp. Her dark hunter let loose a murderous stream of bullets from a submachine gun clipped to her harness, and the blond woman had to dive for her life among the embers at the edge of the fire pit. The black man got off a single shot but it was off target and he had to scramble for his life as the SIG was turned on him, and then the dark bitch was hurtling for the cover of the trees. The blond was up in seconds, her first thought to press down Jonathan Laird who'd momentarily raised his head, and then she fired at the fleeing woman, and if Alicia was right, firing to miss, maybe in the hope the warning would be enough to halt the fleeing hunter. The black man also fired, but his intention was definitely to take the dark woman down, though his shots weren't dead-on. Alicia was sorely tempted to add her bullets to the volley, but from this distance they'd be wasted. Instead, she decided she'd done what she could, and began to back away, hoping to lose herself in the woods while chaos reigned.

Something hard and cold pressed into the flesh at the nape of her neck. 'Make one sound, you bitch,' hissed a woman's voice, 'and it'll be the last thing you ever do.'

TWENTY-FOUR

P o was at his most dangerous, his most uncompromising, when his loved ones were threatened, but he'd no qualms about unloading half a dozen bullets into a sumbitch shooting an assault rifle at him either. Two bullets in the shooter's body hadn't stopped him, and Po had to run for cover as the guy loosed a barrage of rounds in his direction. Keeping his head down would have been the sensible course of action, but once his switch was flipped Po was rarely sensible, if Tess's opinion was to go by. In any case, he knew that if he'd stayed put now, it would have only stalled the inevitable. The shooter wasn't alone, and wounded or not would have coordinated with the others to shoot every last one of them in camp to death. Po had taken the fight to the gunman, and in doing so had forced his would-be killer into a close quarters battle, alleviating the assault on Tess, Pinky, and the others. Targeting the assault rifle's muzzle flashes Po zigzagged his way through the woods, shooting and drawing fire, and finally found a home for another bullet in the guy's throat. Moving in, he stripped the assault rifle from lax fingers and shoved away Frank Lombardi's silenced pistol in his belt, then made a swift check for other weapons: there were none, but Po grabbed extra ammunition magazines and shoved them in his pockets. He took the head-mounted goggles off the guy and checked them out. They worked a treat, but Po felt they were unnatural, and worse than that they interfered with his peripheral vision, so he slung them away. It didn't occur to claim the dead man's phone or radio, and Po was already moving through the woods, relying on his natural stealth to approach the other shooters at the head of the camp when he thought one or the other could come in handy. It was too late to return to the body; he continued on because already the battle lines had shifted.

Thirty feet away a figure slipped as silently as he did between the trees. He was sorely tempted to try to blast the figure with the liberated assault rifle, but that would make him a target of the sniper, and currently the latter enemy was the most dangerous to those in the camp. Pinky was running disruption with the hunting rifle, but his ammunition was limited, and soon the sniper would be able to pick and choose his targets unhindered. Po must engage the sniper and trust his partner and best friend to defend the camp. His resolution to take on the sniper was instantly challenged, because from the opposite side another gunman joined the fray. But Tess won him a few moments: she must've found the bottle of bourbon that had been passed round at supper and dumped it on the fire because suddenly it roared and Po was glad he hadn't worn the night-vision goggles otherwise he'd have been blinded by the glare. Next all the lights went out. The attackers would be hard put to adjust to the sudden changes.

More shooting from the far side of camp was followed by an abrupt cessation. Po had to ignore what was going on back there, concentrate instead with singular purpose.

The low murmur of voices came to him, and he guessed that there was some sort of confrontation happening beyond the fire. If Tess, Pinky, or any of the others were limned in its glow, they'd be dead the next instant. He began a reckless jog, teeth clenched in anticipation of a sniper's bullet striking him down, hoping to draw fire at him.

His plan worked.

If he were a praying man, Po would've thanked God that he was up against a two-bit punk and not an experienced, trained marksman, because the sniper's shot was hurried, a response to Po's crashing advance through the undergrowth. The bullet snapped by his side, tugging at the material of his jacket, and striking a tree behind, but Po wasn't slowed. Po was less experienced with military grade weapons than his enemy though, and he too had made an amateur's mistake: he'd taken the assault rifle without checking how many bullets were left in the magazine. He pulled the trigger, and the Remington spat a single round before it was dry. His bullet missed too, although it caused the sniper to duck behind a fallen tree. He'd no time to reload. As the man bobbed up again, Po swirled the assault rifle around his head and hurled it at him. Po followed the flying rifle with a dive, even as behind him a battle roared anew in camp. He crashed into the sniper, and they rolled together, the M110 locked between them. Branches and rocks dug into Po's body as the gunman tried to ram his rifle up under his chin. Po wrenched his head aside as the gun went off. The muzzle was inches from his face, the explosion of superheated gases almost blinding him, but miraculously he'd dodged another bullet. Neither could hear a damn thing, but his opponent must be severely hindered because his face wasn't much further from the barrel when it fired.

They rolled in the dirt. Eyelids screwed, Po clawed for his pistol. It was jammed in his belt. While he tried to pull it free he could feel the gunman trying to wrench the M110 aside so he could bring its stock to bear as a club. Po forced his eyes open and found he could see. He ignored the pistol and instead swung an elbow into the gunman's face. The man kneed for Po's crotch but luckily only found his inner thigh. Po slammed him a second time with his elbow, this time connecting with the bony tip on the man's jaw. He felt strength flee the man, and they broke apart a few inches, except the gunman rallied quickly. He bucked like a landed fish, and this time tore free the sniper rifle. Immediately he struck with the butt at Po's chest, even as he kicked at Po to force them apart. A dull white agony rode Po's right thigh where a boot heel had found the nerve. The stock of the rifle came at him again, this time angling for his chin. Po batted it aside, with a slap of his palm that left it stinging. He scrambled, but so did his opponent and they both came up, legs splayed, bent at the waist. The guy jabbed once again at Po with the rifle stock, forcing him back on his heels, and a cold smile pulled at his lips: his rifle could now be reversed, and this time there'd be no dodging.

There was only one way Po could go. Forward. As the barrel swung towards him, he swooped almost eagle-like as he scuffed the earth with his knuckles, then he rose up again casting twigs and needles in his opponent's face. His hands never slowed, his left clasping the muzzle of the M110 and forcing it skyward as it flashed fire, while his right palm crashed under the man's chin. Po kept the momentum going, ramming a knee into the man's guts, taking him backwards and forcing his spine tortu-ously over the fallen tree trunk. Then Po was atop him, and his knee had transferred to the man's chest, pinning him long enough for his right hand to dart to the sheath in his boot. Three times he stabbed as his knife traveled the length of the gunman's body: groin, armpit, throat. The latter Po didn't release. He screwed the blade in place, opening veins and arteries and he felt a hot liquid gush over his hand, as spatters of arterial blood rained on his face and upper chest.

The man's death was imminent, but Po didn't release him until he felt the life fully ebb from his body. All tension leached from the three wounds and the man slumped over the log. Po finally withdrew his knife, wiped it clean on the guy's jacket and sheathed it. He studied the dead man . . . a stranger. Fate had thrown them together as enemies and only one of them could walk away alive; Po was grateful he was the one on his feet, moments ago it could have been a very different end to their woeful tale. He reached forward, took the man's lapels and eased him off the log onto his backside, and watched as the head flopped forward, his hands now crossed in his lap: he was less of a target for the birds that'd peck out his eyes. He'd slain the man, he didn't have to disrespect him afterwards.

That done he took stock. Their battle had been short but savage, and Po hadn't come out of it unharmed. He ached in several places, and when he checked how close the bullet had come to hitting his side he found more than his jacket holed: the bullet had nicked a strip of flesh out of his hide and he bled profusely. He wadded the bottom of his shirt over it; he wasn't going to bleed to death. His face stung from the close call and he knew the muzzle flash had burned him. Ironically the injury that troubled him most was the kick to his thigh: his leg was stiff, aching like a bitch, and it hindered his movement as he searched around, gathering the M110 and Remington. He searched the body and found a pistol in a holster under the man's jacket. If he had used the handgun at such close quarters the likelihood was he'd have won the short scuffle. Po took it, tucking it in his belt alongside the silenced pistol. Only then did he limp towards the camp, where everything had fallen silent. Silence, of course, did not mean the danger was over, but armed now and their enemies' numbers culled he and his companions were better equipped to repel it.

TWENTY-FIVE

S he should have obeyed her inner voice and ran away. Now look at what had happened. Captured, and with the evidence in her backpack. She'd made things easy for her hunters, when all she had to do was run and keep on running. *Damn it!*

Alicia eased out her hands, showing her sidearm. She dangled it loosely in her right hand. Without removing the barrel of her gun from the nape of Alicia's neck the woman stripped it from her hand, then tossed the gun into the underbrush. Alicia squinted sideways, noting where the gun fell, hoping that she could perhaps distract her captor and make a lunge for it again. The ease at which her captor had reached for her weapon, while keeping hers tight to Alicia's neck told Alicia an important fact: the woman was left-handed – or perhaps ambidextrous – to disarm her with such ease. Alicia surreptitiously transferred her weight to her opposite foot, readying to spin and control her captor's weapon.

'Don't,' warned the woman at a low whisper. Further explanation was unnecessary. She expected Alicia to attempt to disarm her, but it was clear she was ready for any move. Was she prepared to shoot Alicia dead though, so close to the others in camp, and draw their fire? Almost as if she'd read Alicia's mind, she whispered, 'You just killed my friend in cold blood. *Don't test me.* Take a step backwards, turn and then walk into the woods. I'll be right behind you.'

'Which direction?'

'The same way we just came in.' The woman nudged her with the gun, and Alicia complied, first stepping back, then turning, and following the same route through the woods she'd approached by.

So the woman had followed her here from the crash site? She must have been nearby after Alicia recovered the holdall, but hadn't gotten an opportunity to capture her when Alicia rushed towards the sounds of conflict. She could kick herself; she'd been so intent on helping the biologists that she'd neglected to check she wasn't being followed. After shooting dead the gunman she'd totally allowed her guard to drop and now she was a prisoner. She was fatigued, in almost constant pain; she should forgive herself for the lapse in attention but couldn't. She should have damn well run away!

But she would've no sooner run away than she could now forgive her lapse in discipline. The first was a matter of the heart, the second of the mind, and both were intrinsic parts of her. She said, 'After what's happened here tonight your employers are going to prison. They're finished. Whether you take me in or not isn't going to make a difference now.'

'I don't give a damn about my employers' liberty,' the woman spat, 'or whatever damn evidence you have against them. All I care about is that you shot Hubert like he was a sick dog. He was a friend, a good man, and he didn't deserve to die.'

'Bull shit! He was a scumbag who was trying to murder innocent people,' Alicia countered. 'He got exactly what he deserved.'

'So what gives you the right to decide who lives or dies?'

'Ask yourself the same question. It's why you're taking me out here in the woods, right? You're looking for a place you can execute me and leave before the people in the camp can catch up.'

'Believe me, after what you did to Hubert, I want nothing more than to see you punished. But I'm not going to kill you, not yet. Not unless you try anything stupid. I'm taking you to Locke: she can decide what happens to you.' Alicia felt the woman tug at her backpack, before she added, 'She wants what's in here. Once she has it, maybe she'll let me kill you then.'

'Locke's the dark-haired bitch?' Although she'd never personally come across Virginia Locke during her mission, Alicia knew of her reputation as a stone-cold operative, and now why her hunter had struck her as familiar. They'd met, years earlier, during basic agent training at Quantico. Locke's inclusion in this confirmed the reticence she'd had of approaching anyone in law enforcement. Virginia Locke – a fake legend designed and built for her by the Drug Enforcement Administration – was on a deep-cover assignment to investigate the movement of narcotics across two international borders. Tempted by the glitz, glamour, and reward of an international criminal ring, any agent was at risk of being turned. For some months now her handlers had feared her allegiance might have changed, which was why Alicia Coleman – also a fake legend – had been tasked by the DEA with infiltrating the same group without Locke's knowledge, to test the validity of intelligence being fed to them by their first deep-cover agent. To be fair to Locke, her role as hunter could partly be about Locke protecting her legend, and to her, chasing Alicia was necessary to do so. But that didn't excuse her murderous intention towards those in the camp. However deep an operative was undercover, it didn't give them *carte blanche* to murder with impunity. As far as Alicia was concerned, Locke had become so deeply entrenched in her legend there was no coming back from the monster she played.

Her captor didn't confirm her assumption about the dark-haired woman. There was no need. When Alicia accepted the assignment, she'd never believed that the two deep-cover operatives would be thrown into direct conflict, and yet here they were. It was a frightening scenario, not simply because she knew Locke was a dangerous adversary. If Locke learned she too was deep-cover DEA, the bitch would be able to discover her actual identity, and her daughters could be targeted as she'd feared. Alicia was estranged from her ex-husband and two children, but she still loved the latter two dearly. Locke wouldn't balk at using them to force her to hand over the evidence she'd gathered during her mission. She wondered about the others in Locke's team. When first she'd spotted them in Medway, she'd concluded they might be mercenaries – ex-military or law enforcement – and her opinion hadn't changed. Alicia guessed her captor was the red-haired woman who'd shared a car with Locke and the recently deceased square-faced guy, Hubert. Though she'd said she wouldn't shoot her *yet*, she had to assume the redhead was well trained, and as ruthless as Locke. In fact, by shooting Hubert she'd stung the redhead, who was aching for revenge . . . perhaps she was more dangerous than Locke in the moment.

She took care as she walked not to make any sudden movements that could be misconstrued as an act of rebellion and invite a shot. At the same time she absorbed her surroundings, and the terrain underfoot, waiting for an opportunity to turn it to an advantage and disarm the woman. The redhead couldn't shoot her close to the camp for fear of retribution from those within, but now they were a good hundred yards out, Alicia was unsure why the woman didn't simply kill her, take the backpack, and return to Locke with the evidence. In her shoes, anyone willing to kill in cold blood would do so, and the redhead's reticence gave Alicia hope.

But for muted conversation from camp, little noise traveled through the woods. The redhead's breathing was noisy to Alicia. Perhaps it was no louder than hers, but being so close she had fixated on it. She tried calculating the distance between them using each rasp as a guide, but it was an untrustworthy method. Alicia clambered over a tree trunk fallen across the path. As she moved on her captor called a halt: she was also straddling the trunk. Alicia sneaked a glance. Her vision had adapted to the gloom and she confirmed that her captor was the redheaded woman, and that she was also ungainly in this type of terrain. For a moment Red got hung up on the stub of a branch extending from the trunk, and she looked down, reaching to unsnag her trousers . . . her right shoulder was forward as she reached, gun in the left, partially obscured by her body. It was the moment Alicia had prayed for. Without telegraphing her intention she stepped back subtly, bending and loading up her right leg. As soon as her left boot settled in the earth she kicked out, her right heel slamming Red's shoulder. The kick was clean, delivered with desperate power, and it knocked Red over. The way she fell, she had to grab at the trunk to save from tumbling to the earth on the far side, but that left her with one leg extended awkwardly, and her gun hand swinging wildly for balance. Alicia considered leaping on her and taking her fully to the ground to wrestle with her for control of the gun. That'd be the wrong strategy. She did what her inner voice had extolled all along: she ran!

She couldn't stick to the path; Red would be up in a few seconds and would easily shoot her if she stayed between the trees. She broke through the foliage to the left, using the untamed underbrush as camouflage. She crashed through it, but Red didn't send a random bullet after her. Alicia heard a series of short curses as the woman struggled up and gave chase. The woman was reacting to outrage instead of good sense. Alicia kept going, trampling through waist-high shrubs, breaking a path through the lowest hanging boughs. She ran, yes, but not without purpose or direction. If she continued on the path Red was following, she'd be back at the ridge, below which was the crash site, but she surmised her captor intended to take her another way to some meeting place with Locke, probably to the northwest. Alicia ensured she raced southeast.

Her run took her obliquely through the forest, close to the rear of the camp. Through the gloom she spotted the lamps flicker to life again, and the geometric shape of tents began to take form among the randomness of nature. A flashlight stabbed the forest, but to her left. She was tempted to break off to the right, avoid the camp altogether, but Red was moving after her, and her pursuer would only have to cut to the right to shorten her lead. Alicia wondered at the consequences of such an action. She believed the woman incapable of cold-blooded murder, despite her anger at her friend's death. She couldn't take the chance; besides, maybe Red's reluctance to shoot before was because Alicia was more valuable as a hostage. Now that Alicia had taken that option away, Red might shoot and make do with snatching her backpack before the camp could be roused. Whoever had joined the biologists had done a half-decent job of protecting them from Locke's first assault; would they extend their assistance to her? She swung left in a tight arc and hurtled towards the tents.

A figure stood up sharply before her.

Alicia almost collided with a man, whose weapon was extended at her. In reaction she chopped at the man's wrist with the side of her hand, sweeping his weapon aside, and then shouldered into him. He grunted at the impact, folded around her shoulder and went down as sharply as he'd stood, but unfortunately not without tangling his legs with hers, and bringing her with him. She struck at him again, this time pounding a fist into his gut while she kicked to loosen her feet. She was part-way standing when she noted the glowing screen he'd dropped, and took a longer look at the man beneath her. His youthful features could be made out in the backwash from his tablet screen. Hers too must've been recognizable in the same glow because he croaked, 'Alicia, it's me, Grant! We met last time you were here!'

She frowned down at the young biologist. Her gaze traveled

to the weapon he'd aimed at her and she understood her mistake. It wasn't a gun but some kind of thermal scope. The youth had been plotting her run through the forest due to her overheated thermal signature. Quickly she spun around, checking for Red but she'd fallen silent, perhaps going to ground when hearing Alicia's brief scuffle. Curtly, Alicia ordered the biologist, 'Use that scope of yours and tell me if anyone's behind me.'

Grant McNeill struggled up to one knee, already sweeping the scope along Alicia's back trail. He came to a halt, checked the screen, and then adjusted the angle of the scope. 'There,' he breathed.

Alicia made a quick perusal of the screen.

Red must've taken cover behind the bole of a sturdy tree. All that Alicia could make out was a dim glow that was marginally brighter than the ambient temperature of the forest. But as she watched, Red couldn't resist poking out her head for a better view and on the tablet screen she lit up like a firecracker. Her left arm also flared as it came into view and Alicia shoved McNeill down in anticipation of a shot. It didn't come.

Behind Alicia there were footsteps and she jerked around. A huge man approached from camp, watching her warily. She was tempted to run, but McNeill's ease in his company assured her he wasn't a foe. They exchanged brief nods and then his gaze skipped between the picture on the tablet and the corresponding woodland fifty yards distant. He brought up a hunting rifle and loosed a single round. The sound of the woman crashing back through the wood was all Alicia needed to tell Red was running for her life.

'You must be the mysterious plane crash survivor, you,' said the man in the strangest of dialects.

Alicia looked from him to the young biologist, frowning at his lack of discretion because she was pretty certain McNeill was the one who'd given up her secret, before returning her attention to the big guy. He held his rifle at the ready, and yet there wasn't a hint of menace in his bearing. 'That'd be me,' she admitted, 'but why'd you want to know?'

He made a grandiose nod of his head. 'People are dying, good and bad, and it's all to do with you, girl. That makes you kinda interesting in my book.'

TWENTY-SIX

Tess tended to think she was a levelheaded person, not usually the type to panic under fire, but there'd been a moment there when she'd feared the worst and only her natural instincts had saved her life. When she smashed the bottle of bourbon on the fire, causing it to flare up, it was with the intention of confounding the sniper, stopping him from using his scope, but the tactic had worked in her favor only for a few seconds. Shortly after, the fire's illumination had become her enemy, and she was fortunate not to have been killed when she and Pinky had confronted the dark-haired woman who'd strode into camp full of confidence and the desire to kill. How she'd survived being shot to death by the sniper would have to wait for explanation, but it was only a reckless dive into the ashes at the edge of the fire that'd saved her when the woman let loose with her machine pistol. If the woman had taken a second or two longer to aim, Tess would be dead. While the woman's attention was turned to Tess, Pinky swung round his rifle and shot at her. She'd been forced to shoot wildly to keep both their heads down, while retreating to the woods.

Singed, clothing soiled with ashes, and her ears ringing, Tess had taken a few potshots after the fleeing assassin but had come nowhere close to dropping her. Pinky's shots hadn't been successful either. Tess had moved to cover Jonathan Laird again, hushing the biologist who was torn between his personal misery and the murder of Elsa Carmichael. Tess daren't take her attention off the fleeing woman yet, because there was always the possibility she'd return, or try again to shoot from the perimeter of camp. Her eardrums were still compressed from the recent volleys of gunfire, and her pulse was racing, so it was difficult pinpointing any movement through the woods but she soon grew satisfied that the woman had hightailed it out of there.

'You OK, pretty Tess?'

'I'm OK, Pinky.' She thought of her singed hair and the ashes staining her clothes. 'Though not so pretty, right now.'

'Ha! That flush in your cheeks only adds to your allure.'

Tess offered a strained smile. Usually his charm worked on her, but how could she dredge up more than the weakest of smiles when so many people had died? Elsa's forlorn corpse drew her attention, and Tess's eyelids slid shut as she shuddered in regret. She looked up again, reminded that another had died. Frank Lombardi cradled his young cousin in his arms, and Tess was assured that even a man she'd previously thought of as a cold-hearted criminal had feelings, and grieved for those close to him. Tess was sickened: Carlo had been shot ruthlessly by the unseen gunner on the east side of camp. He was a terrified youth running for his life and he'd been gunned down with impunity.

What'd become of his murderer? The last she knew, Po had gone after him.

Her heart hitched in her chest. To hell with the shooter, what had become of her man?

As the dark-haired woman fled, her SIG roaring, and Tess leaped for her life into the fire pit, she heard more gunfire from the front of camp. Tess hoped that it had been in response to an attack from Po – it meant he'd survived his encounter with the first shooter with the assault rifle, but what had been the outcome of his next battle? The sniper hadn't tried again to shoot her or Pinky, which gave her hope that Po had forced him to retreat. But if that was the case, then where was Po? Had he pursued the sniper, or changed tactic? Somebody had stopped the shooter on the opposite side of camp, but who? Po couldn't have been in two places at once. The only person unaccounted for was Grant McNeill, though Tess didn't believe he'd the fortitude, or the weaponry, to take on a gunman. Except, he must have been the one to turn off the lights. That meant he'd made it to the generator, but where had he gotten to after that? For all she knew he too was dead.

Pinky moved away, standing over Frank Lombardi, his rifle a menacing presence, but even Pinky wore a look of regret at the youth's death.

'I'll watch him,' Tess said. 'Can you check where McNeill

has gotten to? Last I saw him he was tinkering with his thermal imager over that way.'

Pinky nodded, relieved not to have to listen to Frank grieving for his cousin. It was difficult not to feel pity for the man, despite what Frank had come here to do. Tess stood with her revolver hanging loosely by her side. She was unsure if it still held any ammunition, but made no attempt to check. Frank wasn't a threat to them now. Jonathan Laird had also stumbled over to Elsa. He too had pulled a corpse into his lap and was crying over his loss. Tess had gained the impression that Elsa was infatuated with the man, but had thought her affection unrequited: apparently Laird had held similar designs on Elsa, but now it was too late for either to act. Momentarily Laird had forgotten that he was missing fingers, but his injury must be tended to soon or he'd be joining the roll call of the dead if infection took hold.

Tess had traveled here to substantiate a rumor, and instead she was standing waist deep in death. Out there in the woods, she suspected the numbers of dead or wounded outnumbered even those in camp. The lamps flickered on. Pinky, having checked the area of the generator for McNeill, had used his savvy to light up the camp to aid his search. He waved a flashlight in the air, then turned to probe the darkness where Tess indicated she'd last seen McNeill using the thermal imager. She checked on Frank again – he hadn't moved from Carlo's body – then on Laird. Her attention was then snatched to the head of the camp when she caught movement there. Her heart had made a leap earlier, now it almost swelled to the capacity of her chest as she recognized the tall figure limping into camp. Po carried an assault rifle in his left hand, and a longer sniper rifle over his shoulder. He spotted her in the dim glow from the fire, his forehead creasing at her disheveled state, but he smiled in relief when he saw she was otherwise unharmed.

Tess waited for Po to approach and sling down the liberated weapons to the earth, before she caught him in a brief hug.

'Thank God you're all right,' she murmured alongside his ear, then sought his mouth with hers.

'My leg hurts like a sumbitch,' Po told her after they kissed, 'but I've gotten outta this better than most.'

He checked out her singed hair and the smudges of ash on her forehead. 'You get burned?'

'Not much. I can't complain. Poor Elsa . . .'

'Yeah,' he intoned. He also took stock of Laird's hand. 'He's gonna need some help with that.'

'There must be a medical kit around here some place . . .' She looked pointedly at Frank Lombardi.

Po took out a pistol from behind his back. 'I've got him covered if you want to take a look.'

Tess, as had Pinky before her, was relieved to be doing something other than listen to the sounds of grieving. She crouched alongside Laird, consoling him, but also urging him to follow her to the mess tent. Laird was reluctant to leave Elsa but it was as if his pain and shock returned at once, and he let out a different-sounding wail. By the time Tess helped him lie Elsa down, then assisted him across the camp, Laird barely had the strength to stand.

After rooting around, she discovered a fully stocked medical kit. The injuries the biologists usually contended with were minor cuts and abrasions. When Tess was a sheriff's deputy she'd gained valuable experience in treating injuries, some as traumatic as Laird's. Suddenly she couldn't think straight. A series of flashbacks sent her back to when she'd almost lost her hand after a robber desperate to escape had chopped her wrist with a hunting knife. Back then she'd been on the verge of blackout through shock, and she couldn't have saved herself. Luckily her patrol partner had a clearer head and he'd shot the robber before he could strike a killing blow. Tess gave herself a mental shake: right now, she must be the one with the clear head. Laird's injury must be dressed, and she must also be of a mind that the danger wasn't over, not while the dark-haired woman and who knew how many other enemies were still out there in the woods.

A rifle barked on cue.

Laird almost dropped to his knees in terror, while Tess sought protection behind stacked equipment crates. When there was no more gunfire she rose up tentatively, and craned to check what was going on. Nearby Po had also come to attention, having snatched up his pistol, and she could tell from his stance that he fully intended protecting Frank Lombardi as much as anyone

else. He gave her a meaningful look, and she shrugged her
bewilderment. Seconds later the mystery of the rifle shot was
solved when Pinky strode back into camp, leading before him
the missing biologist, and a small, thirty-something woman
carrying a cumbersome backpack. The woman was a stranger
to Tess, but she knew exactly who she was. This was 'Alicia',
and the reason why so many people had died and been injured
in the past few minutes. Tess was unsure if she wanted to embrace
the woman, promise her she'd help, or punch her in the face.

TWENTY-SEVEN

Alicia sensed there was something wrong before the Cessna
172 Skyhawk had even taken off from a corporate airstrip
north of Quebec City and it had nothing to do with the
plane's mechanical integrity. The flight was a short one, due to
land at Portland Jetport in a little under an hour, and apart from
an overnight bag and a holdall she toted, Alicia had boarded with
little luggage. Her concern over her traveling companions was
spiked when the copilot, Claude something-or-other, acting as if
he was a steward, attempted to wrest the holdall from her on the
pretense of assisting her to board: he'd never done so on previous
flights she'd taken with this crew. She'd held on to it, put on an
affronted air and told him she was perfectly capable of carrying
her own bags, thank you. She'd received a stern glare in response,
and she was positive he was about to demand he stow her bags,
but then Claude's eyes had flicked around, and he nodded, coming
to some other decision. Alicia was the sole passenger. She placed
her overnight bag between her feet, the holdall on the seat next
to hers, in reaching distance, and strapped in. Her overeager
steward climbed into the copilot's seat, and leaned across to
converse in whispers with the pilot, who she knew only as 'Foy.'
For some reason Foy's back grew rigid and she noted the flush
of blood brightening his neck. Right then and there she should
have made an excuse and fled the plane, but out on the strip of
asphalt stood her driver. He rested his backside on the front door
of his car, arms folded across his chest, face set in a grim rictus.
Not for a second did she believe he'd hung around to wave her
off; his presence was to ensure she didn't get back off the plane.

She'd heard an unsubstantiated rumor. A bagman suspected
of skimming cash off the top of his collections was allegedly
drugged and taken up in a plane and dropped from several
thousand feet into the frozen wilderness beyond Saguenay. The
same punishment could be planned for her. She was extremely
nervous as the plane climbed, and only felt slight relief when it

didn't detour towards the polar circle, but banked over the Saint Lawrence River and continued its scheduled route towards the US border. It was dark, the only landmarks the pinpoints of civilization below. The Cessna continued into the States, very possibly monitored by Border Control, but with no reason to raise any alarm, as this was a scheduled flight repeated twice weekly. Alicia noticed the deviation in route only when ahead the horizon became a tract of impenetrable darkness. Instead of taking a beeline for Portland, Maine, the Cessna curved out towards the Allagash wilderness as if its destination was in New Brunswick, and for an unspecified reason the Cessna dropped steadily in altitude.

She asked what was going on, but was resolutely ignored. Foy and Claude communicated by way of headsets, but the noise inside the plane wasn't such that she couldn't hear, except they continued to converse in whispers, and more than once Claude turned around in his seat to squint at her. His gaze slipped towards where she'd placed the holdall on the spare passenger seat. The plane descended further. She unclipped her seat belt, reached across and grabbed the bag. It was as if the action was the spark that set Claude on fire. He gave a wordless shout, and lurched up, twisting quickly to grab at both the holdall and Alicia. Foy's head snapped between the two as they grappled for the bag. Then he was bending down, and from somewhere between the seats he dragged a pistol. This was no pressurized cabin, but the discharging of a firearm was still incredibly dangerous: perhaps he only meant to threaten her with it. Alicia got under Claude's groping arms, and she lunged to tackle Foy's wrist. The gun fired. Where the bullet ended up Alicia didn't know, but at least it wasn't in her. She shouted in alarm as she tried to wrestle the gun out of the pilot's hand, and then Claude had latched onto her hands and the threesome were engaged in a contest for the gun. Another bullet exploded through the cabin, and Alicia fell back against her seat, stunned by its proximity.

Claude had the gun. He aimed it at her, cussed blue murder in French – somehow his curses sounded singsong, unlike the coarser Anglo-Saxon cuss words her ears were more accustomed to, and less effective. He hollered instructions at her. Give him the holdall. What else? Was he ordering her to jump or he'd

shoot? *What kind of ridiculous warning is that?* Alicia kicked
out with both heels into the back of Claude's chair. He'd gotten
himself twisted around, so that he was half in, half out of it. The
backrest slammed his extended right forearm, knocking the barrel
of the gun aside, and again Alicia lunged for control of it. She
threw all of her weight into the backrest, jamming Claude
between the seat and the instrument panel, and they both wrestled
for control of the pistol. The gun fired a third time, and Foy
slumped over the control yoke. The Cessna nosedived towards
the forest canopy below.

Claude slammed her face with his elbow, breaking her teeth.
Alicia fell back into her seat, hands cupping her jaw, moaning
in agony, but only for a moment: Claude had control of the gun
and she'd only seconds to live. On instinct, she ducked and
threw her shoulder into the back of his chair. Claude shot again
and she felt the bullet pass by her skull to end up drilling into
the bulkhead. Mouth filled with blood, Alicia screamed in frustration and fear as she lurched up and snaked an arm around
Claude's throat. She throttled him, but he barely gave her notice.
The plane was plummeting towards the vast blackness below.
Foy was dead, a bullet through his skull, and Claude was the
only person capable of saving their lives now. As he wrenched
free, she fell backwards, driven by the forces of gravity on her
body. Alicia gasped out droplets of blood even as Claude
scrambled to take control of the second yoke.

He almost saved the plane. Rearing back on the yoke, he
pulled up the Cessna's nose, and it would have soared clear but
for one particularly tall tree. The Cessna's landing gear struck
branches, which dragged on the wheels before they tore loose.
The nose dipped again, propeller thrashing the uppermost
branches of other trees to kindling. The engine cut out.

Terrific, unimaginable forces took hold of Alicia's body as the
Cessna plowed a track through the branches of trees seemingly
intent on dragging them to the ground. The plane shuddered,
screamed, giving up pieces of its body. Out of her sight the tail
was ripped off. Alicia felt the entire passenger compartment
shift, and then the plane was surfing deeper atop the branches,
slowed but not yet ready to halt. The wings tore free and Alicia
closed her eyes in anticipation of the final impact. Never had she

heard sounds as loud as those that surrounded her. It swallowed the scream of terror that erupted from her throat. Claude's cries of defeat added to hers but they too were engulfed by the greater cacophony. The plane juddered, a behemoth in its death throes.

Immediately a weird sense of peace enveloped Alicia. She was about to die and there was nothing more she could do to stop it. Why rail any longer against the inevitable? Incredibly the holdall had ended up back in her lap. She drew it into her arms and hugged it lovingly to her chest, a surrogate for her daughters she'd never see again.

Glass and metal exploded around her. The passenger door was sheared clean away. Behind her the bulkhead opened its maw and sucked her backwards out of her disintegrating seat. Alicia had no sense of falling at first. Her body drifted feather-light and she experienced clarity of vision that was astounding – each nugget of glass was a tumbling, scintillating diamond she felt she could reach for and grasp, each twisted piece of metal a ribbon of gossamer. She struck a branch and the illusion passed. Everything grew chaotic; sight, sound and pain became one, she suffered a thousand bruising impacts as she was spun and jolted and turned over time and again. She hit an embankment; luckily it sloped steeply and in the same direction she plummeted. Her body finally came to rest, but her mind continued its riotous tumble for what seemed an eternity afterwards.

She'd climbed to all fours before she was conscious of doing so. Around her leaf litter fell from above, among it smaller pieces of torn metal. The Cessna must have caromed to earth while she was still dazed because the only sound now was the patter of detritus falling on her back. She pushed to her knees, afraid to open her eyes in case she was in hell. She was in pain everywhere, no spot more painful than any other, so she felt she could still move, except she was too afraid to try in case by moving she'd undo the final bits of glue holding her together and shatter into a million pieces. Yet she must. She pried open gummy eyelids, and she was blind. No. Not blind, only enveloped by the darkness of a wild forest at night. Her mouth was equally gummy and tasted of copper. By concentrating on it, her mouth immediately became the source of her worst pain, and it flashed through her in a wave of phosphorous bright agony that caused her to cry out.

She was standing, using a tree for support. Her knuckles were rubbed raw, as were her fingertips. She stood alongside the trail she'd torn down the embankment, a scar in the earth that stood out as a paler shade of gray against the hillside. She began the climb, unsure at that point why, but knowing only that she must. Her struggle was titanic, but then she was at the top and she collapsed in relief as she found the holdall. She hauled it into her embrace. It wasn't a surrogate for her children any longer, it was exactly what it was, the key that'd convict those who'd ordered her thrown to her death from the plane.

Smoke and the stench of aviation fuel rode the air. She hauled her body the final few yards to the top of the embankment, collapsed there once again. How long she lay there she'd no concept of. Then she was moving again, the holdall hooked over one arm, and the stink grew stronger. In the darkness were flashes of dim color, where dry bark had been ripped from tree trunks to show the moist innards. She was tacky with resin and her own blood from myriad scratches and cuts. Her foot scuffed something from under a pile of forest litter. The chances of tripping over the pistol used shortly before by Claude to try to force her from the plane were astronomically small, and yet there it was at her feet. She stooped and retrieved it, knowing that there was reason for finding it. She peered between shattered tree trunks, and there was the cockpit of the Cessna, bellied up against a pile of broken boughs, barely recognizable now as the plane she'd taken flight in. She weighed the gun in her hand. She'd survived, and so might have Claude. She staggered on with single intent, and it was moments before she realized the flashing of lights ahead had nothing to do with the crash.

There were people, and in her dazed state she couldn't discount them as others sent to kill her.

It was a man and woman, torches on their heads that blinded her as they swung around at her clattering approach. Blinking at the intrusion of light she raised the pistol. 'Hold it,' she snapped.

'We . . . we're only trying to help,' the man croaked in dismay as his gaze settled on the gun.

She snorted, exhaling blood from her nostrils, a shower of red droplets in their torchlight.

'I don't need your damn help. Now move aside, before somebody gets killed.'

'*You* are hurt,' the woman pointed out. She was tiny by comparison to the man at her side.

'I'm not the one you need to worry about.' Alicia gave a sharp swipe of the gun barrel and the pair moved aside.

Alicia aimed the pistol at the shapes inside the crumpled cockpit. She had to brace a hand on the sill of the missing door. Claude's corpse was nearest her, looking largely untouched by his death, but she could tell by the way his chest surrounded the control yoke that it had crushed his ribcage, making Jell-O of his innards, his heart had probably been pushed up into the back of his throat. Foy was dead before the impact, and it was as if fate had conspired to hide the fact: shot in the head, the evidence had been obliterated by the spearing branches that'd destroyed his skull, and rammed through his body. Unless anyone searched specifically for a gunshot wound, they'd never notice it among the immense traumas he'd suffered.

Alicia regarded the couple. Then, without warning she sat down hard on her backside, the gun hanging loose between her thighs. The couple started forward, and Alicia's head jerked up. They halted. She ignored them as a third figure appeared, a young man with a dusting of whiskers who aimed a small video camera at her.

'Turn that off,' Alicia warned him.

The young man only gawped at her.

Alicia found the strength to lift her pistol. 'If you know what's good for you, you'll stop recording me right now and hand me the memory card.'

TWENTY-EIGHT

Alicia Coleman's survival verged on miraculous, not only because she'd walked away from a plane crash but also because men were already trying to slay her before it went down. Tess was contemplative as Alicia had narrated her tale, but by the end of it she no longer wanted to thump the woman, she felt only the urge to help her bring down her enemies.

'Those men were under orders to drop you out here where your remains would likely never be found. What kind of psychos order anyone to do such a thing?'

'The type of psychos I was investigating.'

'You're a Fed, right?'

'I think you already know I am, Tess.'

'Drug Enforcement Administration?' Tess glanced at the backpack Alicia had kept close to hand once the briefest of introductions had been made, wondering what was inside. Tess had invited the woman to join her while she field-dressed Jonathan Laird's injured hand: it gave them both an opportunity to explain their presence in the north woods.

'Undercover, I was inserted into a ring suspected of transporting narcotics from Central America across two borders into Canada,' Alicia explained as she observed Tess bandaging Laird's hand. Po and Pinky were on guard duty, while a stunned Grant McNeill had retreated to the sanctuary of his monitors as he absorbed the news of Elsa's death. 'Initially I was tasked with verifying intelligence fed to the agency by a long-term DEA transplant called Virginia Locke – you've just met *her*.'

'That was the crazy bitch that tried slaughtering everyone in camp? She's DEA too?'

'She's been suspected of going rogue for some time; I think her actions here speak volumes.'

'Yes, I think we can agree on that. What's in the bag, Alicia?'

The backpack was at Alicia's side. She reached and dragged it closer, placed a hand protectively on the flap. Alicia pondered for a few seconds, wondering how much she could trust Tess and must've decided that truth was the best policy. 'Through digging into the veracity of Locke's intel, I uncovered more than my bosses could've dreamed of. In here's the key to evidence proving that local government officials, cops, and business people on both sides of the US and Canadian border are involved in the transportation and distribution of cartel narcotics. It's become apparent that I didn't cover my tracks sufficiently enough and my snooping was discovered.'

'Why'd they allow you to get on a plane if they suspected you of carrying evidence against them? Why not just take it from you up in Canada?'

'Maybe because they already had a tried-and-tested method for making their problems disappear. I was never meant to make it to Portland. Claude was supposed to take my holdall off me, and I was supposed to be thrown from the Cessna, but I fought back and the flight crashed.'

'I still find it hard to believe you walked away from a plane crash,' Tess said.

'I've thought the same thing every morning I've woken up since. Maybe I was just incredibly lucky; the trees slowed the plane enough so that when I fell out I wasn't killed. The branches I fell through, and then the slope I skidded down, dissipated most of the impact.' Alicia shrugged in disbelief. 'Who can say what might've been the outcome if I'd fallen a second earlier or later than I did?'

'Yeah, I'd say you had luck on your side,' Tess said. 'I think some of it might've rubbed off on us: how Locke's team didn't slaughter us all when they had the advantage, I'll never know.'

Jonathan Laird snatched his hand from hers. She'd been perfunctorily going through the motions of dressing his wounds while engaged in conversation with Alicia. 'How can you say we were lucky when poor Elsa was *murdered*?' he snapped.

Abashed, Tess glanced to the tent where Po and Pinky had carried Elsa and Carlo Lombardi, and respectfully covered their bodies, employing the unused sleeping bags from their backpacks as death shrouds. 'I'm sorry if that sounded insensitive,' Tess said to the biologist. 'You're right. We weren't lucky, but things could've been much worse, and that's why we must get moving soon. Locke has tried killing us once already, and now that Alicia has joined us, I'm certain she's going to try to finish what she started.'

He glared daggers at Alicia. 'I wish we never agreed to help you. This is your damn fault!'

Alicia bowed her head. 'I'm sorry for what happened to your friend. You're right. I'm partly responsible for Elsa's death. I shouldn't have put any of you in danger like this, and I should've done more to protect you after I did. I warned you to keep silent about me because it might attract dangerous people and—'

Shaking his head savagely, Laird jolted upright and stormed away, heading towards the mess tent, where Elsa's body was laid out. Alicia opened her mouth to offer another condolence, but Tess shook her head gently: Laird needed time to come to terms with what had happened, and no amount of apologies would soothe him just then. Instead, Tess prompted other answers from Alicia. 'After you survived why not just contact your DEA handlers and be brought in safely?'

Alicia placed a hand on her backpack again. 'Like I said, I discovered that several corrupt cops and Feds are involved, and I've no idea how deeply embedded some of them are. For all I know, Virginia Locke isn't the only DEA agent involved. I couldn't take the chance of reaching out to somebody who might hand me over to the people who want me dead. Worse than that, I was afraid my true identity would be discovered, and my daughters targeted. I didn't walk away from that plane crash untouched; I was injured, and desperate. I was too weak and in pain, and needed to hide in order to heal first, so I buried the evidence and begged Laird and his team to keep my secret until I could return and recover it.' She shook her head morosely. 'If McNeill had kept his mouth shut none of this would've happened. Instead I've had Locke's team dogging my trail the past couple of days, and then this . . . this *atrocity* happened.'

'I can help bring you in,' Tess offered. 'I work indirectly with the Portland District Attorney's office.'

'When first we spoke you introduced yourself as a private investigator. You were sent here to hunt me down?'

'Not the way that Locke's hunting you. I was only engaged by an insurance company to investigate the rumor . . . oh, shit!'

Tess hadn't considered it before, but she'd just realized that the same criminals that owned the plane probably controlled the insurance company. Had she inadvertently been working for the same monsters that'd ordered Alicia thrown to her death from an airplane, and who'd sent Locke in all guns blazing to wipe out everyone in the camp? 'Listen, whoever's behind this, they don't own my boss, Emma Clancy, and they don't own the DA. I can help bring you in safely, and from there ensure the evidence is secured and only disseminated to the right people. In return, you can help me get Laird and McNeill out of here safely.'

'Who are the dead guy and the one your men have zip tied?'

'Long story,' Tess replied.

'You just sat through mine,' Alicia countered, 'I should do the same with yours.'

The problem was, Tess was unsure how much she should impart to a federal agent: Pinky's criminality could come back to bite him if she shared his past. Then again, Pinky had made no bones about his past with Jonathan Laird's team, and she knew how easily they'd spilled Alicia's secret. She said, 'Pinky Leclerc is in a position not too dissimilar to yours. He's a good person being chased by bad guys. The man tied up, and his cousin – the young man lying alongside Elsa – came up here to claim the bounty on his head.'

Alicia wasn't overly surprised by the admission. She knew now the reason behind the dark-haired man's furtive actions that time she'd spotted him. Perhaps her own situation trumped Pinky's because she merely nodded in acceptance and her gaze slipped to Po. 'What about that guy?'

'What about him?' Tess replied defensively, raising a smile from Alicia.

'Oh, I get it. He's *your* guy, eh?'

'Yes. He's my fiancé.'

'He managed to take out two heavily armed attackers single-handed: he's a good man to have around, I bet.'

'The best.'

'Does he know how to use those?' She was referring to the M110 sniper rifle and the Remington assault weapon taken from their ambushers and stacked in reach. Po had also dumped the spare magazines and a handgun liberated from one of the shooters, being already burdened with the silenced pistol taken from Frank Lombardi.

'He isn't conventionally trained, if that's what you're asking?'

'I didn't take him as military or law enforcement, yet he knows his stuff in a fight.'

'Skills taught to him during a tough life,' Tess said, and that was all she'd say for now.

'What about you, Tess? I get an ex-cop vibe from you.'

'I was a sheriff's deputy.'

Alicia nodded. 'You can handle a gun. I've already seen Pinky shoot so trust he knows his stuff, too. Between the four of us we should be able to protect the other three. That's if you intend taking your prisoner out with us. Wouldn't blame you if you decided to leave him here, tied to a tree until we can send back reinforcements to arrest him.'

'Frank's coming with us.'

'He could slow us down.'

'Then we'll move at his speed.'

'Whoever's tasked with guarding him can't also watch for Locke or her people.'

'I'll keep an eye on him. Between you, Po and Pinky, we should have the others covered.' Tess weighed their options a second time. 'Po already killed two of them, and you shot another. Pinky said he only shot above the head of another of Locke's people and she escaped. We've no real idea about how many are out there in the woods, but I'm guessing it's just the two women now.'

'Yeah, of those I've seen to date, there's only Locke and Red left. If there were more we'd have known about it before now. We should get moving before they can consolidate their position and stop us getting to the vehicles.'

'Yeah, they might try another ambush en route.' Tess exhaled sharply. 'What about your vehicle? It can't be far away?'

Alicia gave an unsure wave of a hand towards the south. 'It's about five miles that way. But it's no good to us. There's room for five of us at a push, not seven,' she glanced at Pinky, 'and there's a guy here who might need a couple of seats to himself.'

Tess raised a finger in sudden epiphany. 'Locke had Laird's

sat phone destroyed to stop us calling in the cavalry. But how was her team communicating with each other?'

'That's a good point, Tess. We should check the bodies.'

Alicia rose to her feet, and was about to turn towards the woods. She halted, stooped and dragged up the backpack that she shrugged into. It was apparent she didn't trust its security to anyone else. She next stooped and selected the Remington assault weapon, slapped in a fresh magazine, primed it and seemed satisfied.

'Wait up,' said Tess. She also checked her revolver and found only one live shell left in the cylinder. She beckoned over Po.

'Whassup?' he asked, as he eyed Alicia's assault rifle.

'Those men you fought, did you notice if there was any comms equipment on them?' Tess asked.

'I recall they were wearing throat mikes. I searched 'em both, but I was lookin' for weapons not radios.'

'Walkie-talkies won't be much use to us out here, not to reach the outside world, but at least we could listen in if Locke uses them to communicate with Red,' Alicia offered.

'I was hoping to find another sat phone. We'll check the man Alicia shot,' said Tess, 'will you go check the others?'

'F'sure. I'll let Pinky know the plan, he's gonna be the only able-bodied man in camp till we get back.'

'There's always McNeill,' Tess reminded him.

'Nah,' Po countered. 'The kid should go with you guys and use his heat-seeking gizmo to check out the lay of the land for enemies.'

'There are two of us to watch each other's backs, he should go with you.'

Po squeezed out a smile. 'Y'know I work best alone, Tess.'

Before Tess could argue, Po limped off; Pinky's ears pricked up as Po ran the plan by him in a southern patois nobody from north of the Mason–Dixon line would follow. Being the last armed man in camp, Pinky stood to attention; Frank Lombardi huddled at his feet, still solemn at his young cousin's demise. Tess considered telling Jonathan Laird where she and Alicia were going, but he was kneeling alongside Elsa's shrouded body within the tent, and safely out of sight of a sniper. She beckoned McNeill to join them.

He came, red-eyed, but equipped with his thermal scope, and, Tess noted, the hatchet discarded earlier by Elsa tucked through his belt. She never intended forcing the blame game on him, but McNeill seemed to have concluded that if he'd kept his lips sealed about Alicia's survival then none of this would have happened, and Elsa would still be alive. Perhaps he'd picked up the axe in some hopeful act of atonement, using Elsa's hatchet to focus his mind.

'Scan the woods for any heat signatures,' Tess told the youth.

He did as asked. Shook his head when no warm-blooded figures showed up. 'I've been watching the monitors,' he added, 'none of our cameras have been tripped again. We should be safe to go.'

'You sit tight here,' Tess said. 'Holler if you see anything.'

Alicia led her unerringly to where she'd shot the square-faced gunman dead. It was instantly apparent that they'd been beaten to the body. His weapon was gone, as was any radio or phone he might've been carrying.

'It had to have been Red,' Alicia whispered. She was the woman chased off by Pinky. Instead of running for her life though, the red-haired woman must have circled back to where her colleague had fallen and stripped him of his weapon and comms equipment. Whether that was through her initiative or by order of Virginia Locke, Tess thought Po was probably wasting his time searching the two men he'd fought as they'd probably also been stripped. There'd be no phone and no cavalry charging to the rescue. Bile burned up her throat.

'Let's get back to the others,' Tess urged.

'One moment.' Alicia strode further out into the woods, followed by Tess. She crouched over scuffmarks in the dirt barely discernible in the darkness, peering to her right. Tess wondered what the hell she was up to, but the woman began rooting around in the underbrush and came up with a semi-automatic pistol she must have thrown there earlier. She handed it, butt first to Tess. 'You must be short on ammo for that revolver. We're going to need all the extra firepower we can bring along.'

TWENTY-NINE

P o was back from his forage by the time Tess and Alicia returned from the woods. His nonplussed expression confirmed what Tess had already assumed: no phones, no radios. While she'd been busy catching up with Alicia's tale, Locke or her last remaining helper must have snuck to the corpses of their colleagues and stripped them of both.

'Their night-vision goggles were gone too,' Po said. 'Not that we need 'em.'

Pinky had swapped the hunting rifle for the M110 – there was more ammunition for it – and had passed the rifle back to Laird, who was in no shape to fire it, but could carry it over his shoulder for when it was needed by one of the others.

Tess checked on Laird. His face was downcast, his lips set in a tight line and his shoulders rounded. He wasn't in a fit state to lead them back to their vehicles, but they had McNeill for that. Also, Po had become acquainted with their surroundings and could probably lead them with as much confidence as either biologist could.

McNeill joined them, still carrying his thermal scope and hatchet. He stared momentarily at the mess tent, where the shrouded bodies of Elsa and Carlo were obvious. Tess clasped his biceps and gave them a reassuring squeeze. 'I swear we'll come back for them.'

'Unless the bears get to them first,' Laird muttered in desultory fashion. 'I'm not happy about leaving Elsa behind like this.'

'And what about Carlo, you asshole?' Frank Lombardi piped up. 'Is my cousin just fuckin' bear food to you?'

'I think the difference between them is patently obvious,' Laird countered.

'How? Carlo was a kid, not a dog turd you stood in.'

'Carlo was a murderous son of a bitch, just like the monsters that shot him.'

'Shut your damn mouth,' Frank snarled. 'If my hands weren't tied I'd shut it the fuck for you.'

'Oh no, wait!' said Laird, gaining momentum. 'Carlo's inno-cent! You're the murderous son of a bitch, right? Well, isn't it a shame it isn't you being left behind as bear bait?'

'Shoulda been you that died instead of the woman, you worth-less coward,' Frank snarled. 'Look at you, whining and moaning like a bitch, and good for nothin'.'

Their bickering had been permitted to play out for a moment. Both men had lost people close to them, it was understandable that their passions were high, but the argument couldn't be allowed to progress.

'All right, that's enough, you,' said Pinky, interjecting between Frank and his target.

'I told ya,' Frank aimed at Pinky instead. 'Carlo was my driver, nothin' else. You got a beef, Leclerc, it's with me not with Carlo. The kid deserves the same kinda respect as any other innocent victim that died here today.'

'Frank,' said Pinky, his voice calm, 'if I had a real beef with you, you'd be keeping your cousin company over there. Now hush, you; stop getting all bent outta shape, and maybe you'll get to come back and collect Carlo's remains.'

Frank's chin rose slightly. He'd absorbed Pinky's words, recognized the hope within them. 'When I came out here, it was nothin' personal, man. It was a job, that's all, and I failed. We ain't enemies no more.' He nodded towards the woods. 'Our real enemy is out there. How's about you cut me loose; I'm more good to you all without my hands tied.'

Pinky's unperturbed expression didn't waver.

'C'mon, man?'

Pinky rolled down a lower eyelid with the tip of his thumb. 'You see any green in there, Frank?'

Frank exhaled in frustration, turned his appeal on Tess. 'Those animals murdered my cousin and they tried to murder *you*! C'mon, you must see it'd be better for us all if we worked together?'

'Sorry, Frank, the cuffs stay on. You can prove you can work with us by giving us no problems.'

'They killed my kid cousin,' he tried again. 'D'you think I'm gonna cause you problems when all I want is to skin those bastards alive?'

'If you get the chance,' Po interjected, 'you'll have to skin 'em with your teeth, Frank. You heard the lady, those cuffs are stayin' on. Now, c'mon, let's get movin'. Kid?' McNeill snapped to attention at Po's summons. 'You get up near the front, use that thermal scope of yours to check the trail ahead.'

'Yessir,' McNeill said and moved forward.

Po grasped him by his shirt collar and reined him back. 'I said "near the front". Pinky . . . will you take the rear?'

'At any other time that might call for a lewd retort, Nicolas.' Pinky gave a wicked grin. Then he settled the M110 in his arms and was all seriousness. 'I've got you covered, me.'

Po said, 'Tess. Alicia. Stay between us, Frank and Laird between y'all.'

Alicia exchanged a glance with Tess, and Tess nodded. Neither woman was usually the type to be lorded over by a man, but Po's plan made sense. 'I'll be watching Frank,' Tess said, reiterating her promise from before, 'you can look after Laird.'

Alicia checked out the biologist. He had his injured hand cupped to his chest as if comparing the pain of his bullet wound to the grief in his heart. She adjusted the backpack, never taking her eyes off him, then said, 'Stick close to me.'

They went without headlamps or flashlights, which would make them targets in the dark. Beyond the camp they were immediately swallowed by the darkness as they left the perimeter lights behind. Unconsciously, they strung out along the trail, Po limping ahead, Pinky stalling at the rear until distance grew between them. To bunch together made them sitting targets for a single strafe of a submachine gun.

Second from the back, Tess had one eye on the forest and one on Frank Lombardi. Since his release had been denied he'd kept silent, and he moved along the trail as obediently as Laird did in front of him. Tess didn't believe he'd cause them any problems while they could be under the crosshairs of Locke or the other dubbed 'Red' by Alicia. She'd felt he was sincere when naming them their shared enemies, but that did not make him an ally. She must stay alert to him trying to make a break for it, or worse, trying to get his hands on a weapon. She took a moment to check on Pinky. An errant spark of light flashed off his teeth as he grinned in reassurance. His looming figure was a comforting presence. Barring Po, she'd trust no other person with her life as much as she did Pinky.

She couldn't see Po. Too many other figures were between them. If not for the occasional dim glow from McNeill's thermal imager she'd be unable to tell how far ahead he was either; Po was ahead of him, but still in earshot in case there was a hit on the thermal scope. Occasionally the dimness of the trail was broken by gaps in the canopy, and the ambient light from a billion stars spilled to the forest floor. Alicia plodded ahead, burdened by the weight of her backpack, and, Tess suspected, the aches and pains she'd carried with her since her miraculous plane crash survival. More than once Tess found her gaze alighting on that backpack. Whatever was within it was heavy, but Alicia toted it without complaint. Tess understood her tenacity, because its contents had the power to bring down an international drug smuggling syndicate . . . allegedly.

She'd like to study the backpack's contents, see exactly what proof there was to incriminate 'local government officials, cops and business people on both sides of the US and Canadian border,' not to mention the evidence that corrupt law enforcement and DEA personnel were involved. It hadn't escaped her that she was taking Alicia's word without challenge, and for all she knew the woman was a mule who'd returned to the scene to collect a bag of drugs or cash. She was in no doubt that Alicia was a DEA deep-cover agent, but so was Locke. It'd be easy to conclude that the two agents had colluded together, only for Alicia to betray her partner in order to steal whatever was in the bag. Locke could have chased Alicia here on a revenge kick, and to recover her take from their criminal proceedings.

No, that theory just didn't feel right. Alicia had helped defend the camp against Locke's ambush, but that could just be part of an effort to defang Locke. She'd shot dead the gunman who would otherwise have stormed the camp along with Locke, and her actions had saved innocent lives. But in doing so Red had almost captured her, risking everything. If she were a criminal, she would have dug up her treasure and then ran in the opposite direction, not towards her enemies. Duty had won out, not greed, and that reassured Tess. But she'd still love to see what was inside the backpack.

THIRTY

Crouching, catching her breath, Greta Peterson was wary of admitting to losing Coleman. Virginia Locke was stone-hearted, and bloodthirsty, and Greta had no intention of turning the woman's ire on her. She was afraid Locke would spot an outright lie, so a twisting of the truth was in order.

'I spotted Coleman on her way to the camp, drawn there by the gunfire, but didn't get an opportunity to capture her. Before I could stop her, the bitch killed Hubert.' Greta swallowed at the memory, and emotion stung her eyes. 'All hell was going off in camp, and I was unsure if you'd want me concentrating on Coleman or backing you up. I chose to back you up.'

In the dimness Locke regarded her, silent, unmoving. Wearing night-vision goggles she was reminiscent of an alien creature, devoid of a soul and human emotion. Greta swallowed again.

'I was forced off by that big black guy . . . but only after I'd watched you get away.'

Locke stayed silent.

'I'm sorry,' said Greta.

'Sorry for backing me up?'

'No, not that. I'm sorry I failed to save Hubert, and that Coleman got away from me.'

'James and Whyte died too, and I didn't catch Coleman either.' This wasn't Locke forgiving Greta's failure, it was her way of saying she had no intention of apologizing. She'd made it clear before that her team was expendable, and she would lose no sleep over their collective demise. 'Shit happens, Peterson. Get over yourself, and forget about Hubert, or you're no good to me.'

Now it was Greta who fell silent. Locke's coldness hadn't stunned her; it was best to quit while she was ahead. She'd sold the lie of what had happened back there at the camp and bringing it up again would only serve to layer more lies on top of the first. The more lies she wove into her tale the harder it'd prove to keep track of them.

'They're on the move,' said Locke. Without warning she stood and crept off between the trees. Greta stood, peering through the shadows to where the target group was strung out along a defined trail. It surprised her that Locke hadn't planned a second ambush on the trail, and was instead heading off at a tangent away from them. Wary of making any noise, Greta turned slowly, and then crept after her. Only once they were a hundred paces out did Locke turn to the northeast, urging Greta to follow.

After Greta fled from the guy with the rifle, she'd beelined to Gabe Hubert's corpse, sent there by a snappy order from Locke to strip him of any comms equipment and weapons. Locke's attack on camp had been launched with the intention of silencing witnesses, and also to deny them any contact with the outside world. Locke had also collected the radios and sat phones from Whyte and James, but apparently the tall, brooding character who'd ended their lives had already snatched their guns. The group was without working phones, but was now more heavily armed than Locke and Greta. Locke evidently did not want to test them in an open battle again, and had come up with an alternative plan. She just wasn't sharing it with Greta yet.

Greta followed with some trepidation.

The trouble with any black-hearted bitch like Virginia Locke was that she made no bones about her disregard for Greta's welfare. She was as expendable as all the rest, as long as Locke got her way. How in God's name had she allowed herself to get caught up in Locke's orbit? Locke was not her friend, and Greta owed her no loyalty beyond the fact she was being paid for her services. Well, it was tempting to dispense with her promised reward, cut her losses and slip away while she could. The only trouble was, once she was done with Coleman, that'd bring Locke in pursuit, and Greta didn't wish to run forever. As she followed the woman through the gloom, she weighed her gun in her hand against her chance of survival. It'd be easy to sneak up on Locke, shoot the insane bitch and have done. Except – even if she could bring herself to shoot her – Greta wasn't confident her plan would work: Locke was so hard-skinned it was doubtful a bullet would penetrate her frickin' hide!

Greta put away thoughts of murdering her boss. They'd been stupid to begin with. She'd fucked up, and she was as much at fault for Gabe Hubert's death, for allowing Coleman to close in on him when she could have caught her as she left the crash site. If she'd saved Hubert's hide, he'd have been there to assist Locke when she stormed the camp, and all of this would have been over with by now. *Knuckle down*, she told herself, *and do your damn job.* Locke would recover the evidence against their employers, and there was time yet for Greta to avenge her fallen comrade. She felt no pity for James or Whyte, they were assholes the world wouldn't miss, but Hubert – as far as violent guns-for-hire went – was a decent guy and she'd miss him.

Mentally hitching up her pants, Greta moved with more determination as she followed Locke through the north woods. Ahead of the group from camp, she was unaware exactly of where they were going, and was reliant on Locke on getting them there. She stuck close, working hard to match Locke's tireless stride, and they ate up the miles.

They spilled out into an open glade. Overhead, the clouds had cleared, and the stars were sharp against the depthless backdrop of space. A fingernail clipping soared high overhead, casting enough wan moonlight to earth for Greta to make out a trio of vehicles about a hundred yards to their right. One of the vehicles belonged to the field biology team, another must have carried the strangers here, and she recognized the third as the one Locke, Whyte and James had arrived in – it was an identical model Ford to the one she and Hubert had abandoned miles to the south. Locke headed directly for them.

Greta bent at the waist, heels of her hands on her thighs, and sucked in a few grateful lungfuls of air, then jogged after Locke. She caught up as the woman took off her night-vision goggles and squinted inside an SUV sporting wildlife decal, checking for a radio set: there was none. Locke paced to the next, an Escalade, and also peered inside. Greta took the moment to suck in more air. Untouched by the labor of trekking through the woods, Locke turned to her.

'Disable both these cars,' Locke instructed.

Greta didn't ask why. It was obvious. Except Locke then added, 'If they get back to Brayton Lake, they'll get signals on their phones. The place will be swarming with Border Patrol in no time.'

Greta fleetingly considered shooting out the tires on the cars, but immediately discarded the idea. This close to Brayton Lake the gunshots might be heard and attract unwanted attention; besides, it'd be a waste of ammunition. She drew a knife from a pouch on her belt and went to work. Locke left her to it; she took out her satellite phone and made a call.

THIRTY-ONE

At first Tess was unaware when Po halted in his tracks. Concentrating on scanning the woods for heat signatures, Grant McNeill walked with his head tilted down, eyes on the screen. He almost collided with Po, but a hand was thrust back and brought the young biologist to a stop. His head came up, and Po shushed him. Po leaned past the young man, signaling Alicia, and she sent the message down the line, signified by an upraised fist. Everyone behind Po crouched, except for Frank Lombardi, until Tess tugged him down by his jacket collar.

'Whassup?' Pinky's voice was pitched just loud enough for Tess's ear. She glanced back at him, offering a shrug he most likely couldn't discern. It was enough for her that Po was alarmed though, and she began peering into the deep shadows at either side of the trail, checking for snakes in the grass – snakes of the human variety.

'Got something,' McNeill announced, his voice carrying to Tess in the sudden hush. 'It's at two o'clock, but it's difficult to tell how far out.'

Tess, like everyone else in the group, followed his direction, but all she could define was a wall of trees against a drop cloth of blackness. She recalled Po's words about not needing any night-vision goggles to see by, but she could have done with the technology because she was virtually blind. She rose up a few inches, peering over the heads of those in front of her, and caught sight of McNeill in the backwash from his screen. Beyond him, Po was a broad-shouldered silhouette astride the trail. He was as still as the tree trunks that surrounded him.

'It's moving,' McNeill announced.

There was a clattering sound, and everyone tensed. Tess aimed the pistol in the direction of the racket, tracking movement. A few paces behind her, Pinky had the M110 braced to his shoulder, finger on the trigger. The sound diminished.

Tess breathed in relief, and Pinky lowered the sniper rifle.

There was a surge of motion to their left, and Tess spun to confront the new danger, dreading a black bear launching from the undergrowth. There was no way possible a single shot from her pistol would halt a determined carnivore. She prepared for the inevitable. With a crackle of breaking twigs something hurtled out of the undergrowth, and Tess wasn't the only person to cry out in alarm. She half fell into Frank Lombardi, her gun coming higher, trying to follow the blur of movement. Then the shape was past her and bounding out of sight on the opposite side of the trail. All around them other deer took flight, some following blindly across the trail and causing the humans to bunch together in twos and threes to give them clear passage. High-pitched mournful calls marked the herd's progress through the woods. Tails flicked white, tiny explosions within the gloom.

Tess snatched her attention to Frank. His face was so close to hers to be intimate. She felt his breath, ragged and swift on her cheek. She reared back, stumbling on a hidden root, and was surprised to find his hands, though cuffed at the wrist, grasping her elbow to steady her. With her feet planted again, she felt ungrateful aiming the pistol at him, and brusquely urged him to his feet.

Behind her Pinky quipped, 'I used to love Bambi, but I don't now. Deer aren't so cute when they come at you like that. I almost filled my damn boxer shorts, me!'

Tess was relieved that she hadn't become bear fodder, and was equally relieved she hadn't needed to shoot one of the magnificent beasts in defense.

Down the line, people checked on their nearest neighbors, ensuring nobody was hurt by the flashing hooves and antlers. Po signaled them to continue on and his instruction was passed back.

'Got to empty out my sneakers, me,' Pinky whispered.

Tess halted Frank, waiting while Pinky propped the M110 against a tree trunk. He performed an awkward dance, shuffling from foot to foot as he tugged off and spilled the contents of his Converse sneakers on the trail. He had to squirm and stamp his feet into the shoes again, almost falling over at one point. He picked up the rifle. Out of breath, he announced, 'Good to go, pretty Tess.'

A distance had grown between them and the others. She could

barely make out Jonathan Laird as he trudged in Alicia's steps. Stalled at the back, the three of them were vulnerable to attack, easily picked off by Locke or Red if they were out there in the forest. 'C'mon,' she said, and grasped Frank by his elbow to usher him forward. 'Close the gap.'

'No need to be so rough,' Frank said, a sly smile forming. He held her gaze, his sclera dimly reflecting the starlight filtering through the canopy. 'I told ya, I ain't gonna give you no problems.'

'Just move.' She shoved him.

'Steady on,' Frank said. 'We can stay civil, right? No need for the rough stuff?'

Pinky loomed in. 'You want to see rough, Frank? How's about I ram this rifle up your ass and carry you over my shoulder like a hobo's bindle?'

Frank sucked air through his teeth. Made his decision. He moved on with no further resistance.

Tess exchanged a glance with Pinky, and he shook his head. 'Don't trust that slick mofo an inch, Tess.'

'Don't worry,' she said, loud enough for the subject of their discussion to hear, 'I can be civil *or* rough. However *he* wants to play it.'

Frank rolled his neck but didn't comment.

Tess pushed the pace until only a mere few yards separated them from Laird. She could hear the biologist moaning with each labored step. He was struggling: blood loss, pain, shock and grief, a cornucopia of misery to contend with.

'How are you faring up, Jonathan?' she asked. 'Need to take a rest?'

'I want this to be over with,' Laird groaned. 'I only want to get back to Elsa before the bears find her.'

'You and me both, brother,' Frank intoned.

'I'm not your brother!' Laird's face contorted, his eyes feverish. 'You are scum to me!'

'Hey, kiss my scummy ass,' Frank snarled.

Tess wished she'd never asked.

They trudged on, every clot of shadow pregnant with possible danger. Wildlife was startled to flight on more occasions, mostly birds, and their clattering and squawking eruptions had everyone on tenterhooks, anticipating a flurry of bullets to follow, but finally

Po led them unerringly to the glade and they all crouched at its perimeter while they checked for an ambush. Under the pale light of the waning crescent moon Laird's SUV and the Escalade were visible where they'd left them hours earlier. Tess took out her cell phone. She cupped her palm over the screen to hide the glow: not that she need fear the glow giving her position away when Locke and Red had night-vision technology. No signal. Others followed her example, and their reward was equally frustrating.

'We're still in a dead zone,' McNeill explained. 'Nearest place to here to get any cell reception is Brayton Lake, and even there the service can be patchy.'

Po sidled up to Tess. 'I'll go ahead, check things over. Keep everyone's heads down till I give the all clear.'

'Be careful,' she said. For all they'd been alert to and feared ambush in the woods, this was the optimum location for Locke to mow them down.

'I'm always careful,' he said, with a wink at the irony.

His leg still troubled him, but he didn't allow it to slow him. He kept to the edge of the tree line, moving at a steady lope for the cars a hundred yards or so distant. Tess, Alicia and Pinky braced for trouble.

Po's shadow blended with the SUV as he crouched alongside it. He moved on, dipping down beside the Escalade. He stood slowly, making a scan of his surroundings, not yet waving them forward. Still wary of a trap he'd selflessly gone ahead to spring it, but everyone was aware that Locke would wait until she had all of them in her sights before shooting. Po waited, then stepped out into the muddy clearing, forcing Tess to cringe in worry. Sometimes she thought he'd the instincts of a wild thing, as if he'd honed his senses to a higher than normal level. He raised a hand and beckoned them to join him. Tess had learned to trust his instincts.

'OK, let's move, but stay close to the trees, and keep your heads down.'

McNeill led off, then Alicia bustled forward, the backpack bobbing with each step, followed again by Laird. Now that they were out of the woods, Pinky took a knee, covering Tess while she pressed Frank towards the cars. Once he was reasonably certain they weren't in any gun sights he rose up and followed, while Tess now covered for him.

'It's too quiet, I don't like it,' said Tess as Pinky joined her.

'I prefer the silence to the alternative, me,' he confessed.

A dozen feet away in the open Po stood like a sentinel. His attention was concentrated to the east.

The others were already muttering in dismay or poorly subdued anger at the way the vehicles were sunken almost to their axels in the dirt.

'The tires have been slashed,' Alicia announced as Tess approached her.

'All of them?'

'Every last one of them, including the spares.'

'Have they been disabled in any other way?'

'Not that I can tell.'

'It won't be easy going, but can't we still drive out of here on flats?' Tess wondered. 'We only need one car to get us near Brayton Lake then hopefully our phones will work.'

McNeill pitched in. 'If we'd a solid base to set off on, maybe, but not with the hubs sunk into the soft dirt. There's no way either car's moving.'

'So what's our alternative?' Alicia asked.

'We keep walking,' said Tess.

Po returned. His face was set in concrete, the dim moonlight emphasizing its angles, planes, and furrows. 'There's fresh tire tracks leadin' outta the glade. Looks like Locke's skedaddled. Y'all can wait here,' he suggested. 'I'll run ahead, an' I'll raise the cops soon as I get a signal on my cell.'

Tess shook her head. 'No, Po, we must stick together.'

One side of his mouth jumped up in endearment. Unlike Po, Tess often wore sentiment openly. Locke and Red must be hours ahead of them by now, with plenty of time for preparation. She was worried that if he ran on ahead, then he was alone and at the mercy of an ambush. There was no way she'd willingly allow him to go alone without any backup. Besides, what would happen if Locke and Red returned while he was gone and they were without their strongest asset in a fight? Pinky, Alicia, Tess, all were capable fighters, but Po was the natural warrior.

'You suggestin' we all sit here on our thumbs an' hope they've given up?' he asked.

'Of course not. We all go on together. That way we stand a chance at protecting each other until we can phone for help.'

Po checked out the worn aspect of the group. McNeill looked fresh enough, as did Tess, but the health of the others was in question. Alicia was still carrying injuries from her near-death experience during the plane crash: she hid them well, but she was in constant pain, and the weight of her backpack had begun beating her down. The moonlight added to Laird's deathly cast; he stood almost zombie-like, pale and listless. Pinky winked at him, but wasn't kidding Po.

'How you doin', Pinky?'

'There isn't a pinch of flesh left on my heels, but I'm good for a few miles yet, me.' He hadn't complained, but his poor footwear had added up during the latter part of the trek out, and his feet were rubbed raw and blistered.

Po's scrutiny went to Frank Lombardi. He was an encumbrance, but fit enough. Though, Tess realized, that wasn't why the man had drawn Po's attention.

'Where's the GMC you and the kid rode in?' Po asked.

Frank scowled. Perhaps he'd been concocting an escape plan where he could make it to the GMC alone and drive away, leaving the others to their fates. Tess doubted that escape might not be all that was on Frank's mind though, because he could still have designs on the bounty on Pinky's head, and also have a need to avenge his cousin. Perhaps abandoning them all out in the wilderness and returning home wasn't an option for him; Carlo had a father – Frank's uncle – and Frank had let slip he wouldn't be forgiving of his nephew if anything bad happened to the kid.

'Cat got your tongue?' Po asked.

'Why should I help any of you?' Frank replied and held up his cuffed wrists.

'Why shouldn't we put a bullet in your head?' Pinky reminded him.

'Who's to say you won't after we get outta this mess?'

''Cause we ain't murderous scumballs like you are, Frank,' Po said.

'I haven't murdered nobody.'

'Which is to say you've murdered somebody,' said Po, 'but I'll forgive you the double negative for now. Where's the GMC?

Can't be far off, but you'll win a few brownie points if you tell us and don't waste our times making a search. We'll find it; it's in your best interest that we find it sooner rather than later.'

'Who's to say it's any more roadworthy than your cars, man?'

'Who's to say it isn't? Let's go check, shall we?' Po galvanized him by bunching a fist in his collar and shoving him ahead.

Alicia groaned as she straightened under the weight of her backpack. She took a couple of deep breaths, preparing for the fresh effort of walking again.

'I could take that load off you if you'd like?' Tess offered, now that she was no longer in charge of guarding Frank.

'Thanks, but no thanks, Tess.'

'How're you holding up?'

'I'm sore *everywhere*, but I've a couple of broken teeth that take the damn trophy. What I wouldn't do for some Novocain right now.'

'The offer's open, I could help.'

'I've got this,' Alicia said, with a nod over her shoulder, 'and it isn't leaving my side till I know it's safe.'

'I get you, but you must say if you need any help, OK?' Tess didn't push the issue any further.

McNeill looked embarrassed that he hadn't offered to take the burden off Alicia, and as an excuse held aloft his thermal scope and screen. He looked towards the SUV, as if contemplating leaving them with the car.

'We might still have need of those,' Tess told him. 'Keep them handy.'

This time as they moved on, Tess fell back to walk alongside Pinky, who tiptoed on his raw feet over the troughs and mounds in the dirt.

'Are you happy you demanded to join us on our camping trip?' Tess smiled to show she was joking.

'There's no place on earth I'd rather be right now, pretty Tess,' he replied with a smirk, before launching into a half-decent impression to paraphrase Bruce Willis's most iconic character: '"Let's go camping," she said. "We'll have some beers, cook some hotdogs, have a few laughs and sing 'Kum ba-freakin'-yah' round the fire." I'm telling you, by comparison, this is a joyful way to spend my first night in the woods.'

THIRTY-TWO

'Aw, c'mon, man! You've got to be freakin' kidding me!' Everyone in the group shared Frank Lombardi's sentiment, and though she'd been partly expecting it, the sight of his cousin's GMC sunken on its rims momentarily disheartened Tess as well. They'd all hoped, with it hidden up the forest trail, that Locke's team would've missed it after disabling their vehicles. But whoever had slashed their tires had also gone to town on the GMC's. Even the back window had been smashed in order for the vandal to reach the spare wheel in the rear compartment.

'It isn't the end of the world,' Po announced. 'It was different back there on the soft dirt; our cars were bedded down deep but the GMC's standing on hard pack here. I think I can get it moving, and once we're back on the road it should get us aways.'

'You'll buckle the hubs in minutes, man!' Frank argued. 'You'll have no control of the steering, and those rims will just dig into the asphalt.'

'You seen much asphalt since you got off Route 11, Frank?' asked Po. 'These roads are built for utility vehicles and agricultural machinery. They're iron hard and built to last. The GMC's rims will barely scratch the surface.'

'Shit, man,' Frank went on, 'it's gonna cost me a fortune to replace the hubs after this: it's not as if Carlo can claim against his damn insurance, is it?'

'And you already out of pocket, you,' Pinky smirked.

Tess assessed the damage to the tires. 'Are you certain this can carry us, Po?'

'We won't know until we give it a try. While we've still got rubber we'll still have traction.'

'Please tell me you remembered to bring the keys after you first searched them.'

Po tapped an index finger to his forehead. He then dipped a hand in his jeans pocket and pulled out a set of keys that weren't his own. 'I thought ahead. Had a feelin' that Locke might mess up our rides, but hoped she'd miss this one.'

Pinky sidled up to Tess, without his attention leaving Frank. He spoke out the corner of his mouth. 'Tell me you also thought ahead and grabbed some of those Band-Aids outta the med kit. I sure hope Nicolas can get this heap moving, I'm not sure I can walk much further on these blisters, me.'

Tess scowled at her own lack of forethought. She'd been the last person to use the medical kit when patching up Laird's hand: it should've been on her to bring it with them considering she already had one patient to contend with. She shrugged an apology.

Po used the key fob to bleep open the locks and pulled open the driver's door. Pinky squinted through the tinted glass into the passenger compartment. 'There isn't much room in there for seven of us. Hell, there isn't much room on that back seat for my fat butt and one other.'

'We'll dump the junk outta the trunk,' Po suggested, 'and a couple of us can ride in there.'

'Better than us all cramming inside like the goddamn Ant Hill Mob,' Pinky agreed.

'I'll climb in the back,' Tess said. 'Somebody has to keep an eye on Frank, and I'm sure there's nobody else here who wants to get crushed up alongside him.'

'I'll ride in the back with him.' Alicia had pulled out of her backpack, but still held it by its straps. What had gone unspoken was she didn't want separated from it, and there'd be no room in the front for it with her.

With their seating arrangements agreed, Po hauled open the rear hatch, reached inside and began yanking out the random items that had accumulated inside. He dumped them at the side of the trail, then set about unscrewing the bracket holding the deflated spare tire in place. He tossed it away, and then broke off a small branch from a fir. He used it as a broom to sweep out the worst of the broken glass. There was plenty room for Frank, Alicia, and her backpack, though they wouldn't be traveling in comfort.

The engine started with the first turn of the key. As people began jostling for position, Po said, 'Hold it, y'all.'

He set the GMC rolling and it juddered and shook, the ruined

tires almost instantly beginning to misshape. 'Should be good to
go, but walk on down to the main road. If you all get in now,
I'm unsure it'll make it.' Po reconsidered: the road was only fifty
yards away, but it was another hundred painful steps for Pinky.
'Pinky, jump up front with me. Tess, you OK watching Frank
till y'all get to the road?'

'Sure.' She appraised Frank, her chin raised to meet his gaze.
'There's going to be no funny business out of you, right?'

'Huh! I'm the one gets to lie in the back of my own cousin's
car like a damn sack of turds, what's to fuckin' laugh about?'

Once Pinky settled in the front, the GMC trundled forward at
walking pace, and the group on foot shuffled in its wake. Alicia
hauled the backpack along with one hand and the assault rifle
with the other, her body canted to the opposite side from the
pack to even out the weight. She was puffing and panting with
each step. Laird countered her with gasps and moans, mercurial
drops of sweat shivering on his brow: his wounds must've grown
agonizing. McNeill still scanned the woods on both sides, his
head only rising from his screen to check the amorphous shapes
picked out by the scope. Tess walked with Frank, one hand grip-
ping his elbow as if he was under formal arrest; she kept the gun
out of reach of a sudden lunge, but ready should he try anything
stupid. She'd noticed that his gaze kept going to the hunting rifle
slung over Laird's shoulder, as if plotting to go for it, except he
wore a pinched expression of regret, and she wondered what
exactly was going through the would-be hitman's mind. Despite
the way both men had gone at each other's throats, they were
alike in that they were both grieving, and perhaps Frank felt
some kinship with Laird. She pitied him his loss, but she wasn't
a fool. *Don't trust that slick mofo an inch,* Pinky had warned,
and she wasn't going to allow herself to be lulled by Frank's
fleeting display of humanity. He'd come here to murder her and
Po's best friend, so didn't deserve pity. She gripped his elbow
tighter, reminding him that she wasn't to be messed with by
flashing him her pistol. He almost buried his big chin in his chest,
and his unkempt dark locks covered his eyes.

A squeal announced the GMC's arrival at the road. One of the
front wheel rims had cut through the rubber tire, biting into
loose gravel instead, and Po responded by giving it more gas:

the big 4x4 jostled up the tiny incline onto the hardpack and he brought it to a halt. He got out to oversee their prisoner while the others chose their respective seats. Tess ended up squished between the biologists, Laird juggling around the rifle one-handed so it sat across both his and Tess's laps. Tess leaned past him, thumbing the window control. 'Poke that thing out of the window,' she told him, but had to help him when he fumbled the task. She craned to watch behind, her neck aching. Frank was making a meal of his predicament, complaining that it was difficult clambering in with his wrists cinched. Po grabbed him by his shoulder and the seat of his pants and threw him in.

'Shift over and quit bellyaching,' Po growled at him. Frank rolled on his side, pulling up his knees, cussing vilely at Po and the world in general. Po assisted Alicia, cupping a palm under the backpack and taking the weight while she dragged it inside. She squeezed into the opposite corner to Frank, the backpack seated between her thighs. She settled the assault rifle on top, and made Frank a silent promise. Frank cussed again, but turned his face aside. He peered out the side window, his view a tinted picture of the omniscient forest juxtaposed by his own reflection.

Alicia met Tess's eye. She looked thoughtful. Randomly, she asked, 'Are you a reader, Tess.'

'Sure I am, when I get the opportunity. Why?'

'Did you ever read Heinlein's *Stranger in a Strange Land*?'

'Can't say as I have. Never was one for sci-fi.'

'Once this is over with, maybe you should give it a try. But it must be a first edition, printed in nineteen sixty-one.'

Alicia said no more about books, and Tess was left wondering if the recommendation was some kind of metaphor for Alicia's predicament . . . no damnit! It was a key! Before she could give it more thought, Frank growled, 'Gimme some room, will ya? You've got your damn toes up my ass.'

Alicia shoved him away with her foot. 'Keep to your own side, asshole.'

Twisting around in her seat, Tess left them to it. She took out her cell phone. The *No Service* message from her provider was in the top left corner of the screen. She clucked her tongue at her stupidity. Even where a network provider's signal was unavailable provisions were made where emergency calls could piggy-back on another service provider's signal where one was present: maybe another's was wider ranging than her own. Having trekked miles closer to a town there was always the possibility. 'Everyone check your phones,' she instructed, even as she dialed in 9-1-1. Her call didn't get bounced through via available cellphone masts, but that wasn't to say—

'Holy shit!' McNeill cried out. 'I've got the "emergency calls only" message. D'you think I—'

Without asking permission, Tess snatched his cell out of his hand. At first she'd no idea what to say – there was still the issue behind the reason for Frank Lombardi's presence, as well as retaining Alicia's anonymity to consider – but to hell with it! She needn't mention either of them; all that was important was that she summons the cops as rapidly as possible. She dabbed in the numbers, held the phone to her ear and waited breathlessly. She heard a ringtone.

A droll-sounding dispatcher asked the usual questions, but Tess spoke over her in a rush. 'My name is Teresa Grey. I'm a licensed private investigator from Portland. I'm with six other people about ten miles northwest of Brayton Lake in Aroostook County. We are under *armed attack* by unknown numbers. Two of our party have already been murdered, and we have one injured. *We need urgent police assistance*—' She stopped speaking abruptly, as the connection had quit. She glanced at the screen. *No Service.* 'Damn it!'

She tried again, hoping she could hook onto a different signal. No luck. Po got the GMC rolling. It rumbled along the hardpack, shuddering at the effort. Hopefully the nearer they approached Brayton Lake, the stronger a signal would get. She was bombarded by questions, words coming at her rapid-fire from all directions; her companions mostly wanted to know the same answers. Did she get through? What did the dispatcher say? Are the police coming? Tess had tried to impart her call with enough urgency and key words to ensure the desired response, but she couldn't say how much of her message had been heard or understood by the dispatcher. 'I got through, they should be coming.'

'*Should* be coming,' Laird croaked in dismay.

'They should be able to ping our location from the call log,' Tess reassured him. 'They'll find us.'

'We should stop moving then. We should wait here for the police.'

'I ain't stopping.' Po flicked a glance at Tess in the rearview mirror. His swift look was enough to convey what he meant: they might not get moving again, and besides, crammed inside the stalled GMC they presented a single target if Locke returned. Hell, for all they knew, she was out there in the woods stalking them, planning the best moment to strike. It was better that they kept moving and not make things easier for her. Crawling along at under ten miles per hour was still moving.

'Keep trying your cells,' Tess reiterated. 'We'll get a clear signal soon.'

'Locke's probably waiting for us at Brayton Lake,' McNeill piped in.

'We know,' said Tess and Po in unison.

'So why are we going there?'

'She's less likely to try another ambush where there are so many witnesses.'

Laird gave a short but hysterical laugh. 'This is the same monster who attacked our camp, walked in while the bullets were flying to slaughter us all. Do you really think a few locals seeing her will concern her? She'll only kill them too!'

'Not if we stop her first,' said Tess.

'Yeah, well, how'd that work out for you before?'

THIRTY-THREE

Virginia Locke studied the lakeside community from the safety of her Ford. Opposite the V formed by the roads intersecting at the post office was a broad strip of ground on which some of the residents parked their vehicles. At the eastern end there was what might be termed a lumber yard, only if you suffered delusions of grandeur. There were a few trucks, some propane tanks and even a couple of gas pumps, plus the ubiquitous stacks of felled lumber awaiting transportation. A rowboat was the only craft moored at the pier jutting out into the marshy lake. Dawn would arrive within a couple of hours, and if there was something she knew about homesteaders they were the type to rise early. Presently Brayton Lake slumbered under the blanket of night, and not one soul was abroad, but that would soon change. A few pinpricks of light, where porch lights had been left on overnight, picked out the separate structures and one bathroom window was limned by a pearlescent glow as a resident's weak bladder was emptied. She estimated that half a dozen families made the small hamlet their home, and there were other, more remote houses scattered throughout the woods between the lake and airstrip. The airstrip was a glorified strip of grass, used primarily by aircraft from the local bush service to bring in essential supplies, to collect and deliver mail from the small post office adjacent to the lake. Occasionally it might be used in medical emergencies to fly the sick or injured to hospital in one of the larger cities to the southeast. She wondered if state troopers had access to aircraft to get them here, and decided they would if the magnitude of an emergency demanded it. Otherwise, she reckoned, the community might receive a visit from a mobile patrol once or twice a week at best. As far as she'd been able to determine, the nearest manned police station was at Greenville, from where she'd traveled to meet with the old fisherman Arthur Jackman yesterday. Driving from Greenville, even under emergency conditions, they'd need a few hours' travel time to arrive at the isolated backwater. She assumed there were cops nearer by, but not in any great number, so wasn't concerned. She could handle a hick cop more used to checking lapsed hunting licenses and dealing with the occasional domestic drama than confronting skilled combatants.

Locke had chosen the settlement as her battleground. There were other directions the group from the camp might flee, but she sensed that first they'd try for their cars, and when they found them disabled, their next move would be to try to reach Brayton Lake in the hope of raising assistance by way of their cell phones. They were going to be in for a nasty surprise when they discovered the cellphone network was down. Locke had that covered. She'd summoned reinforcements and they'd made use of the town's airstrip. The same operators, who'd set a small explosive charge to disable the town's cell mast, were currently moving from house to house cutting phone wires and disabling radio antennae. Soon their incursions on Brayton Lake would include home invasions, during which the residents would be immobilized and contained. Locke knew that she should only choose a battleground that she could control, a hard lesson learned after the clusterfuck that went down at the camp.

Another rule of combat she'd been sorely reminded of was to never underestimate an enemy. She still had no clue why Guido Lombardi's son was present in the camp, but it had grown apparent that she'd presumed wrongly that he'd brought a bunch of trig-germen after Alicia Coleman. Carlo Lombardi had proved himself just a terrified kid. She'd given his corpse little notice after Billy James had cut him down, but she had spotted the restraints he'd worn. A second restrained man, she'd concluded, was Carlo's only friend in camp, a possible triggerman, had proven as inept against the trio of strangers as her own team had. Who were the blond woman, the black guy and, most importantly, the tall man on whose shoulder Death rode? When she had stormed the camp the former two had almost ended her life; single-handed, the latter had slaughtered her best two gunmen. She thought they must be allies of Alicia Coleman, summoned there to ensure she escaped unharmed with her prize. But if that were the case, then why had they answered her summons unequipped for war? Of course, they'd soon rectified the situation, first using what they'd scavenged, and later adding to their haul with the sniper and assault rifles stripped from Whyte and James. For a time there they'd been better armed and outnumbered Locke and Peterson, and it irked her that she'd had to retreat. But that was then and this is now. She'd summoned fighters of her own, and they had arrived armed to the teeth. If Coleman and the trio of strangers thought they held the upper hand now then they must think again.

Locke had stationed Greta Peterson a mile to the west, in the only house between Brayton Lake and the glade where she'd disabled the group's vehicles. She had her orders to sit tight and watch for the group's approach. Locke had warned her not to engage with them unless it was absolutely necessary, her only duty to report on the group's progress, and then to fall in at a safe distance behind them if she wanted to join the fight here. Locke had dangled a carrot before Peterson, promising that she could have Coleman once she was finished with her: for some reason Locke didn't understand, Peterson thought it was her right to avenge Gabe Hubert – had they been screwing each other? It mattered not to Locke, other than that Peterson's desire for revenge meant she would not shirk from the battle. She'd been suspicious of Peterson's version of events at the camp, and wondered if the woman truly had it in her to murder in cold blood, so Locke had tested her response. The house they'd chosen as Peterson's hiding place was a ramshackle old thing, with few modern comforts or amenities, and a single elderly resident. While the old man had knelt in his boxer shorts and wife-beater vest on the threadbare carpet in his living room, begging for his life, Locke had put the barrel of her SIG to his head, and watched Peterson's reaction as she'd pulled the trigger. To Locke's satisfaction, Peterson's eyelids had barely flickered when clots of bloody brain matter spattered her clothing. Perhaps a better test would've been to order Peterson to slay the old man instead, but Locke had been aching to kill since she'd been forced to flee the camp, and the old goat's murder was something to be coveted not given away. Had Peterson flinched, or worse tried to stop her slaying the man, she'd have executed her as a worthless piece of crap.

Not counting Peterson, she had another six assets on the ground in Brayton Lake, and also there was a second clean-up team due to move in on the abandoned camp. Their mission was to recover the bodies of Whyte, James, and Hubert. Once everyone with Coleman was dead, nobody must be able to identify their killers: if left where they'd fallen the corpses of her former colleagues would inevitably be identified and sooner or later the investigation would lead back to Locke and then to her employers. If that were to happen, then all of this would have been for nothing. Why go to so much trouble to recover the key that'd convict dozens in their network when leaving bodies around would do the exact same thing?

She'd discarded the previous bullshit radio protocol, electing instead to trust they were now far enough from the international crossing to be monitored by the Border Patrol, though she was still careful about using given names. Each of her assets had been designated a call sign corresponding to the NATO phonetic alphabet – Bravo through to Golf – of course, she was Alpha. From the comfort of her car seat she demanded a status check, and the answers rolled in. The team was all criminals, but they worked with almost military precision, and unlike Hubert and Petersen, they'd already proven they were unafraid of killing. She should have brought them with her in the first place, instead of making do with the first useless fools she'd been allocated.

Alarmed voices filtered to her from across the green belt between the road and town. Startled from their beds, the inhabitants of Brayton Lake were being rousted from their homes and herded towards a single structure adjacent to the lumber yard. It was a storage shed, currently empty, with only one egress point one of her team could guard. When it came time to clean shop, it would serve as a crypt for the town's residents, but first she chose to keep them alive as bargaining chips. Most of the captives went quietly, too terrified to resist, but one woman was vocal in her outrage and received a smack to her face from 'Echo.' When her husband flew to her defense he was callously shot in the chest and died instantly. While Echo forced the screeching wife away at gunpoint, 'Bravo' dragged the husband's body out of sight of the road, and pulled down a stack of empty wooden pallets over him. Locke observed the antics unperturbed. Once the survivors were all inside the shed, and Echo on guard duty, she drove her Ford and parked it out of view behind the post office. Greta Peterson's voice chimed through her earpiece: 'They're moving toward you in that GMC we found.'

'I thought you crippled all the cars.'

'So did I. But they've got it moving . . . slowly.'

'They're all in it?'

'I counted seven.'

'So Coleman, too?'

'Affirmative.'

'Good. What's their ETA?'

'They're crawling at a snail's pace, so you're good for a quarter hour at least.'

Locke noted the current time and when they were due to arrive in Brayton Lake.

'Fall in at a safe distance behind them. If they deviate from their current path I want to know.'

'Copy that. Where'd you want me once they're in town?'

'Move in and shut them down. I don't want them getting out again the way they come in.'

'Understood.'

Locke heard the note of satisfaction in Peterson's tone. Maybe she'd misjudged Peterson's appetite for murder, because she sure sounded keen to join the party.

'Remember I need Coleman alive . . . the others are fair game.'

'Understood. But I still get her after you're done with her, right?'

'Weren't you listening the first time I said so?'

'Just checking the plan hadn't changed.'

'It hasn't.'

'Cool.'

Locke didn't respond further. She got out of her car and moved towards the back of the post office, kicking open the flimsy door. The postmistress, an elderly woman so ancient and with legs so bowed Locke wondered if she'd once ridden for the Pony Express, had already been ushered across to the storage shed by 'Delta.' This was not a regular post office, but an old lady's house that doubled as one. She cut through a cramped kitchen, then a living room cluttered with a lifetime's trinkets and gewgaws, into a small extension built on the front of the house. There was a waist-high wooden counter, stained and scratched, on which sat an old weighing scale and beneath there were dozens of individual shelves stacked with envelopes and other sundry items. Posters decked the wall behind her, one carrying the tariffs for sending mail of varying sizes. The front of the make-do office had floor-to-ceiling windows, the glass aged and warped, and gave her a clear view of the road where it entered town at its western end. She checked the time. The GMC should limp into her crosshairs within the next ten minutes. She rested her reloaded SIG MPX-K on the counter, and waited.

THIRTY-FOUR

Tess scrunched onto the back seat, forcing McNeill to shift over and squirm against Laird, who groaned in pain. Their positions had changed when Tess elected to be the person to go and check the old house for a telephone line. Armed with the pistol handed to her by Alicia, she'd approached the house that sat back off the roadside on a half-acre of cleared ground. The house was dilapidated, the roof sagging, windows so dusty there'd be no clear view inside even if she pressed her nose to the glass. Parked at one side was an ancient pickup truck, loaded with plastic drums. Briefly she'd considered it as a more viable mode of transportation than the disabled GMC, but a quick check showed that Locke had beaten them to it. Its tires were slashed.

Approaching the dwelling she kept close to the trees, near enough to dive for her life if she was walking into an ambush. Pinky had stepped out of the GMC, leaning over its cab with the M110 to offer her cover, but his shot would be reactionary only and by then Tess could be dead. Her stomach gurgled, and acid forced a path up her throat, but she kept moving.

Deathly silence hung over the house. Sunrise wasn't far off, but night still held sway, and the house was in its grip. There was no hint of lights behind the windows, no sounds of life. Thankfully there was no gunfire. She got within twenty feet of the front door and halted. She listened, swept each filthy window with her gaze, but the tableau didn't alter. She took out her flashlight last used during their walk to the camp yesterday evening. She brushed its dim glow over the house, checking the roofline and eaves, but there was no evidence of the residents ever having access to a telephone line. She assumed that if whoever lived there needed to contact the outside world they'd perhaps drive into Brayton Lake and use the phone of a neighbor.

She switched off the flashlight. Began a slow retreat. Stopped. If Locke had beaten them to this house, what had become of its occupants? Had they been harmed? Was there somebody inside mortally injured and in need of urgent medical assistance? She stepped forward again, but halted in her tracks when the small hairs prickled on the back of her neck: a quiver ran the length of her spine. Her gaze snapped to the window furthest to the right from the door. Had she noted movement in her peripheral vision, or was it just a play of dim starlight on the dirty glass as she'd altered position? She sank down a few inches, and brought up the pistol as she stared, watching for the slightest movement that might betray an ambush.

Nothing happened.

Perhaps the movement had been the homeowner peering out at what amounted to an unwanted night-time visitor. Pointing her pistol at them wouldn't endear a warm welcome.

'Tess.' Po's call came to her as he leaned out of the GMC's window. 'Come on back now.'

Tess didn't move. She was certain she was being observed, but whether that was by friend or foe she couldn't determine. One or the other, it didn't matter. There was no hope of calling the police from the house, and taking on another person would only add to their burden and slow them down getting the necessary help. She began retreating once more, not taking her attention off the window.

Back at the car, McNeill was about to climb out to allow her to sit in the middle, but she asked him to shift over. Her pistol would be little use if she stayed wedged between the two biologists.

Once she and Pinky were inside Po set the GMC trundling once more. Most of the tires had shredded, and overheated metal squealed as it dug furrows in the road.

Tess continued to spy at the house, until it was again hidden by the woods.

'It was wasted time but we had to check,' she said. 'The pickup was out of commission, and there never was a telephone line. I've no idea if they had access to a bush radio, but if there was one, it's a certainty it's been disabled.'

'No harm done in checking,' Po reassured her.

'I couldn't tell if there was anyone inside or not.'

'If Locke was there, I'm sure we'd have found out.'

'I'm more concerned about who lived there.'

'When Locke was there they probably slept through her visit, the way they did yours.'

'I should've made sure. The way Locke attacked our camp . . .'

Po exhaled. 'Tess, if Locke went inside, the folks in there are probably dead. There's not a darn thing you can do to help the dead. We can only hope to get justice for them.'

Pinky shifted his weight in the passenger seat. He twisted as far as he could to catch Tess's eye but she was seated directly behind him now. She reached over his chair and gently squeezed his shoulder to show he'd gotten her attention. His words were meant for everyone, though.

'We're driving directly into a trap, us.'

'That's inevitable,' Po said. 'But we have to, if we hope to draw the crazy woman out.'

Jonathan Laird shook his head, his pale features stricken at the idea of another gun battle. 'This is insane! You're all insane!'

Tess said, 'The insane one is the woman who wants to murder us all for what's in Alicia's backpack.'

'Just give her the damn backpack then! We don't need it anymore. We are witnesses to murder and we can send her to prison without the evidence in the bag.'

'That's *exactly* why we can't *just give her it*,' said Tess. 'Do you think she's going to allow any witnesses to live?'

'We could make a deal with her . . . we could—'

'*There isn't going to be any deals*,' Alicia snapped behind Laird. 'Don't you get it, Jonathan? Locke's a single pawn in this and even if I give back the evidence and she disappears, it won't make a damn difference. The people she works for have far too much to lose to let any of us live. For all they know I've shared their names and their involvement with you all, and they won't allow any of you to implicate them in the drug ring. The only way any of us will ever breathe easy again is if I can get this into safe hands and all the key players are rounded up. That's the only way we can ensure all of them, Locke included, are behind bars and can't hurt us.'

Laird shut up. Yet he wasn't the only person who had an opinion that differed from Alicia's. After first moaning about his mistreatment, Frank Lombardi had sunk into brooding melancholy. Now he pushed up onto an elbow so he could stare directly at her. 'If I get my way, that murderous bitch isn't going to prison. First chance I get I'm gonna blow her guts out, the way Carlo's were.'

Alicia rocked her head at his plan, didn't reply. Pinky did. 'You aren't going to do anything, you. You're just going to sit right where you are. Now shut up, or I'll have to zip tie your lips as well, me.'

Frank snorted at the lame threat. 'So I've to just lie here like a trussed hog while the bullets are flyin'? You may as well put a bullet in my head right now and save Locke the trouble.'

'As tempting as that idea sounds,' Po said, and he exchanged a glance and nod of agreement with Pinky, as he maneuvered the car around a tight corner, 'we haven't kept you alive all this time to execute you now. You said you could be helpful to us, Frank, well, you're gonna get a chance to prove it.'

Tess wasn't party to their plan for Frank Lombardi, and was mildly miffed that she hadn't been included in whatever decision they'd come to, but she trusted Po, and knew that whatever was in mind for the hitman, it was for all of their good. Before she could ask, Po's attention went to his rearview mirror, and he grunted under his breath.

Tess twisted as far as she could in her seat, trying to spot what had caught his attention. Alicia also looked out through the shattered rear window, and immediately adjusted the assault rifle.

'Don't let her know you've spotted her,' Po warned.

In the distance, a figure stood alongside the road, believing she was hidden by the gloom, except her silhouette was a deeper shadow against the hardpack that almost glowed silver beneath the starlight.

'Is it Locke?' Tess asked.

'No,' Alicia replied, 'it's the other one I call Red.'

'She musta been hiding in that house, waitin' for us,' said Po. 'She didn't shoot at us, which means she was only there to watch and report.'

'Confirms there's a trap up ahead, right?' said Tess.

'Yup.' Po aimed a grim smile at her. 'There's a turn in the road comin' up, but I doubt it's gonna be there. Here's what we are gonna do . . .'

THIRTY-FIVE

When Locke callously shot dead the innocent old man, Greta's heart had shriveled in her chest but she was careful not to allow her revulsion to show. She understood she was being tested, and if she'd exhibited any weakness she'd have been gunned down with equal impunity. She had serious misgivings about working with Locke, whom she now understood would as soon put a bullet in her head as she would Alicia Coleman's and was sorely tempted to throw away her radio and disappear, leaving the cold-hearted killer to get on with slaughtering those in the car. Two things stopped her from running away; first, she wanted to avenge Gabe Hubert, he'd been her only friend and she felt she should *try* to set his soul at peace; second, she was too afraid of the obvious repercussions if she betrayed Locke. Obeying Locke's instructions would place her in danger, but not to the same extent as she'd be in if she made an enemy of the crazy bitch. Following the plan – by helping Locke kill Coleman – she'd at least get a chance at a normal life afterwards.

Who was she kidding? Her life after this could never return to normal. As yet she hadn't hurt anyone, but through her inactivity, by failing to stop Locke from killing, she was as culpable of murder as Locke was. She'd be a fugitive, whether or not her part in the murders, past and future, was ever determined; she'd know it in her heart and mind and would forever run from her guilt, fearing that knock on the door, or the officious hand on her shoulder.

What was normal anyway? Who could ever have guessed that a bookish girl from Cedar Rapids, Iowa, once voted 'most likely to succeed' by her fellow high school friends, would have ended up here in this desolate backwoods carrying a gun and ushering victims to slaughter while contemplating normality? When she'd enlisted it had been with the noble intent of serving her country, protecting her fellow Americans, never *this*! Her military career hadn't lasted – she'd experienced similar contempt for her gender as she later had from the likes of Billy James and Lance Whyte – but the skills gained had landed her a sweet job as part of a protection detail for Tyson Kelly, an ambitious politician based out of Buffalo, New York. His climb to office had been derailed by a sexual scandal involving a minor, but through contacts made while in Kelly's employment, Greta had joined the staff of a mega-rich businessman called Gerard Pattyn from Toronto. Being intelligent and organized trumped her physical skills as a body-guard, and before long Greta had become more an assistant than a guard, and she was trusted to conduct certain tasks not in her original remit. Pattyn's, it turned out, was not entirely a legiti-mate business, or more specifically, he conducted alternative dealings not associated with what went through his books. Greta was wise enough to know that what she'd gotten involved in was criminal, but her side of things never saw the narcotics Pattyn helped flood into Canada, so she was happy to turn a blind eye. As with any involvement in criminality it goes two ways: either you are that way inclined and throw yourself fully into its nefarious ways, or you are pulled incrementally to the dark side by one seemingly inconsequential act after another. Before the latter type know it they are fully immersed, and can't see a way out. A girl who once wished only to protect the innocent and helpless had become what she'd originally loathed, a monster . . . and there was nothing she could do to change that. That was her current normalcy.

From the confines of the death house she'd observed the blond woman approach. It was the first time she'd gotten a good look at the one Locke had told her came close to killing her during the incursion on the camp. Greta had expected a tough-looking bitch, a mirror of Locke's pinched face and wiry strength, but instead saw a pretty, if unremarkable, woman carrying a few more extra pounds than expected of a deadly enemy. Greta didn't fear her . . . not immediately. But her opinion changed when she noted the manner in which she approached and carried her gun; the woman was trained. More so she was fearless. She was wary, took her time and made no reckless moves, but was unafraid. For a breathless moment Greta thought she was going to come all the way inside, forcing Greta's hand, but something had stalled her in her tracks. The blond noted that the old man's truck was out of commission, and that he'd never had a telephone installed on his property, and was about to back off. She'd set her jaw though and stepped forward. Greta had shifted, and the woman's gaze snapped on her, the barrel of her gun aimed directly at her. Greta held her breath, remained stock-still, confident she was invisible in the deep darkness behind the filthy glass. The woman stared, and Greta stared back, only then realizing she was silently pleading with the woman to turn around and walk away. Anger urged Greta to avenge Gabe Hubert, but it was targeted towards Alicia Coleman, not this stranger, and the thought of shooting her without pity – the way Locke had the old man lying dead behind her – curdled her blood.

To Greta's relief one of her companions called the woman back to the GMC. The woman looked torn by the instruction, and Greta guessed it was because she was concerned for the welfare of whoever lived here, but she retreated, backing away so her gaze stayed glued to the window. The GMC was being driven without the use of headlights, but as the woman went to climb inside, the interior light briefly illuminated those within. Greta made a head count, and more deduced than confirmed that the seven known to have survived the fight at the camp were now squashed inside. The GMC moved on, passing the end of the drive and was hidden by the trees.

Greta hurried to leave the house. She glanced back at the forlorn figure lying on the floor, a halo of blood encircling his head where he lay, and wished she hadn't. A shudder ran through her, but she fought back another wave of revulsion. 'I'm sorry,' she whispered to the unheeding corpse, and slipped out the door and onto the down slope. The car's progress was noisy but dwindling. Greta jogged down the drive, and then tentatively leaned out beyond the last of the foliage to watch. She keyed her radio and Locke responded. Without taking her gaze off the receding GMC she reported on its occupants and the time she expected it to arrive in Brayton Lake.

'Fall in at a safe distance behind them,' Locke ordered curtly. 'If they deviate from their current path I want to know.'

Greta confirmed she understood as she edged further into the road. 'Where'd you want me once they're in town?'

'Move in and shut them down. I don't want them getting out again the way they come in.'

Greta gritted her teeth, steeled herself, and even forced a note of enthusiasm to her answer. 'Understood.'

The GMC was approaching a bend in the road, swallowed by the shadows where the overhanging boughs converged. She began pacing forward. Locke's next words were delivered like a warning. 'Remember I need Coleman alive . . . the others are fair game.'

'Understood,' Greta said. 'But I still get her after you're done with her, right?'

Locke's reply was as sarcastic as ever, and Greta assured her she was only checking the plan hadn't altered.

'It hasn't,' Locke snarled.

'Cool.' The word wasn't wholly appropriate, but she at least sounded enthused by Locke's confirmation. She didn't feel cool, she felt downright chilled to the core. All seven of those people in that car were traveling blindly to their deaths. Not something she wished to dwell on, and she again challenged the idea of what had become *normal* in her life. She'd facilitated deals for Pattyn, had arranged the delivery and wider distribution of narcotics on his behalf, had even witnessed the terrible effects of addiction on some of his clients, but all through the process of compartmentalization. The awful slaughter she was about to help facilitate was not something she could remain even one step removed from, but she'd already convinced herself that there was nothing she could do about it. Regrettably she must play her part or pay the consequences.

The GMC was out of sight. She could still detect the grumble of its engine and the rasp of steel on gravel. She hurried to close down the gap. The bend in the road was sharper than she initially thought. The road then doglegged back on itself and the GMC was beyond the second turn. She cut through the S-bend at an oblique angle, shortening the distance, and came up against the trees on the right-hand side. The GMC was a swaying, blocky form about a hundred paces ahead. Greta allowed it to roll on until it again met a corner, and felt it was safe to pursue. She came out of hiding, loping in a semi-crouch. The engine never halted its groaning, and closer now she could also hear the thwacking of torn rubber on the road surface. She matched her steps to each revolution of the tires. Before the next bend she cut across the road, again heading for the trees that would help conceal her from view.

She jerked to a halt as Alicia Coleman stepped out of the forest to meet her, aiming an assault rifle directly at her chest. For a fleeting second she thought she'd been served a chance at revenge and Greta's gun began to rise.

'Don't be stupid, Red,' Alicia growled.

There'd be only one outcome if they traded bullets, and not in Greta's favor. Her gun began to lower, even as she felt the caress of steel on the nape of her neck.

'Drop it,' said another female behind her, and she knew without looking that the blond had crept from the trees on the opposite side to close the trap. The barrel of her pistol dug into Greta's flesh, emphasizing the threat. Greta couldn't exactly explain why at that moment, but a sense of relief flooded her. She dropped her gun, and raised both hands, placing them on the back of her head. She didn't resist when the blond tugged down her hands behind her back and cinched them together with plastic zip ties. She was forced to kneel.

Alicia approached, still with the assault rifle raised, and Greta couldn't forget how calmly she'd shot Hubert dead . . . Except then Hubert had been in the act of shooting at innocent people in the camp. Greta, on the other hand, was disarmed and trussed up. Somehow she didn't think they would kill her. 'I never wanted to be involved in this,' she said.

'Yet here you are,' said Alicia. 'And here *we* are. What do you think's going to happen now?'

Greta said nothing.

Behind her the blond leaned in close to her ear and said, 'If *you* want to live you're going to help *us* stay alive.'

THIRTY-SIX

F ingers of mist rose from the lake that gave the tiny settlement its name. In the darkest hours before sunrise there was a definite drop in temperature, and moisture condensed on windows and wispy tendrils rose from the mouths of her team with each exhalation. Within the storage shed the dozen or so townsfolk huddled together, but not in an attempt to keep warm. Terrified they clung to each other, each seeking support, each offering support, against the faceless monsters that'd invaded their homes and dragged them there. All but Virginia Locke concealed their faces behind ski masks, through which only their eyes and mouths were visible. She didn't feel the need to hide her identity the way they did: after all, there wouldn't be a living witness after she was finished in Brayton Lake.

She waited patiently, sequestered behind the counter in the makeshift post office, her SIG in easy reach. If Greta Peterson had approximated the GMC's speed correctly then it should show within the next few minutes. She expected to hear it before it trundled into view between the trees at the edge of town. She keyed her radio. 'Heads up, and get in position.'

She received affirmations from all six members of her team in town but nothing from Greta, who was on a different channel. Locke switched over.

'Sit rep,' she demanded.

'They're about five minutes out,' replied Greta. 'The car's not making very good speed . . . tires are totally gone.'

'They're still moving though?'

'Yes.'

'No stops, no deviations?'

'None. They seem intent only on reaching town.'

'You're certain they haven't spotted you.'

'I'm positive.'

'Switch channels. Let us know when they're on the last

approach.' Locke switched back to the dedicated channel. 'Stay frosty, they're inbound,' she announced.

The man codenamed Bravo spoke up. 'We've incoming from the east.'

'Say again: *east*?' said Locke. The GMC was to their west.

'Confirmed. East.'

Locke's face pinched. In these hills, sound could easily be distorted. She briefly wondered if Bravo was hearing an echo of the GMC's noisy approach. From within the post office she couldn't determine for sure. She grabbed her SIG and back-tracked through the house, exiting at the rear onto the narrow road that led to the airstrip. She had a clear view across the open ground to where the road entered town next to the lumber-yard. A vehicle was approaching at speed. Blue-and-red lights flickered among the trees.

'We've got company,' she warned. 'I'll handle it.'

Instead of retreating she moved further into the open, placed her SIG down behind a hummock of couch grass erupting from the hardpack, and doffed her bulletproof vest, hiding it too. She yanked her hair out of its ponytail, tousled it, did the same to her shirt so that it hung awry and concealed the sidearm on her hip. Lastly she slapped her cheeks repeatedly to get a blush glowing and the sting set tears in her eyes. As an Aroostook County sheriff's patrol car rushed into Brayton Lake she stumbled towards it, throwing her arms in the air and waving as if in a mad panic. The deputy behind the wheel slammed on the brakes. Locke stumbled forward a few more feet and collapsed over the hood of the patrol car. She slid off it, going to one knee.

There was a moment where she worried the deputy's first reaction would be to call for assistance before checking her, or he'd use the loud hailer in his car to instruct her from the safety of the cab. He did neither. The deputy threw open his door and stepped out, his attention fully on her as she grabbed for balance at the fender, dragging herself up. 'You have to help me,' she wailed.

He didn't immediately approach but he stood by the open door, right hand hovering over his service weapon, his other hand extended towards her. He glanced around, momentarily confused. It struck Locke that somehow the group with Coleman had gotten out a message to the police before the cell tower was taken out, and this deputy had been deployed to investigate and report; it appeared he wasn't expecting trouble here in Brayton Lake, but much further out in the wilderness.

'Ma'am,' he said, 'show me your hands and step away from the vehicle.'

'You must help me!' Locke's face was practically concealed behind her loose dark hair. Strands of it had caught in her mouth and only added to her distraught appearance.

'Step away from the vehicle,' he reiterated. He unsnapped his holster, but didn't yet draw his weapon.

She lowered her face into her hands, her shoulders jerking as she sobbed. Through her interlaced fingers she moaned, 'I was the one that called for help . . .'

'I'll help you, ma'am, but first I need you to—'

A chorus of cries rose from the storage shed as the townsfolk tried to warn the deputy of his impending doom. He spun towards the racket, his hand momentarily leaving his gun as he reached instead for the radio mike clipped to his uniform shirt's epaulette. Echo stepped into the open door of the shed, his assault rifle braced to his shoulder. The deputy croaked in alarm, and began bleating an unintelligible message into his radio, even as he was torn between diving inside his cruiser, and going to assist Locke. In the next instant he was dragging out his gun. His head snapped back and forth, first on the gunman in the ski mask, then on Locke, and back again, and he understood he'd been fooled. He swung towards Locke.

It was too late.

Her hand had already crept to her right hip. She snapped up her sidearm and fired into his chest. Shock distorted his features, and he slumped, almost sitting down but was held in place by the body of his patrol car. He was hurt, but not dead. He was still in the fight even. He tried to get a shot off at Locke, but she again beat him to it. She caressed the trigger of her gun, this time shooting him higher in the chest . . . above the bulletproof vest concealed under his shirt. The bullet took him in the hollow above his sternum, punching through his throat and blowing blood and bone tissue out the exit hole at the nape of his skull. The deputy slumped to the ground, miraculously with an iota of

Matt Hilton

life still in him. His gun had never fully left its holster. His trembling hand reached for his mike. 'Officer down . . .' he attempted to gurgle but his fingers lacked the strength to depress the button.

Locke leaned around the open door and stared down at him. His eyes rolled up, full of condemnation. 'Sorry, buddy,' she said and shot him again, this time in the head, 'but you were in the wrong place at the wrong time.'

She holstered her weapon, and then with the same perfunctory attention, pulled back her hair and tied it back. The tears had already dried on her cheeks. She turned and perused the storage shed. Inside the hostages whimpered in dismay, while Echo only stood staring back at her. Maybe he was contemplating the kind of trouble he'd gotten into through his association with Locke. Killing a few civilians would cause a public outcry, killing a cop would ensure a hard and fast response from the entire law enforcement community.

'Shut those fuckers up,' she snapped – meaning the hostages. She keyed her radio. 'Foxtrot, get over here and move this body. Charlie, I want you to drive this cruiser to the end of town and block the road, leave the lights on and stay with it. If there's a dash camera, I want it scrubbed and turned off.'

The two men came out of concealment, rushing to comply. She caught their exchange of wary glances as they approached the dead deputy, and snarled, 'Get on with it.'

Foxtrot slung his weapon. He was a huge guy, thickly muscled, the best fit for the task. He crouched and grabbed the deputy by the shoulders of his shirt. He tugged the corpse aside so that Charlie could get inside the cruiser and reverse it. Once the car was clear, he took the deputy's gun and shoved it in his belt. He dragged the body towards the lake. On the down slope, he kicked the body the last few feet and the corpse flopped face down. Murky water flooded over it, enough that the body would be unnoticeable from the road.

Foxtrot backed away, then turned to Locke. She'd collected her SIG and vest from their hiding place. 'Back to your position,' she told him.

'Coleman must've got out a call for help,' he cautioned her.

It was unlikely that the deputy had driven all the way out here in the wilderness for any other reason, she concurred, especially using his lights. But the fact he'd arrived at Brayton Lake alone reassured her that a second response would take time. The deputy – the nearest available patrolman – had most likely been sent to evaluate and report on what could very well be a false alarm before other cops were deployed in numbers. She'd killed him before he could get out a clear message, but nevertheless, his abrupt silence would speak volumes to his dispatcher. The cavalry would be en route.

'We'll be long gone before any more cops get here. Now do as I said.'

Though unsure of his order, he nodded, then jogged away to concealment behind one of the stacks of lumber. Locke checked on the cruiser. Charlie had positioned it as instructed, blocking the entrance to town from the east. Its headlights glared and the rack of gumball lights danced. Spotting the sheriff's vehicle would offer hope to Coleman and her new friends, and help lure them into Locke's trap. They believed they were up against two enemies only – Locke and Peterson – and had no idea a team of gunmen waited for them. The presence of a deputy would give them the wrong impression that they were safe, because *surely* Locke would have made herself scarce, right?

'Wrong.' She smiled nastily at the thought of the forthcoming killings. In an hour tops, she'd have Coleman dead at her feet, and the evidence against her employers safely in her hands, and she'd be aboard the plane waiting to extract her and her team at the airstrip. An hour after that she'd be back in Toronto, and Gerard Pattyn would be the first of a number of uber-rich people spread across the North American continent happy to pay the inflated reward she'd command for her future services.

'Alpha! They're less than a minute out.'

Greta Peterson's warning had come late, but Locke had to cut her some slack. Greta had no real way of approximating where she was in the woods, and it had possibly surprised her how close the GMC had gotten. At least she'd come through and given a warning with time for Locke to prepare herself.

A rumble warned of the GMC's imminent arrival in town. Locke strode, watching for a hint of the car as she headed again for the post office. This time she didn't enter the building – time didn't allow it – but took a position in its shadow. She clutched her SIG, her right shoulder pushed tight to the wall. From her hiding place her view of the road as it entered town was partially concealed by the tiny office annex tacked on the front of the building but through the stained glass she was happy she'd see enough while she'd remain hidden. She inhaled deeply, held the breath in her lungs for a long count of three and then exhaled slowly. All tension left her body.

The GMC trundled out of the forest, approaching at the pace of a fast walk. It arrived without its lights on, but as it was brought to a halt they flared to life, causing Locke to squint against the sudden glare. The headlights flashed repeatedly. She assumed those within had spotted the sheriff's vehicle and wanted to summon it to them. Without being told, Charlie gave a brief warble of his siren and began rolling forward, getting in a better position to join the ambush. Locke let him come, and she stepped out from concealment to spring the trap.

'Alicia Coleman,' she hollered, 'you've five seconds to step out of the vehicle or die with the others.'

The headlights continued to flash erratically, making it difficult to view the car, let alone make out the position of those inside. Any one of them could be aiming a weapon at her, preparing to shoot.

'I'm waiting,' Locke yelled. 'You're down to three seconds. Two . . . ah, fuck it! Light them up.' Her latter words were snapped through her radio, and to emphasize her point she let rip with her SIG, strafing the engine compartment with a barrage of bullets.

THIRTY-SEVEN

To Tess, the old proverb 'forewarned is forearmed' was proving to be true, but it was still extremely risky to spring Virginia Locke's ambush. The capture of Greta Peterson had given them a tactical advantage: they now knew that Locke had bolstered her forces with a team of recently arrived reinforcements, under which circumstances they should have turned tail and fled for the relative safety of the woods to wait them out. But they'd also learned how Locke had taken the villagers of Brayton Lake hostage. Greta Peterson turned on Locke, not only giving up vital information on numbers, but also the frame of Locke's mind. She had totally lost touch with reality, in Greta's opinion. She'd backed this up by revealing how Locke coldly executed the old man as a test of Greta's resolve, and how she planned on slaying every possible witness in Brayton Lake – man, woman, or child – in order to conceal her activities here in the north woods. Greta admitted that she'd held a misguided grudge against Alicia Coleman for shooting her friend, Gabe Hubert, but also that her thinking had undergone a paradigm shift after witnessing the old man's death. She willingly offered to help them stop Locke from executing her plan, and had needed no coaxing to say the right thing when communicating over the radio with the woman, effectively setting her up.

Stripped of weapons, radio and her liberty, Greta was now sitting in the woods two hundred yards outside of town, under the watchful gazes of Jonathan Laird and Grant McNeill, who Tess and her friends had deemed too injured or too inexperienced to assist with the hostage rescue attempt. Tess had used the woman's radio, patching into a Border Patrol monitoring channel and requesting immediate assistance, but it was imperative they help the villagers before Locke went through with her plan to salt the earth with their blood. Initially the plan was for Alicia Coleman to sit tight with Greta and the biologists, but her intention of staying safe in order to get the evidence safely to the

DEA was trumped by her need to help. She risked falling into Locke's hands, but, she reasoned, if not for her, none of those innocent people in Brayton Lake would be in this mess, and she was determined to help make things right. Tess didn't argue against her decision; an extra gun would help, and undeniably Alicia knew how to handle herself. Po, still lame, wouldn't let a sore leg hold him back, any less than Pinky would a few weeping blisters. Remarkably, they gained an extra ally.

It was Frank Lombardi who drove directly into Brayton Lake, drawing the attention of Locke and her team. He brought the car to a halt, pretended to hail the sheriff's deputy by flashing his headlights repeatedly, but really to stop Locke from seeing that the car held only one occupant. Tess had to concur that Frank's willingness to help was spurred mainly by his desire to avenge his young cousin, but it was a brave move nonetheless, and incredibly risky. As Locke let loose with her submachine gun, destroying the GMC's engine, she genuinely hoped that Frank had made it safely out of the car and found somewhere safe to take cover. As the SIG lit up the predawn darkness with strobing muzzle-flashes, she took the opportunity to rush from the edge of the forest towards the rear of a house alongside the narrow road leading to the airstrip. Fifty feet to her right, still lugging her backpack, Alicia also moved across the fallow ground heading towards the rear of the post office. Alicia had her part to play, Tess her own. North of her she knew that Po had already streaked ahead, and taking the dampest option, but the least that required running, Pinky had made his own move.

As she ran, Tess waited to be gunned down by a remorseless enemy. Each step she survived moving forward received a wordless prayer of thanks to God. She came up against the back of the small home, breathless and feeling sick with anxiety, but no less determined to free the hostages. In that moment she didn't care about bringing an international narcotics ring to justice, or about securing the evidence, or about Locke, only saving innocent lives. Reinforcements were coming, but she and her friends had feared they wouldn't arrive in time to save the village people from Locke's demented plan to kill them all, so they must act. She was armed with a partly loaded handgun, going up against better armed criminals who had no compunction about committing murder;

any sane person would be nervous, and she was, but she was also resolute.

From Greta Peterson she'd learned that, including Locke, there were seven killers in the field. Tess only knew the locations of three of them. Locke was out front, another was in the deputy's car, and one man wielding an assault rifle terrorized the hostages. That left another four who required locating and stopping . . . no mean feat. It wouldn't be achieved by staying put, hidden from the battlefield by the house. She crept around it, keeping the house between her and Locke. The woman was shouting periodically punctuating her words with gunfire. That the shooting continued was hopefully a good sign that Frank hadn't died in the first barrage. As she approached the narrow lane, she hunkered against the side of the building, watching for any sign of movement. Distantly she saw a ski-masked figure bob up from behind a pile of stacked logs, to lend firepower to Locke. He covered the GMC while Locke danced to one side, trying to ascertain who was inside the now steaming wreck. Locke spun in a half-circle throwing up her left hand in an exclamation of irritation. The gunman was too far away for Tess to trouble with her pistol. The deputy's car had halted, the driver keeping a safe distance between him and Locke's bullets. He too was out of range for Tess. Only Locke presented a viable target . . . except she'd her back to Tess.

Shoot the bitch and this would probably end. Without their leader, the self-preservation instincts of her team of gunmen would kick in and they'd flee, and the hostages would be saved. Tess's finger paused on the trigger. Before she was a private investigator she was a sergeant with the Cumberland County Sheriff's Department, and then she had been governed by protocol and procedure. She would've warned before shooting, and always attempted to wound before resorting to a fatal resolution. But she couldn't forget what Po often reminded her: she was no longer a cop, and this was not a police scenario; the only rules here were to kill to survive. It soured her stomach, but she again tracked the woman with her gun. One bullet could end it all.

She leaned forward, aiming down her sights, and—
Crack!
Splinters of wood stung Tess's face. She ducked, and a second

bullet struck the wall of the house inches from her. Another man in ski mask and nondescript black clothing had abruptly appeared less than ten yards from her, adjacent to a dwelling on the opposite side of the lane. He too was armed with a semi-automatic pistol but he showed no pause in shooting a victim without warning. *One bullet could have ended it all!* Not in the right way, though. It was only the unexpected shift as Tess had leaned into her shot that had saved her. She scrambled, having no way to go but around the front of the house – if Locke turned she'd be in the woman's gun sights. Her would-be slayer was forced to follow her by stepping fully from concealment alongside the neighboring house. He fired. This time his bullet nipped cloth and skinned her hide. Tess returned fire, but her shot was errant and had more chance of killing a night-flying bird than it did the man on the ground. It didn't matter: it gave him a second's pause and then she was hurdling over a waist-high railing onto a front porch. The house's front door hung open from when its residents were forcibly marched to the storage shed. Tess rushed for it. Bullets tore into the house in front of and behind her, and she understood more than one killer had made her a target. Continue for the door and she'd run directly into a fresh hailstorm of bullets. She collapsed down, throwing out her feet so she slid on her side across the planks. She checked up against the front of the house, bullets punching through the aged wood above her, and smashing glass. Shards from a shattered window rained on her. Tess ignored them, rolling fully onto her belly, offering the smallest target as she aimed back through the railings at her nearest attacker. She fired.

The gunman dodged aside, returning fire on the run. His bullets showered her with more splinters. He ducked alongside the same porch that sheltered her. He was out of sight for a few seconds, and then bobbed out again, directly where she'd positioned to take a shot at Locke only a moment ago. Battlefields were dynamic, ever changing. She had a slight advantage, lying prone and shooting up was always easier than targeting something on the ground. She fired and he grunted and disappeared behind the wall. Was he dead? She had no idea, and no time to check. The second shooter was firing at her from somewhere to her right and Tess had few places to hide. The open door, behind her to the left, offered the only escape. She began snaking backwards, using one elbow and her squirming legs to propel her for the opening.

A bullet struck her right thigh, and the shock sent a scarlet wash over her vision. She cringed in agony, waited for blackness to take her fully, but only dots of oil swarmed behind her eyelids. Nipping her bottom lip between her teeth she cursed inwardly at the pain, fighting against an urge to submit to it: she wasn't going to allow it to stop her. She jack-knifed her body and rolled and was within the house. She came up onto her knees, trembling with the flood of adrenalin coursing through her. Bullets cut through the open doorway and the flimsy walls. Tess scrambled for cover. She was in a neat sitting room – or it was before the bullets chewed through the furniture. She crawled behind a settee, hoping the upholstery would take enough force out of the bullets to stop them killing her. Gasping for air she checked on her leg wound. It was a mass of hurt, but thankfully a ricochet must have hit her with most of its force spent, because she was bruised but not pierced. The first injury she'd taken still stung, and a quick check showed her that she'd lost a couple layers of skin, and the wound wept plasma tinged with blood: it was more of a burn than anything else. Splinters had also embedded in her cheek, and tiny slivers of glass tinkled from her hair and clothing as she shifted. Her eyes flicked back to the doors and window. She couldn't forget potentially two gunmen had her penned down and it'd be moments at best before they assailed the house. She made a quick check of her gun, dropping the magazine, and doing a quick count of the rounds. There were only four in the mag and one in the chamber. Not great. She quickly reinserted the magazine and checked around her. Pockmarked blinds covered the shattered front window, but Tess spotted a shadow flicker between the slats. She fired, and heard a curse in response. Immediately a second figure bobbed around the open doorframe, and an assault rifle swept the room with bullets. Tess ducked low, going down on an elbow so she could reach around the edge of the settee.

Outside, a clamor was growing louder throughout Brayton Lake. There were gunshots and shouts, screams, and the roaring of an engine. There was also the singular crack of an M110 sniper rifle. The man intending to kill Tess from the doorway suddenly crashed down across the hearth, dead. Pinky – thank God – was in position and had joined the battle. Tess ignored the glassy expression in the corpse's eyes, the way the mouth was twisted askew – the only features visible behind the ski mask – and instead grasped his fallen rifle and pulled it to her. She'd fired few assault rifles in her time, but she knew the basics. She carefully inserted her pistol in her belt, then readied the rifle for action. As an afterthought she patted through the corpse's pockets and found spare magazines. She pocketed them in her jacket.

Beyond the walls of the house a different assault rifle roared. She wondered about her first attacker. Twice now she believed she'd hit him, but he was far from dead. Tess wasn't stupid, there was no way possible she was going to poke her head outside to check. She backed through the sitting room, seeking another exit, and found a kitchen. A door led out back, near to where she'd first checked up against the house after her breathless run from the forest. She'd lose ground going out that way, but it was better than losing her life. Besides, she'd done her part for now, causing a distraction while Po saw to the truly dangerous bit of the plan. She threw the bolt, and eased open the door. She led with the barrel of her newly acquired rifle as she took a quick glance left to right outside.

She should have checked right to left instead.

As her gaze turned to the right, the stock of a handgun was already flashing towards her face. She flinched in anticipation of the impact, but it didn't help. The gun butt slammed her above her right eyebrow, and she fell back against the doorframe, emitting a yelp of pain. Consciousness threatened to abandon her, and she raged against it, tugging on the trigger of her rifle as the first gunman charged in behind the strike of his gun butt. He'd slipped within the barrel's range, that or he was impregnable to gunfire, because he wasn't slowed a second. His left hand caught Tess around the throat, squeezing so hard her windpipe was about to collapse, and he hove in with the pistol in the other, intending smashing her face to pulp. Knees collapsing, there was nothing Tess could do to stop him from beating her to death.

THIRTY-EIGHT

S luicing dirty water from his clothes, Pinky grabbed the floundering Frank Lombardi and dragged him bodily into the rowboat moored alongside the pier. Frank spluttered and hacked up a lungful of lake water, eyes rolling wildly. It was a struggle for him to breathe, and panic grasped him and he reared up to try to clear his airway. Pinky thrust him down again, and both men lay top to toe in the wildly rocking boat he'd swum across the lake to reach.

'Chill out, you,' Pinky rasped. 'You'll be OK in a second or two, all right?'

'Thought . . . I . . . wus . . . gonna drown.'

'Can't believe you never learnt to swim, you. Jeez . . . isn't that supposed to be my racial stereotype?'

Frank spluttered again, earning a shake of Pinky's head.

'If you're going to die, do it without all that damn movin' around, you. You're going to end up capsizing us, an' if you do that, I won't be haulin' your ass outta the lake again.'

Frank was gaining control of himself, breathing a little steadier; he craned up so that he could sneer at Pinky. 'Woulda been easier swimmin' if my friggin' hands weren't tied.'

'Never expected you to end up in the drink, me,' said Pinky. 'Truth is, I never expected you to make it out of the car alive.'

'I very nearly didn't, man. That crazy bitch lit it up like it's the Fourth of July!'

'Good job we didn't tie you to the wheel like I first wanted, huh?' Pinky had never really made the suggestion: Frank had actually won kudos for volunteering to be the one to drive the crippled GMC into town. Granted, he was probably looking at it as his best opportunity to escape captivity, but nevertheless, it took some *cajones* Pinky wouldn't have credited him with before. Nobody expected Locke to let loose on the car, thinking she wanted to take Alicia alive so wouldn't fire blindly at it. As she blasted the engine to scrap, Frank had made it out by the

skin of his teeth, lurching out the passenger door on the far side
from Locke and tumbling down the slope into the lake. He'd
floundered and splashed, clawed his way through the reeds. Locke
hadn't bothered pursuing him, but the bogus deputy had been
dispatched to finish Frank off. The guy had sped forward, then
jogged from the cruiser, laughing at Frank's attempts at swimming for his life, and had run directly into a bullet from Pinky's
M110. The dead guy flopped in the lake. Frank clung to the dead
body until Pinky had fished him out, a soaking, coughing wreck.
   Pinky checked on Locke.
   She was busy casting around, trying to pinpoint Alicia or the
others, and had no idea the gunshot signified the death of one
of her own rather than Frank. Pinky lined her up and was about
to drop her too, and that's when a riot of muzzle flashes and
gunshots drew his attention. Even in the dark, there was enough
sporadic light from the flashing of guns to see that Tess was in
dire peril. He watched as she made it inside the open door of
a house, but was being pursued by two of the ski-masked
sons-of-bitches. One of them reeled away from the shuttered
window, and Pinky gave Tess a silent cheer for winging him
with a blind shot. The injured man retreated, going back over
the porch railings and taking cover at the side of the house. The
other moved in and he was carrying an assault rifle . . . Tess
would never survive a trade-off of rounds with him!
   Pinky's scope left Locke, tracking tight toward the house.
The boat rocked under him.
   'Goddamnit, Frank! Lie still!'
   The boat still wallowed, making his shot less than perfect,
but Pinky took it anyway. Better he try to slow the gunman,
give Tess a chance at escape, than nothing. The man dropped,
poleaxed. He fell dead in the doorway.
   'Well, would you look at that?' Pinky wheezed in surprise.
He'd killed the man more by fortune than design, but dead was
dead and that was all that mattered. 'Go, pretty Tess,' he said
under his breath, 'get outta there, you.'
   There was no more he could do to help her in that instant,
so he swung his scope back to Locke. Or where Locke had been
a moment ago. The woman had made herself scarce, aware now
that she and her helpers were under fire from various points in

Brayton Lake. Two of her heavies were dead, and she no longer held the upper hand. Pinky searched for other targets, spotted movement behind a stack of lumber but had no shot. Further to the right another dude in a ski mask popped in and out of the doorway of a storage shed, from where a number of voices rang out in fright. The boat wobbled. Pinky wasn't for trusting another lucky shot. 'Hey!' He kicked in frustration at Frank, a glancing blow with his heel. 'Lie still, you!'

'Gimme a gun, Pinky,' Frank said.

'Like hell I will.'

'C'mon, man. What've I got to do to prove whose side I'm on?'

'You've gotta lie still, shut the fuck up and let me help my friends.'

A gunman broke cover, streaking across the lumberyard towards the far corner. He took shelter behind the parked truck, assessing his next run. He was going to go for the Sheriff's department cruiser, use it for cover while he flanked Pinky's position.

'Yeah,' Pinky whispered encouragement as he lined up the crosshairs on the front of the truck, 'go for it, you.'

'Pinky . . . man?'

Pinky gritted his teeth, refusing to answer Frank's exhortation as he waited for the gunman to show his masked face.

Frank was persistent. 'At least cut me loose, man. I'm lyin' in the bottom of a boat, and can't do a damn thing to save my ass if one of them gets past you. C'mon, man, gimme a fighting chance.'

Pinky was about to tell him to shut up, and his split second of inattention was all it took for the gunman to hurtle out from concealment. Pinky squeezed the trigger, but even before the bullet left the muzzle he knew he'd missed. The gunman crouched at the rear of the cruiser, blocked from sight. Lying belly down in the rowboat, Pinky's view of the deputy's car was obscured by the tall reeds at the lakeshore. He'd no option but scramble up to his knees, despite the fact he was offering his head and torso as a target in return.

An assault rifle chattered, and not the one toted by Pinky's target. Bullets chewed the pier alongside Pinky, casting splinters and ricochets that whined past his head like angry hornets. Pinky ducked, and the boat rocked wildly, and he had to drop the sniper rifle to grasp the sides to avoid falling over. Something clattered and Frank squirmed. More bullets cut into the prow, and it was a miracle none made it through to Pinky's body.

'To hell with this, man, you're on your own!' Frank abandoned ship, rolling over the gunwale in an unceremonious fashion, no longer afraid of drowning. He grasped for the pilings and dragged his body out of sight beneath the pier. There he crouched, hip-deep in soupy mud, hidden in the inky darkness where the pier met the shore. He set to on his plastic bindings, rasping them on the burred end of a metal retaining bolt protruding from a piling. More bullets sent Frank floundering in the mud again.

Pinky gave Frank no further thought; he'd two shooters to contend with and they had him in overlapping arcs of fire. More bullets smashed into the pier and boat, and then the second gunman joined in, shooting blindly from hiding at the side of the cruiser: his bullets came closer to nailing Pinky than the other's did. Pinky grabbed the sniper rifle, and went over the opposite side of the rowboat, into the same churned-up mud as Frank had a moment before. The pier offered momentary sanctuary at most. Without eyes on his attackers, he'd have no way to defend against them if they came in on opposite sides. Even if he managed to drop one, the other would tear him and Frank to ribbons.

Pinky surged backwards, going down on his back with the M110 clutched to his chest, and kicked away from shore. When first he'd volunteered to be the one to swim across the lake he'd joked he wasn't naturally buoyant, a self-deprecating joke at his extra weight, but as a kid he'd regularly swum in the bayous, and after his incarceration in Louisiana State Penitentiary, and the onset of his health issues, it was a pastime he took up again, favoring Olympic-sized pools over boggy waterholes and sluggish rivers. Despite his build, Pinky was a strong and accomplished swimmer. He allowed the natural turn of his body to send him deep into the lake, away from the bullets striking the planks he'd be expected to take shelter beneath.

He resurfaced a dozen yards away, hidden from those on shore by the mist pooling around him. He rose slowly and silently, allowing the water to gently sluice off his head and eyelashes, breathing through his nostrils only. His feet were planted under him, buried deep in centuries' worth of silt. He raised the M110 so it was only inches above the shimmering water and waited . . .

THIRTY-NINE

Alicia spotted Locke's dark blue Ford parked to the rear of the post office-cum-old lady's house, and judged the chances of escaping in it against the probability that Locke's fury would be terrible. Tess and her partner, Po Villere, were currently attempting a daring rescue mission to free the townsfolk before Locke had them slain. Taking the bitch's car and fleeing town was possible now that the sheriff's cruiser no longer blocked the route out to the east but Locke's wrath would be instantaneous. She barely gave the thought more than passing attention, because she'd already dedicated herself to helping her new friends. The Border Patrol was en route – how would it look to the world if she, a federal agent, abandoned the others and they failed to save the hostages before help could arrive? Demolishing an international narcotic smuggling operation wouldn't earn any honors if she were declared the coward that'd run and left behind innocents to die for her sake.

She, or more correctly the key in her backpack, was what Locke wanted most, the lure necessary to give Tess and Po the window they needed. She took shelter in the house. The back door stood open: already somebody had been inside, probably when the post mistress was rousted from bed and led at gunpoint to the storage shed. She couldn't be certain if anyone was inside or not, so went cautiously, clearing first the kitchen, then a sitting room, before edging through another door into the annex office. The windows were aged, warped, murky, but she could make out the muzzle flash near the pier and the crackle of gunfire came to her ears less than a second later. A shadow bypassed the windows, a human shape, and she couldn't tell if it was friend or foe. She crouched behind the counter, tracking the movement with her assault rifle but daren't fire. The figure moved out of sight.

She didn't rise yet. Concealed by shelves stacked with sundry office supplies she thought about her next move. She must draw

Locke to her, but not at the expense of being an easy target, but
if the worst happened and she was killed she must ensure the
bitch didn't get her hands on the contents of her backpack. Should
she die, she'd bequeathed the contents to Tess Grey and earlier
told the private investigator the key to decipher the coded data.
She tugged out of the backpack, loosened the flap and dragged
out the holdall she'd dug up. It was grimy and dirt was stuck in
the zipper, but inside the key would have retained its integrity
as she'd taken care to protect it prior to leaving Canada. Much
of what was in the holdall was useless, simply random documents
and packages among which she'd hidden the important stuff.
She'd been encumbered with unnecessary weight since digging
up the holdall, but this was the first time she'd been able to sift
through and discard the extra weight unobserved. She found the
key exactly where she expected, secreted between other pastel
colored, plastic-wrapped packages.

Outside the gunfire had diminished. That did not mean that
the fight was over, only that the combatants were jostling for
superior positions. She had no idea if any of her allies were dead,
or how many of Locke's people they'd taken out of the fight, but
she expected that more people would die before sunrise. Tess,
Po, Pinky, and even their prisoner, Frank Lombardi, were doing
their bit to defeat Locke and save the innocent townsfolk, but
Alicia wasn't hiding, keeping her head down until the fighting
was over with, she'd best get on with playing her part.

A desperate howl filtered through the building, somewhere
behind her, and it galvanized her into action. It also served as a
catalyst to ignite round two of the battle for Brayton Lake.

She began stuffing the holdall again.

FORTY

P
o was in his element. He never felt more alive than when
danger loomed so close by that it set his blood alight. The
debilitating ache in his injured thigh was not only ignored,
it was totally displaced by the buzz of endorphins coursing
through him. He moved through Brayton Lake almost wraith-
like, a specter of doom to those he'd set his sights on, with Frank
Lombardi's silenced pistol once more in his hand. He'd prefer
to forgo the pistol, but he was neither an idiot nor reckless . . .
he faced enemies with bigger guns and more firepower.

Testifying to that thought was the popping and chattering of
firearms coming from two fronts where his friends had closed with
Locke's people. His turquoise eyes gleamed, and his teeth were
clenched in a grimace; he might be in the kill zone, but that
wasn't to say he was unconcerned about the safety of his loved
ones. But Locke's people must be drawn into a fight in the open
where their numbers and firepower would lose their advantage,
and also serve to clear a passage for Po to reach the storage shed.

There was the briefest lull in the fighting. He crouched in the
lea of a house a stone's throw from where the hostages were
corralled. A man wearing a ski mask and dark clothing stood
guard. He was restless, his attention torn between those he was
supposed to be guarding and a desire to join the fight. As the
shooting suddenly abated, the guard stepped further from the shed,
and his gaze darted, seeking a target. If Po moved he'd attract
attention and a storm of bullets from the guy's assault rifle.

From Tess's direction a scream of unadulterated rage split the
air, and it sparked a return to battle. As gunfire blazed, the guard
backed away so he was once more concealed within the doorway
of the shed. He cursed at his hostages, ordering silence. Po checked
around, then slinked forward another twenty paces and ducked
behind a stack of firewood in a lean-to shelter. From Greta Peterson
he understood that Locke's team numbered six combatants. Pinky
had killed two already – the guy who'd gone after Frank from

the deputy's car, and one of those threatening Tess who'd been dropped in the doorway of the house she sheltered inside – that left only four alive and kicking. Two gunmen approached the pier seeking Pinky and Frank; Tess was fighting another; that meant Po had to contend with a single guard. He couldn't discount Locke, because he'd no idea where she'd gotten to since the first exchanges of bullets but he knew she wasn't near the storage shed.

He could move directly for the doorway the ski-masked thug was stationed at. Wait until the action, and his eagerness to get involved, drew him out and then shoot the punk dead – except Po might be the one torn apart by bullets if the gunman got the drop on him. No, that would not do. He wasn't afraid of a full-frontal showdown, but Po was the best chance for freeing the hostages before Locke gave the order to slaughter them. That wouldn't happen if he allowed pride to get the best of him. He darted away, heading towards the back corner of the shed.

The storage shed was part of the lumberyard. Out of his sight earlier, Po discovered the ground to the rear of it was clogged with redundant tree-felling machinery and more piles of stacked timber. It formed a labyrinth of towering shapes among which he moved without fear of being seen or heard. He exited the mounds at the back right corner of the shed, and placed an ear to the wall. Within the hostages were cowed into silence, but for one weeping woman: she cried for a recently murdered spouse, apparently cut down by their guard. If Po ever had qualms about shooting a man in the back, he shucked off that reticence now. He slunk along the side of the shack, checking periodically through chinks between the walls, and got a good bearing on the position and numbers of hostages despite the darkness though not their guard. Towards the front right corner he paused, looked down at the silenced pistol then across at the propane tanks. In movies he'd seen heroes cause immense explosions by shooting at similar gas containers, but he doubted it could be done. He wasn't about to waste bullets on a Hollywood myth to cause a diversion. Instead he stepped around the corner, and edged up to the doorway.

The guard was yelling into his radio, demanding instruction. It would've been helpful if they'd brought the Peterson woman's radio to listen into Locke's teams' communications, but it had been left with Jonathan Laird to help guide medical assistance to him when the Border Patrol arrived. He heard the codenames Alpha and Echo repeated, and guessed he was about to kill the latter. He had no compunction about the cold-blooded thought when he overheard the next discourse.

Alpha snarled, 'Charlie and Golf are down; we're getting our asses kicked out here. It's time to up the ante. Echo, bring out one of the hostages and put a round in their head. Let these bastards see where resistance is getting them.'

Echo didn't immediately reply, but not through reticence to obey the command. The son of a bitch was choosing a target. He grabbed the crying woman, and began dragging her towards the door – pursued by the cries and pleas of the others. 'Shut your damn mouths, unless you wanna take this whore's place,' Echo barked.

Po had heard enough. He stepped inside the shed.

Echo's back was to him. The thug had an arm around a middle-aged woman's throat. He dragged her unceremoniously to her execution. The woman screeched, kicked, dug in with her heels. Beyond her the other townsfolk suffered equal amounts of horror and shame. An older man, dressed in pajama bottoms and a white T-shirt, made an effort to stand but was pulled down by a woman – his spouse perhaps – who howled at him to *stay with her*. Others spotted Po in the doorway, but for all they knew he was another killer there to assist Echo. They cowered, and even the would-be have-a-go hero sank down on his heels, peering up at him. His partner clung to him in relief.

Echo was unaware of Po's presence until he felt the suppressor dig into the base of his skull.

'Let her go,' Po growled.

Echo weighed his options. The woman had become cumbersome in his grasp, fainting so abruptly that he couldn't hold her up and juggle his rifle in his other hand. Po was tempted to squeeze the trigger, but the son of a bitch deserved to see death coming. He grabbed Echo's ski mask, ripped it backwards so that the man staggered. He met Po's extended leg and crashed down on his butt, his assault rifle falling uselessly at his side. Po stamped down on it, trapping it on the floor, even as he whipped his gun against the man's exposed chin. Echo rolled away, hands cupping his face, and Po leaned down to check the woman. She was out

of it. Po got between her and Echo; over his shoulder he said,
'One of you help her. Get her outta the way.'

He didn't look, but he'd bet it was the older guy who came
to help haul the woman to safety. His gaze never left Echo.

The punk climbed to one knee, rubbing his chin. His ski mask
was askew, and he ripped it fully off to glare up at Po. 'You're
gonna be sorry—'

Po shot him.

Echo yowled as the bullet cut into his left thigh.

'I'm gonna be sorry?' Po asked.

He cast aside the pistol. It wasn't bravado. He was out of
ammunition. He dipped towards his right ankle, came up again
with his knife in hand.

Echo's eyes darted from the knife to his assault rifle back to
the knife. If he tried to lunge, especially with one leg disabled,
Po's knife would pierce his lungs before his fingers reached the
gun. His hand went to a sheath on his belt and he drew a hunting
knife, serrated along the back edge. He pushed up to his feet,
favoring the injured leg. Blood pulsed from the wound, gathering
in the black material of his trousers as a glistening swathe. His
foot dabbed at the earthen floor, the wounded muscle contracting:
Po had leveled the field, taking his own injury into consideration.

Only a couple of yards separated them. Echo tried to close
them down, throwing his weight into an upswing to gut Po. Po
swiveled at the hips and slashed down. His blade sliced through
the material of Echo's sleeve and drew more blood, but the injury
wasn't enough to loosen Echo's grip. The man immediately swung
at Po again, and this time Po sucked back his hips. His riposte
jabbed an inch of steel in Echo's bicep. This time his hand
convulsed and he dropped the hunting knife. Po stepped back.
Nodded at Echo. 'Pick it up.'

Echo's mouth worked wordlessly; his eyes were huge.

'Pick it up,' Po repeated.

Echo reached tentatively for the hilt with his right hand. Then
he lunged, grabbed it in his left and backhanded it at Po's throat.
Po's blade jabbed with a viper's speed, and Echo's left wrist
spilled blood. The blade clattered to the ground, but Echo didn't
care. His back swipe had forced Po to retreat another yard, and
it left room to grab the assault rifle. He snatched it up – he

couldn't care less that the hands he required to control it were both trembling uncontrollably; it was his only hope of survival. He jostled it around with fingers slick with blood, and brought it to bear on Po. Except Po had moved.

He grasped the gun with his left hand, thrusting it skyward. Echo depressed the trigger, and the barrel grew from warm to blistering hot as he discharged most of an entire magazine in one long burst. Po rammed a knee into Echo's midriff, forcing him back against the doorjamb. He met Echo's look of hatred with one of his own. Beneath the blazing muzzle Po thrust in with his knife, digging deep into the man's exposed armpit. He gave the blade a final twist. Po watched the light go out of Echo's eyes, lowered his knee, and allowed the dirt bag to sink to the floor. He kept hold of the rifle until it slid from the man's dead fingers. Po's gun was empty; this one was done too, so he threw it aside. He wiped his blade clean on Echo's shoulder, then spirited it away in its boot sheath. He turned to survey the terrified hostages, and his mouth twitched when he saw that the older guy and his wife had taken charge of the woman he'd just saved. She had come out of her swoon but appeared dazed by the turn of events. Others appeared equally confused. A few of them began to moan in fear.

'Take it easy, I'm here to help, y'all,' Po reassured them. 'Everyone follow me, I'm gettin' y'all outta here.'

They were unsure. They'd just watched him torment Echo before slaying him. Perhaps he was taunting them now with a false promise of freedom.

He raised his voice. 'I've friends out there fightin' on your behalf. I want to go help them, so help me do that by gettin' your butts in gear.'

Po led the freed villagers outside, ensuring they went around the shed on the far side from the battle. 'Back there's a maze,' he reminded them, 'but it isn't safe to hide there. The cops are coming: go further out into the woods, keep your heads down and don't return till you hear the sirens and the shooting stop.'

Without question they began filing past. The older guy supported the woman who'd fainted earlier, while his wife clung to him. He nodded in gratitude, and it was all the thanks Po required. As they scurried away he returned to the fray.

FORTY-ONE

The clubbing blow to her eyebrow plus the squeezing of her throat both vied to rob cognizance from Tess. Her knees liquefied and she slumped, and though her attacker was much larger, she was still a dead weight when held in one hand. He lurched. Instead of his next blow bashing in her skull, he missed his mark. The butt of his pistol still skidded across her head, sending a bright flash of pain deep into her core, but her hair cushioned some of its force. The agony also jolted her out of her swoon and she wrenched to one side, jabbing the butt of her rifle in his side. She had no room to shoot, but the protuberances on the frame of the rifle dug painfully into him, forcing him to also squirm aside. His grasp round her throat loosened, if only for a second. Tess gulped air. Spots danced in her vision and she could taste iron. Then his fist closed again and she squawked as he stiff-armed her against the wall of the house. Her rifle was between them, but despite being at arm's length she still couldn't shoot him – her hands lacked the strength. The rifle fell between them. He raised his pistol, this time in the conventional manner and aimed it between her eyes.

'You fucking shot me, you whore,' he snarled. Hot flecks of saliva sprayed her face.

Tess didn't know where her bullets had hit him, so it was luck that guided her groping fingers to the wound in his shoulder. Blindly, desperately she dug in her nails, gouging deep into a wet hole in his jacket. Her nails raked raw flesh. Her attacker gritted his teeth, groaning in pain, and his pistol left its target. But it was only so he could smash her again with its weight. He swore savagely as he struck at her wrist, inadvertently connecting with the old injury that'd wrecked Tess's law enforcement career. The agony shooting up her forearm exploded a second later in her brain. Her fingers fell away from his shoulder, spasming, useless. The web of his thumb sealed her throat completely. She tried kicking him in the groin – her leg didn't actually move.

There was no need for him to waste a bullet on her; she was dying from lack of oxygen. Except he was hell bent on paying her back. He again raised his gun, settling his feet so that this time there'd be no missing his target.

A wild scream, part rage, part desperation, assaulted his senses. The man twisted to its source, just as a figure flew at him from the darkness, one arm thrown back holding—

Grant McNeill hurtled at him, hacking wildly with the hatchet he'd carried from camp. The man twisted towards him, dropping Tess in order to save himself, and the hatchet struck. It caromed off his gun he'd frantically swiped to parry the blow. McNeill's attack was frenetic though, and he chopped again, and again. Both times steel crunched through flesh and bone. The man cowered in shock, but McNeill continued screaming, and chopping.

Tess kicked out of her slump. It took a few seconds for clarity to return to her while she rasped air in and out of her lungs. The battling figures trampled over her. In reaction she grasped the nearest leg, and used it to yank her forward. She got her uninjured arm under her and pushed up to her knees. *What in hell is going on?* In the dark, her head still swimming, she had no way of telling who was who. She was buffeted again, but this time realized that two men were grappling for control of a single axe. They cursed and shouted, one of them hysterically. Then Tess understood who her guardian angel was. The young biologist wasn't a fighter, but he'd been spurred into action by grief for Elsa.

The man was severely wounded, but he was more than a match for the kid, especially now McNeill had lost the ability to strike with the axe. The ski-masked thug butted his forehead savagely into McNeill's face twice in succession, and the biologist flagged. They swung in a lazy dance, arms extended, each held at the opposite wrist. The man lost his pistol. Tess scrambled for it, and snatched it up.

Unerringly she aimed it at the man's back, despite the hammering agony pulsing from her abused wrist.

'Hold it!' she shouted – her words a faint rasp through her tormented throat. As an ex-law enforcement officer she was loathe to shoot anyone in the back, at least without issuing a warning first.

Whether he heard or not he showed no sign. He was engaged fully in the fight for the hatchet and was winning. He wrenched it free of McNeill, juggled it into a better position and slashed at the biologist's head.

To hell with this!

Tess fired.

The bullet punched into the man's skull. The hatchet fell from his lifeless fingers, dropping as abruptly to the ground as his corpse. McNeill slumped against the house as if an invisible string holding him up had been sundered. He gasped into his cupped palms, as much horrified by his actions as those he'd helped stop. Tess dropped to her knees in front of him, gasping also.

'I . . . I killed him . . . with my hatchet . . .' McNeill refused to look at the huge man lying next to him.

'No,' Tess croaked, 'his death's on me. You saved a life today, Grant, and that's what matters.'

'I wish I could've saved Elsa too.' He sobbed, but then stared at her with clarity. 'You're hurt, are you—'

Tess touched the swelling on her brow; it was as large as a plum, and probably the same color. It was the least of her concerns. Her wrist, her leg, her throat, each gave her more trouble. 'I'm fine,' she lied. 'What about you, Grant? Did he hurt you?'

'I feel as if I just wrestled a bear, but' – he briefly assessed his aches and pains, touched his bleeding nose – 'I'm OK. I don't think anything's broken.'

'Come on, then. It's too dangerous, you can't stay here.'

McNeill searched for his hatchet. It was nowhere to be seen. Tess guessed it was hidden beneath the corpse, and best left there. She was grateful for McNeill's heroic intervention, yet things could've ended differently for both of them. She shuddered at the thought.

She retrieved the assault rifle and handed him the dead man's pistol. 'Do you know how to use that?'

McNeill inspected the gun, weighed it in his grasp. 'I've fired a flare gun before.'

'This one's different.' Tess leaned in and showed him the basics. 'Safety's off in this position. Leave things like that for now. All you have to do is aim and squeeze the trigger, you don't have to pull back the hammer first.'

'I'm not sure I could ever shoot someone,' he said, then thought about how ridiculous he must sound following his frenzied assault with the hatchet. 'Well, I didn't think I ever could before today.'

'You don't have to shoot anyone. That's only for show. Go on back to Laird. If you see any of Locke's people, fire towards them and then run for the woods, OK?'

'I should help you. I can—'

'You'll be helping by staying safe. Things are coming to a head now, and I can't guarantee your safety if you stay with me.'

He blinked at her as though she were nuts. He'd just saved her life, hadn't he?

'Besides, Laird could do with your help,' Tess went on. 'He's hurt, and if Peterson tries anything—'

'Peterson's gone.'

'What?'

'Jonathan told her to leave.' He spotted the apprehension in Tess. 'Peterson isn't like these others,' he assured her, 'she's a decent person who got caught up in something out of her control. Don't forget she helped us fool Locke so we could free the hostages. She's earned a second chance, right?'

Tess glanced around, as if expecting the red-haired woman to suddenly burst out of the trees to join the fight against them, but in her heart knew that McNeill and Laird were correct. Greta Peterson had seemed genuine when she described how she'd ended up there in the woods, and how much Locke's actions sickened her. She only had to glimpse at the corpse to agree that good people sometimes ended up doing bad things for reasons they couldn't govern.

McNeill said, 'She's running for it right now, to get away before the cops arrive. Just let her go, Tess. Please?'

Tess cradled the assault rifle. 'Peterson isn't my concern. Locke and the others are. Now go on, do as I said and get back to Laird. He's hurt, he needs protecting now that he's alone.'

He nodded in agreement and turned for the forest.

'Grant,' she said, and he looked back at her. 'Thank you.'

He shook his head sadly, but accepted her thanks with a brief smile and nod. He ran for the trees bent almost double while she covered his retreat. Once she was happy he'd make it safely to hiding she moved back through the house and peered around the jamb of the open front door. She didn't as much as glance at the other dead man at her feet. She'd no idea how the tide of battle had shifted in the past few desperate minutes, or even if Po's mission had been successful. One thing she was certain of was that Pinky's situation had altered for the worse, if the hellish racket down by the lake was to judge by. The muzzle flashes showed two men converging on the pier, tearing it – and whoever had taken shelter beneath it – apart with machine-gun fire. Without thought for her own safety, Tess lunged from cover and began a limping jog towards the fight.

FORTY-TWO

There has to be an element of cosmic irony involved in this, Pinky thought. That an illegal arms dealer sickened by his actions had turned his back on his trade yet was now using an illegal firearm to defend against a bunch of criminals carrying illegal firearms he could very well have sold wasn't lost on him. Add to that he was about to risk his life trying to save another criminal who'd chased him here with the intention of killing him because he'd foregone his former trade, and he'd admit some divine entity with a twisted sense of humor was having a laugh at his expense. *Ha fucking ha!* It'd be hilarious if it weren't so freakin' ridiculous!

Frank Lombardi was alive . . . for now. But his life expectancy was measured in seconds. Two gunmen – Bravo to the left, Delta to the right – moved on his position with murderous intent. Their assault rifles blazed intermittently, one man shooting while the other reloaded and vice versa, ensuring there was no opening for a counter attack: they had no idea Frank was unarmed. Perhaps due to his lack of involvement in the last minute or more they thought Pinky had perished, or that he was out of ammunition. The truth was, the ten-round detachable box magazine was depleted to the last few cartridges, and Pinky was unsure how few. He hadn't been counting. Before swimming across the lake to get in position he'd discarded his voluminous jacket as soaked it would have dragged him to the bottom; the spare ammunition collected by Po had been stuffed in the pockets. He'd brought a spare magazine for the rifle, but during his scramble for life and rolling out of the rowboat, it had been lost in the mud. Pinky mentally shrugged: he'd either enough bullets or he hadn't. If the same twisted deity currently sniggering at him had marked his cards there was nothing much he could do to deny fate.

The M110 with scope, bipod and partly loaded magazine attached weighed in at around fifteen pounds. It was designed for firing from a prone or supported position, not by a marksman nostril deep in boggy water with the mud sucking the sneakers off his feet. Under normal circumstances its effective firing range was up to eight hundred and seventy-five yards . . . these were not normal circumstances. Pinky took the weight with the stock braced to his shoulder, and supported by his left palm. He was stronger than average, but there was a tremor in his muscles. He wouldn't be sending a bullet downrange to the accepted accuracy of a seasoned marksman. It didn't matter, as long as he hit his damn targets the force of 7.62x51mm NATO rounds through their central masses would ruin their day.

Bravo cut further to the left, seeking a view under the pier. Grass grew tall against the edge of the boardwalk, concealing Frank from sight, but it didn't take a rocket scientist to work out where he was holed up. Bravo fired from the hip and wood splintered and divots of dirt kicked up. While in that position his partner, Delta, couldn't flank the pier for fear of being caught by friendly fire. He fell back, retreating so that he was safe from Bravo's bullets, and instead checked out the rowboat from the sloping embankment. He swayed and dipped, checking around the boat and then under the pier where it jutted over the water. Maybe he expected to see Pinky's corpse wallowing there.

'Surprise, surprise, you,' Pinky whispered internally.

Delta was an open target, but Bravo was the greatest and imminent threat to Frank. Pinky settled on Bravo, knowing that as soon as he fired he'd draw return fire from Delta.

He fired. Bravo dropped like a poleaxed steer.

Pinky swung the rifle on Delta, but already the man had responded to the bark of the M110. In the mist Pinky was invisible, and Delta's counterfire was rushed. Bullets churned the water, but none immediately found Pinky. He remained stoic, lining up his next shot. Delta fired again, and this time water splashed Pinky, and something stung his left elbow. He hadn't taken a direct hit, but his arm jerked and his shot sailed past Delta and lost itself somewhere in town. Delta had a firm fix on his location now. Bullets ripped the surface and Pinky dived beneath it and struck out for safety, kicking like a bullfrog for the depths, towing the M110 with him. Zipping bullets cut phosphorescent bubble trails around him. Pinky trailed blood from his arm.

In his urgency to dive, Pinky hadn't taken a gulp of air. He was forced to resurface within a few seconds, and maybe his spluttering gasp for oxygen gave him away, because Delta had tracked him. Again bullets churned the water to froth, and Pinky again felt the nip of a close call. He dived.

When next he resurfaced it was in the opposite direction to where Delta might have expected. Pinky brought up the sniper rifle, blinking droplets from his eyelashes and tried to get a fix on his enemy.

Muzzle flash drew his gaze, but it wasn't only from Delta's gun. From behind the smoking wreck of the GMC, Tess Grey contested with Delta. With the car between them, neither held the upper hand.

Pinky aimed, got Delta in his scope and squeezed the trigger, just as Delta darted to one side to get a better angle on Tess, whose rifle had fallen silent.

'Damn it, you!' Pinky's curse was for the laughing god who'd made him spend his last round on an engine block. He dropped the cumbersome rifle and struck for shore. As he surged from the depths, losing a sneaker in the process, he didn't slow, but it was as if the conspiracy against him continued. He slipped on the grass and went down on his hands and knees. He slipped and slid over the slick, wet grass but he pushed forward, rushing to Tess's assistance even if it meant going up empty-handed against a foe with a machine gun.

Covered with mud, Frank Lombardi hove up from beyond the pier. His black hair was sodden and tufts of grass and splinters were stuck in the curly locks. In his arms he cradled Bravo's liberated assault rifle. His wrists were bound still, so he held it with his right hand on the grip, his left elbow cocked to balance the barrel. Its muzzle was aimed directly at Pinky.

'You have to be kidding me, you?' said Pinky. Frank was not the foe he'd been thinking of.

'Gimme some credit, will ya?' Frank snorted and he turned to strafe the last of Locke's people as Delta reared around the tail of the GMC to end Tess. Unaware of the new threat, Delta was cut down.

Frank turned to observe Pinky, and they each stared for a long beat at the other. Finally Frank's mouth twitched and turned up at one corner. 'You gonna pick up that rifle, man? 'Cause that crazy bitch that killed Carlo ain't dead yet.'

Pinky was uncertain. Was this turn of events manipulated so that he met his fate to the laughing god's pleasure? He who lives by the gun dies by the gun, right? Was Frank trying to lull him into a false sense of security before ending his life and claiming the bounty?

Tess rounded the GMC. She held her gun loosely, but it could be snapped onto target in an instant. She appraised the tableau.

Frank said, 'Fuck sake, Pinky, twice you saved my ass back there . . . d'you think I'm an ungrateful son of a bitch who's gonna shoot you now?'

Pinky raised his right hand and held his index finger and thumb a half-inch apart. 'A little bit,' he admitted.

Both men waited a beat before laughing.

'Go on,' Frank said. 'Grab that gun.'

Pinky didn't need telling twice.

Assault rifle in hand, he checked on Tess. The lump above her eyebrow was livid. She bled from a leg wound. She held her damaged wrist tight to her abdomen. 'You've been through the wars, pretty Tess,' he said.

She noted the blood on his arm, and the lack of a sneaker on one foot. Frank looked like a swamp monster. 'I think we all have.'

'It ain't over yet,' Frank said. 'Not while Locke's still out there.'

'Where's Nicolas?' asked Pinky.

Tess turned to check the storage shed. The guard had disappeared, and its interior was distinctly silent. Po had released the hostages, but at what price? Tess's chest hitched, and she took an urgent step in the direction of the shed.

'Lookit!' Frank exclaimed.

Po jogged towards them. He appeared unarmed, and more importantly to his friends, unhurt. As he slowed his limp grew more obvious, but it didn't seem to trouble him. Pinky could tell that Tess wanted to embrace Po, but now wasn't the time or place. They were out in the open and although the gunmen had all been killed, there was still a dangerous foe to contend with. They put the wrecked car between them and the village.

'Jeez, Tess,' was all Po said as he appraised her injuries. Concern for her was painted on his usually austere features.

'I'm fine,' she said, convincing nobody. 'Are those people safe?'
Po jerked his head towards the forest. 'All hidin' out there except
for one,' he said. 'We were too late arrivin' to save one fella—'
he glanced at the deputy's cruiser – 'sorry, make that two.'

Po looked Frank up and down. 'So we're allies now?'

'Will be once you cut me outta these.' Frank set down his
rifle and indicated the zip ties around his wrists.

Po appraised Pinky. 'Up to you, bra.'

'Me and Frank have kinda made up,' said Pinky. 'Right, Frank?'

'Just kinda?' Frank joked, holding his thumb and index finger
slightly apart.

'Cut him loose.'

Po withdrew his blade and stepped in, meeting Frank eye to eye.
'The enemy of my enemy, huh? Don't make me regret this, Frank.'

'Only one person I have a boner for, Po, and it's none of you
guys.'

Po's blade snicked through plastic. Frank exhaled in relief,
began rubbing life into his wrists. Out the corner of his eye, Pinky
spotted Tess do the same with hers. She was pale with suppressed
agony. 'Maybe you should sit the next part out, pretty Tess.'

Tess shook her head.

'Pinky's right,' said Po. 'You're hurtin'.'

'I won't slow you down.' She glowered, but the stern look
didn't work well with a swollen brow.

'That's not what I mean, Tess, and you know it. You need to
rest up before you fall over.'

'I'm not letting that maniac get away with this. I'm not resting
until Locke's in handcuffs.'

'Handcuffs?' Frank retrieved his assault rifle. 'I was in handcuffs. That bitch deserves much worse.'

'We take her alive if we can,' Tess said.

Frank indicated the corpses of Delta and Bravo; his response
also took in the other gunmen who'd died on Locke's behalf.
'We'd no qualms about shooting any of these saps, why let her
get away with anything less?'

Tess said, 'This was done in self-defense, and to save the
lives of the hostages. There are four of us against Locke now;
there's not a court in the land will accept a self-defense plea if
we hunt her down and kill her.'

'They don't need to know how it goes down,' Frank argued.
'S'long as we close ranks afterwards, we can do whatever we
want with her.'
'I'd know,' said Tess, in a manner that brooked no further debate.
Frank wasn't done though. 'She had Carlo murdered in cold
blood.'
'For which she'll rot in prison.'
Frank rocked his head. He was trying to fool none of them.
If he got a shot at Locke he was going to take it.
Po once more got in his face. 'I'm just beginning to like you,
Frank; don't go spoilin' our burgeoning friendship.'
'Maybe you won't have to worry about me killing her . . .
ain't we missing somebody?'
Beyond the lake, and the miles of trees beyond it, a new star
rose above the horizon. It brightened as it sped towards them.
'We've got inbound, us,' Pinky said unnecessarily, as it was
apparent to all that a helicopter was speeding in their direction.
The Border Patrol was only minutes from arriving: undoubtedly
other law enforcement officers had also been dispatched and were
en route by road. Brayton Lake was about to be invaded by armed
people for a second time that morning.
'We can sit tight and let the cops do their jobs,' Tess suggested,
'or we go get Locke.'
All four of them moved from behind the smoking wreck and
faced the small town. All four halted in unison.
Virginia Locke had appeared suddenly from behind the nearest
building with her SIG to Alicia's head. 'Not another step or this
whore gets what's coming to her,' she barked.
Pinky's and Frank's guns snapped up, but Tess kept hers
lowered. None of them had a shot at Locke without also killing
Alicia. Pinky glanced at her for direction, saw that Tess's full
attention was on the face of the hostage. Something unspoken
passed between the DEA agent and Tess, who whispered to
them, 'Do as Locke says.'
Locke had Alicia's backpack slung over her left shoulder,
and the compact submachine gun in her right hand. Alicia was
directly in front of her, arms out at her sides, almost as if offering
her enemy extra protection. In no possible way had she allied
herself with the maniac.

FORTY-THREE

Her team had been systematically wiped out by a bunch of civilians! Locke was furious. The six hired guns were supposedly the best on Gerard Pattyn's payroll, but they'd been as useless to her as Whyte, James, Hubert, and Peterson before them. Everything was ruined! Locke had decided that once she was back on Canadian soil, she was going to have to rethink where her future allegiance should lie. With her plan to cover her tracks going to hell in Brayton Lake she was finished as a DEA agent, but neither would she be welcomed back to the criminal underworld once her identity came out. Both sides would hunt her unless she could somehow finish the job and keep the evidence that'd incriminate her employers out of the hands of law enforcement. She'd buy a new life, disappear and fuck everyone!

Bullets flew, and people died violently, while she'd concentrated on finding Alicia Coleman. There were few places the betrayer could be if she'd joined the hostage rescue attempt, and Locke beelined for it, entering the post office via the same door she'd kicked open previously. She found Coleman seated on the floor, backpack between her splayed legs and her back to the shelves stuffed with envelopes. Coleman had set aside the Remington assault rifle earlier liberated from Billy James. She was pale, feverish, and in pain. Peering up at Locke she also appeared resigned. 'I'm tired of running,' she croaked, and pushed the backpack towards her.

Locke stared down at her, the first time they'd come face to face since their cat-and-mouse game had begun and the blood chilled in her veins. 'I know you.'

'You've been chasing me long enough.'

'No. I mean *I know you*.' Before then Locke had only ever seen Alicia Coleman's face on photographs supplied to her by Gerard Pattyn's people. On each, Coleman had resembled the type of clean-cut worker bee you'd find in any office across the nation, anonymous and unremarkable. Seated on the floor, an assault rifle within grabbing distance, scuffed and banged up, she looked entirely different. In that context she looked exactly like a fellow trainee she'd known from when Locke completed her eighteen-week agent training program at the academy in Quantico, Virginia. 'You're DEA.'

'Takes one to know one, huh?' Alicia raised her right hand to her mouth. 'I'd laugh at the look on your face if it didn't hurt so much.'

Locke chewed her bottom lip. Her head was totally screwed up by the denouement.

'You can't get away with this,' Coleman pointed out. 'You must know that by now?'

Locke's head shook, but her arm was steady as she raised the SIG. 'There's still a way out of this for me.'

'Locke, huh . . . I know that's not even your real name. You're done. Any minute now Brayton Lake's about to be flooded by cops and there's no escape for you. Do yourself a favor. Let me arrest you and I'll see you're treated fairly.'

The laugh she spat out sprayed saliva over Coleman. 'Arrest me? Coleman . . . if that's even *your real name* . . . I'm about to blow you full of fucking holes. Then I'm going to take that bag and get the hell out of here. What're the DEA paying you? You'll be GS-Thirteen level by now, right? So a hundred grand per annum tops? What's in that bag will earn me ten times that amount, enough for me to buy myself a new life, a new identity, one that the DEA will never uncover. D'you think I'm going to let you or a bunch of half-assed county cops stop *me*?'

'My new friends might have something to say about that.'

Outside the gunfire had fallen silent. Locke's attention darted to the grimy windows. Dawn was breaking, pearlescent light flooding the landscape. Shapes moved beyond the smoking GMC, and another figure jogged towards them, limping the last few steps.

'I don't fear them.'

'You should. You had some of their friends murdered. They've just kicked the asses of your team; they'll easily do the same to you. Let me arrest you, avoid the inevitable.'

Locke scooped up the backpack and shoved her left arm through both straps. She jerked the barrel of her SIG. 'Get up.'

'I'm exhausted.'

'Get up or die here. I'll take my chances without you.'

Coleman struggled up, using the shelves on the counter to assist her climb. Locke grabbed her collar and dragged her backwards, while forcing the barrel of her gun in the side of her neck. The muzzle bumped her jaw, unnecessary abuse but Locke took delight in it. She forced Alicia through the house and out the back door where her Ford waited. She smiled: she had a contingency in place. On a separate channel on her radio, she said, 'Fire her up, I'm en route. ETA five minutes.'

Voices grew louder, and she knew Coleman's new friends were approaching.

With the SIG to her hostage's head, she pushed Coleman into the open. 'Not another step or this whore gets what's coming to her.'

The response to her command was immediate. Coleman's new friends halted, and two of them raised assault rifles taken from the bodies of her team. Neither had a clear shot, aided somewhat by Coleman who opened her arms almost protectively. Locke waited, and watched as the blond woman spoke briefly and the rifles were lowered. The blond looked as fit to drop as Coleman did, visibly more so with her swollen face and bloody leg. The fight against Locke's team hadn't gone all the wrong way. The overweight black guy and the gaunt Italian looked as if they'd been wrestling with gators. Only the tall man with the seething turquoise eyes looked unfazed. She'd lied when she told Coleman she didn't fear them; never in her life had she feared another human being, but this latter man sent shivers of unease down the length of her spine. *Death rides on his shoulder,* she thought, *and he's the Grim Reaper's agent.* She was tempted to turn the gun on him, drill him full of holes, but that'd invite a lethal response from the others.

A distant chattering raised her gaze beyond the quartet. A bright searchlight cut through the lessening gloom. Helicopter. Coleman hadn't been bluffing about the cops being on their way.

'We're leaving,' she called. 'If anyone tries to stop us, Coleman dies.'

She backed up to the Ford, forced Coleman inside through the driver's door then ordered her to slide across to the passenger side. Coleman gave her no resistance. She threw the backpack into Coleman's lap, took a last look at the others then jumped in. She set the SIG across her lap so Coleman would understand the folly of trying anything reckless. The Ford came with keyless entry – the electronic key was in her pocket – and started the instant she depressed the ignition button. She threw the car into reverse, the tires kicking up gravel as they chewed for traction. Locke hit a turn, stamped the gas. In her mirrors she watched the quartet and they didn't do anything foolish like shoot at the car, fearful of hitting Coleman. The Ford roared between the houses of Brayton Lake, on the narrow secondary road to the airstrip.

'What now, Locke?'

'What do you think?'

Coleman slumped in the seat. 'You've only kept me alive for now as a human shield. You've a plane waiting, right?'

'How'd you think my second team arrived?'

'Don't tell me, once we're in the air, you're going to make me jump out.'

'I was going to take you back and throw you to the dogs, but now that you mention it . . .'

'What if I survive a second fall?'

'You won't. I'll make certain before you go out the door.'

'Karma's a bitch . . .'

Locke sneered at Coleman. 'And so am I?'

'Well, if I'm going to die . . .'

Before she ended her proclamation, Coleman lunged for her enemy. Disarmed for a moment by Coleman's desultory tone, Locke was unprepared for the attack. Coleman's fingernails found her eyes, and Locke squawked in shock. She fought back blindly, elbowing Coleman off her, grabbing for the SIG with her other hand. With no control of the steering wheel there was little she could do when Coleman yanked it to the right, then immediately sawed it left. The Ford left the track, bumping and grinding over the untended ground, and in among the trees. Both women were thrown up and down in their seats. Coleman wouldn't release the steering wheel, despite the elbow rammed into the side of her jaw. Locke's foot had left the gas pedal, and it stabbed for the brake, even as she grabbed for her gun. The roar of the SIG was lost among the greater cacophony of twisting metal and shattering glass as the Ford slammed into a tree.

FORTY-FOUR

'We ain't letting Locke go like *this*?' Po's words were less a question than a statement of intent.

'No way,' said Tess.

Pinky glanced at his feet. One sneaker leaking water, one bare foot reddened with blisters. He wasn't going to win a race with a speeding SUV. 'You guys will have to do the next bit without me,' he said.

Frank checked him out. 'The cops are coming, Pinky. Don't take me wrong, but a black guy surrounded by dead white dudes . . . I don't fancy your chances, man.'

'As much as it shouldn't be true, he's got a point,' Po concurred.

'Don't worry about me, you, I won't pose a threat.' Pinky handed the assault rifle to Po. 'Go get her, you guys. Just make sure you're back before some racist punk demands answers from me at the end of his nightstick.'

'Be careful,' Tess whispered to him.

'Careful's my middle name,' he replied, and winked. 'Y'all be careful too.'

He sat down in the dirt, kicked off his remaining sneaker and began massaging his aching feet. He offered a grin. 'Could I strike a less threatening pose, me?'

Tess considered waiting with him until the police arrived. Pinky would be treated with less suspicion if discovered alongside her, an appointed agent of Emma Clancy's specialist inquiry firm. In her injured state she would only slow down Po and Frank, despite her earlier claim to the contrary. Then she'd expected to seek and capture Locke among the houses of Brayton Lake, not racing to intercept her before she could board a waiting plane at the town's airstrip. However, Po didn't strike out along the road, he turned about, and she understood what was on his mind. After the gunman – Charlie – abandoned the deputy's cruiser with a plan to finish off Frank, he'd left the keys in the ignition. Po roared up alongside them within seconds. 'All aboard that's coming aboard.'

'Me too?' asked Frank.

'I ain't leaving you here while Pinky's unarmed.'

'Jeez, c'mon, Villere! Whadda I gotta do, man?'

'Get in.'

Tess chose the front, relegating Frank to the rear seat. He eyed the secure cage between them spuriously. 'You ain't gonna lock me in here, right?'

Po growled. 'Frank, you're toting a goddamn machine gun, what you got to be worried about? Now get in or get lost.'

Frank piled inside, even as Po hit the gas. The door slammed shut, missing his heels with a fraction of an inch to spare. Frank jostled upright in the back seat. 'Smell's like vomit in here,' he noted. 'Then again, I've never been in the back of a cop car that didn't.'

'That's because it's where the pukeballs normally sit,' Po reminded him with a curl of his lips. 'You should feel right at home.'

Frank laughed with him, guessing it was the first time Po had ever been in the front seat of a cop car, never mind driving one.

The airstrip was less than half a mile from town. They raced between the houses where Tess had contested with the two gunmen, and were beyond the outlying houses within seconds. The forest folded in around them on both sides. Po drove with the lights on high beam, the road rushing at them as a pale ribbon between the trunks of thousands of trees, impenetrable walls it seemed: except they weren't.

'There!' Tess indicated deep gouges in the earth at the edge of the road, and the splintered remains of smaller trees and shrubs. Po hit the brakes, bringing the cruiser to a controlled halt. Between the boughs there were hints of light. Steam and smoke billowed between the trees. It didn't take much to realize what had happened: the Ford had veered out of control and they all knew who was behind the crash.

In her urgency Tess was out of the cruiser and heading into the woods without a thought for her injuries. The Ford's taillights beckoned her with the unblinking gaze of a serpent. She approached the wrecked Ford with her assault rifle held high, alert to movement. In her peripheral, Po was there, moving at a different angle. The hood was buckled, the engine beneath wrapped around the sturdy bole of a tree. Steam plumed and sparks popped and hissed. The driver's door hung open, and a compact submachine gun was abandoned on the seat. Sadly Locke was not inside, but Alicia lay slumped in the passenger seat. The windshield showed where her head had impacted with it.

'Alicia?' Tess called, aware that Po was circling the wreck, checking for Locke. When the agent didn't rouse, Tess dropped her rifle, swept the SIG into the footwell so she could scramble across to her. She checked the pulse in Alicia's throat. It was slow and weak. Blood painted the woman's features, leaking from a network of small cuts on her forehead and hidden within her hair. 'Alicia, can you hear me?'

Her head lolled, then came around slowly as Alicia roused. Her eyelids were glued with blood; they flickered, struggling to open. 'D . . . did I get her?'

'She's gone,' Tess said, 'but don't worry about her, it's more important we get you to a hospital.'

'No . . . she can't get away, Tess.' Her voice was thin, yet adamant. 'She'll disappear. She remembers now who I really am and my daughters will never be safe.'

'She won't get away, not now the Border Patrol are coming—'

Alicia tried to move, as if to give chase herself, but lacked the strength. 'She'll be in the air and over the border before she can be stopped. Once she lands and realizes she hasn't got the key—'

'What do you mean she hasn't got the key?' Tess had already noted that the backpack was nowhere to be seen.

Alicia grunted. 'You thought I'd just given up? I was never going to make it that easy for her.'

'What?'

'Back there before Locke found me in the post office, I stuffed the backpack with empty envelopes,' Alicia explained, and delivered an extra twist: 'I mailed the evidence to your boss's office in Portland just in case none of us got out of Brayton Lake alive. Do you remember the book title I mentioned?'

'Yes. *Stranger in a Strange Land.*'

'It's the key.' Alicia held out her right hand. It glistened with blood, but Tess took it. She gently squeezed the woman's fingers and was surprised when Alicia squeezed back with vigor.

'I'm trusting you with this, Tess. Decipher the notes I've sent you, find the code and login details. The code allows access to a Deep Web database used by Gerard Pattyn and the others involved in his network. It will give you everything you'll need to ensure justice is done. But, Tess, first you must . . .'

'Your children will be safe from her, I promise you.'

Alicia gulped, finding breathing more difficult by the second. Her hand dropped to her side, and Tess saw her clothing was awash with blood. She'd been shot numerous times. She'd hung on long enough to speak with Tess, but was failing quickly. 'I'm in so much pain, Tess . . . ha! No, not the bullets . . . these freakin' broken teeth are sending me nuts!' She hiccupped out a laugh that was indeed tinged with madness, before shaking her head in sorrow. 'No . . . it hurts most that I won't see my girls again.'

Tess held her hand again, offering comfort while she died.

An assault rifle chattered nearby.

Tess snapped around, then scrambled from the car, seeking her gun even if she wasn't in immediate danger.

'She's running,' Frank Lombardi hollered from the road, and he let loose with a second barrage of bullets. His next words were for the fleeing Locke. 'Yeah, you can run, you skinny bitch, but you ain't getting away.'

Tess and Po raced for the deputy's cruiser.

'C'mon, c'mon, c'mon!' Frank was leaning over the roof of the car, hammering his palm on the metal. Evidently his gun was out of ammunition because he'd cast it aside. At the furthest reach of the car's headlights, the soles of Locke's boots flashed as she hurtled towards the airstrip. Tess and Po exchanged glances. 'She *isn't* going to make her flight,' she told him.

'That's for damn certain,' he said as they all clambered aboard.

FORTY-FIVE

Locke had the build of an endurance athlete, and she ran as if unencumbered by her bulletproof vest or the backpack over her shoulder. But she couldn't outrace a supercharged car. They were on her heels as she bounded out into an open pasture. Po could have run her down, but there was no need. Locke stumbled to a halt and Po drew the car to a stop. She stood, hands fisted at her sides, shaking. She turned to face them in the full glare of the headlights. Her face was streaked with blood, her eyelids torn, evidence Alicia Coleman had clawed her almost blind. Her lips writhed and it was the only warning of her intent. Her hand reached to a pistol on her hip.

'Get down!' Po shouted, and he reared across to pull Tess to safety.

Bullets struck the windshield and shards of glass rained on Po's back.

Instantly Po bobbed up to check. Locke was advancing towards the cruiser, shivering in every inch of her being. She fired repeatedly and more glass exploded. A bullet ricocheted off the inner prisoner cage and Frank yelled in alarm. Tess tried to juggle round the assault rifle, but inside the car there was little room. Po sat up, facing their would-be slayer, hit reverse and powered the car away. Locke shouted something wordless at them as they retreated. But sanity returned to her and she scanned around and spotted the airplane waiting for her on the airstrip. It was a Beechcraft twin turboprop, a larger plane than the Cessna that crashed in the woods, this one big enough to deliver a team of six killers and their equipment. Locke dashed for it as it taxied into position for take off.

A door was open near the tail, in preparation for her boarding. Locke jogged alongside it, hefting the backpack up before she grabbed at the opening and sprang inside. She must have yelled at the pilot to get airborne, because the twin engines roared and the plane picked up speed. The airstrip wasn't designed to accommodate larger craft. A Cessna would require less runway distance than a Beechcraft, but the pilot was going for it. Locke stared back at them from the open doorway, a triumphant grin splitting her face.

'She made her flight,' Tess moaned in dismay.

'Not yet,' said Po as he clipped in his seatbelt. 'Buckle up, y'all.'

'What are you doing?' It was a rhetorical question, as Tess already suspected what was on his mind. She took his advice, snapping the belt into its holder, as he shifted gears and hit the gas. The supercharged cruiser kicked up wings of dirt as it surged across the meadow for the airstrip.

The self-satisfaction fell from Locke. She fired from the open door. The bullet caromed off the roof of the car. Tess powered down the window, leaned out and returned fire. Her bullets struck the Beechcraft's fuselage, punching holes in it. Locke disappeared inside, but returned a moment later, clinging to the open doorway. Like a boorish juvenile she flipped them the middle finger, then ducked away and slammed the door behind her, getting ready for take off. The Beechcraft powered for the end of the airstrip and the wall of trees beyond.

'Will they make it?' Tess pondered aloud.

'Not if I don't let 'em.' Dependent on the headwind, a light aircraft's typical take-off speed is around sixty-three miles per hour, slightly more for a twin turboprop: Po had no idea about aviation, but he knew about cars and acceleration, and he'd put his money on the cruiser to beat the airplane in a drag race any day of the week. Now that they were no longer being shot at, he floored the gas pedal.

'Y'all might want to cover your heads,' he warned. It would be preferable to get ahead of the airplane, to block its forward passage, slow it down and force the pilot to abort take off. Po wasn't keen, because then the car could be at the mercy of its whirling propeller and he'd no intention of putting Tess – or even Frank – in unnecessary danger of decapitation. Although what he did do was just as dangerous. He yanked the steering hard left, and rammed the cruiser in deep under the body of the plane, buckling the undercarriage and shunting the plane up and over the roof of the cruiser. Both vehicles, conjoined momentarily, swerved wildly for the edge of the airstrip, Po braking with all his might. The plane tore free, but canted over. Its left wing dug in, furrowing the earth before the crippled Beechcraft pinwheeled away. One propeller ripped away, its blades cutting chunks from the wing, and the plane was suddenly spinning in the opposite direction, powered by the remaining engine. It came to a smoking rest across the field, mere yards from the boundary of the forest. The second engine cut out and puttered as it died. If anyone inside had survived they'd feel as if they'd just been through a tumble dryer on an industrial scale.

Po was first out of the car, grabbing for the assault rifle he'd jammed between the seat and console. Tess, and in the rear, Frank, were too stunned by the insanity of the last few seconds to immediately react. Both had to be wondering if they were alive or dead. Po was more concerned by the state of Locke's mortality. He ran for the cockpit first, and was greeted by the incredulous look of the pilot peering back at him. Po aimed the gun and the man raised his hands: he wasn't a threat.

Tess approached, her rifle raised. Frank had spilled from the car too, but was holding his head in both hands, checking he was in one piece. Po called to him, and indicated the pilot, 'Watch this guy. If he moves, shoot him.' Frank shook his head to clear the cobwebs, as he jogged over. Po handed him the rifle.

Cautious of an explosion Tess kept her distance, but Po rushed alongside the plane. With the undercarriage gone, the plane lay on its belly in the grass and he was tall enough see through the windows. The cabin was filling with smoke. The door swung inward and Locke tumbled from the plane, landing in an unceremonious heap. Alicia's backpack was under her. Po grasped her by the collar of her jacket and hauled her away from the smoking wreck; she dragged the bag with her. Tess moved in, covering her with her rifle.

Locke pushed up onto her knees. She blinked up at the couple looming over her, then settled back on her heels, nodding in an expression approaching admiration.

'You people,' she said. 'I don't know who the hell you are but I sure wish we weren't enemies.'

Tess said, 'We are. You're a murderer and you're going to pay for your crimes.'

Locke shrugged at the accusation. 'I'm not the only killer here.'

'You're the only one that killed innocent folks,' Po told her.

'That's all a matter of perspective. I only killed who stood in the way of getting my job done; they weren't innocent in my book.' She touched the backpack almost reverently, then pulled it against her thighs. The flap was twisted awry, and pulled a handful of the topmost envelopes into view. 'What's in this bag is worth more than a million bucks to me. D'you hear me? Let me go, I promise I'll make you rich.'

'You're going nowhere,' said Tess. She wanted to take some of those worthless envelopes from the holdall and stuff them into Locke's mouth, the way Po had served the warrant to Charles Boswick two mornings ago. 'Get your hands above your head.'

Locke was slow to move. Po said, 'You got crud blockin' your ears? She said, "hands above your head." Do it.'

'Take it easy, big fella. I just wasn't clear on her intentions. Looks to me like she's ready to execute me right here and now.'

'You're going to prison,' Tess assured her.

Locke shook her head. 'I'm DEA, how long do you expect me to survive in prison? Do me a favor, shoot me now and spare me a life of hell.'

'I'm tempted to, but that'd make me just like you.'

'We aren't alike. You're soft . . . you haven't got what it takes to pull that trigger in cold blood.'

'I have though,' announced Frank Lombardi just as Locke's hand flew from the holdall.

His gun barked once and Locke pitched sideways, the pistol she was snatching from the backpack falling from her hand. She must have planted it there before tumbling from the plane. Tess and Po regarded her a moment before frowning at Frank.

'I'd like to say that was for Carlo,' he said, 'but it wasn't. I was saving your dumb asses. Didn't you see she was goin' for her gun?'

'We had her covered,' Tess told him, and eased the pressure off the trigger of her rifle.

FORTY-SIX

'Next time we take a vacation, let's go to Florida, us.'
'You didn't enjoy camping, Pinky?' Tess asked
sardonically. They were seated on the porch of Po's
ranch house, intent on finalizing the paperwork necessary to file
Po's tax return, but not getting much done since Pinky had
arrived for a visit. He'd moved into Tess's vacant apartment on
Cumberland Avenue, but rarely spent a night there alone. The
constant rush of water over Presumpscot Falls formed a backing
track to their conversation. It was a calm night otherwise, a
billion stars scintillating overhead. It was a week since the
incident in Brayton Lake.

'What's not to enjoy about camping? I got to spend the night
in the woods, saw some wildlife, and even got to cool off with
a nice swim in a pond. My greatest regret is we didn't get to eat
much good food; I'd have really enjoyed a deep-fried turkey leg
and a frozen banana, me. A fine cuisine! Best place to find that
combo's Disney World, I hear.'

Immediately Pinky frowned, thinking back to the only time
they'd eaten while in the north woods. Elsa Carmichael had fed
them and she'd been a good cook, a gentle and kind, if unwilling,
hostess. She should be remembered for more than being the first
victim of Virginia Locke's murder spree. Posthumously Locke
had been designated the murderer of five victims: two residents
of Brayton Lake, Elsa Carmichael, Carlo Lombardi and . . . no,
not Alicia Coleman, but of the deep-cover DEA agent, and mother
of two daughters, Alicia Grace. She was also culpable for the
deaths of the ten hired guns that'd been killed during the fights
by Tess and her friends to survive the attacks on the field
biology team and to protect the innocent townsfolk of Brayton
Lake. There had not been a mistake made in the tally of the
dead; as far as anyone knew the only other female involved,
Greta Peterson, had perished in the woods, her remains yet to
be discovered . . . unless the bears got to her first. Jonathan Laird

and Grant McNeill were happy to keep the secret, feeling somehow that they were honoring Elsa's memory by giving another woman a chance at life. Tess, nor any of the others, held a grudge against Peterson; if not for her willingness to help them defeat Locke in the end, things could have gone badly for them all. They all hoped Peterson took their silence as an opportunity to begin her life anew. Similarly they'd all concocted a tale to explain Frank and Carlo Lombardi's presence in the woods that didn't include claiming a bounty on Pinky's head. The story that Pinky and Frank were mutual camping buddies of Po was met with disbelief, but the cops had enough to contend with, and why rock the boat casting aspersions on their characters when the residents of Brayton Lake were hailing them as their saviors?

Po stepped from the house lugging three bottles of beer fetched from the fridge. He handed them around. Pinky clinked bottles with him. Tess would've too, but she held the icy glass to the yellowing bruise on her forehead, and instead gave him a smile of gratitude.

'Shoulda brought you a steak for that eye,' he said.

'Forget her eye,' Pinky said, 'get a steak fried up for me, Nicolas!'

'I would, but I'm all outta steak. Could maybe rustle you up a bag of chips and a jar of pickles.'

'Weren't you listening? I'm a man who enjoys fine cuisine!'

'That was the old Pinky Leclerc,' Po reminded him.

'You're right, Nicolas. If I'm going to rough it with a red neck like you from now on, I'd best get used to redneck food.'

'Stick with me, bra, I'll make you an honorary redneck in no time.'

Grinning, Pinky settled back at the idea, putting up his feet on a low table. He was wearing a brand new pair of expensive sneakers. Some things about Pinky would never change. Tess sat down opposite him. She took care setting down her beer; her wrist still ached from the abuse it had taken during the fight. She studied Pinky, earning a quizzical lifted eyebrow from him.

'You *are* a changed man now, Pinky?'

'You have my word on it, pretty Tess. My old life's well and truly behind me . . . courtesy of a debt repaid by Frank Lombardi.'

Through DeAndre Freeman I found out who sent Frank after me. In return for us keeping him out of prison Frank kindly offered to deliver a message on my behalf.'

Tess's mouth fell open. 'You put a hit on your opponent?'

'*Moi?* Of course not! Can't speak for Frank, of course, he's his own man. I only asked that he say hi from me before . . . well, let's just leave it at that, us.'

Tess placed her face in her hands. 'I don't want to know.'

Po gently squeezed her shoulder. 'Frank did us all a favor.'

'Locke needed killing,' Pinky agreed.

On their arrival back in Brayton Lake, Tess's first stop was in the post office. She'd found a fat envelope secreted among others mailed by the townsfolk awaiting collection. It was addressed to her care of Emma Clancy's office as Alicia had promised. Inside she found a plastic-wrapped sheath of papers, some of them blank pages but others containing rows of numbers, each with five digits. Each corresponded to a specific page, paragraph, line, word, and letter. To anyone they'd be indecipherable who didn't have access to the publication the numbers referred to: a 1961 first edition of Heinlein's *Stranger in a Strange Land*. It was an outmoded method for coding a message, but still valid, and admittedly almost uncrackable without access to the corresponding title. As promised, the code, once deciphered opened a doorway to the Deep Web and disgorged the secrets of the international criminal network: A multi-agency FBI, DEA, and RCMP task force had been busy rounding up dozens of key players, beginning with Gerard Pattyn, various corrupt officials and law enforcement officers on both sides of the US/Canadian and US/Mexican borders and from all points between, including the managers of the insurance company that'd engaged Tess to help them find Alicia who had firmly been in Pattyn's pocket. Many of those arrested had the wealth to attorney-up, and be released on bond while awaiting trial. It would've been awful if Virginia Locke had survived, got word through the network, and sought to punish Alicia posthumously by targeting her children. Now Alicia's daughters were safe from her, and wasn't that what Tess had promised the dying woman?

She'd spotted Locke's gun in the backpack, but hoped Locke

wouldn't draw it and force her to shoot her. Frank had saved her from a bundle of heartache and guilt when he took the shot. He'd served up rough justice, but Tess decided she could just about justify it when weighed against the lives of innocent children.

Tess picked up her bottle, and tipped it to each of them, then to the absent member of their party. 'Cheers, Frank.'

They all drank to him in unison.

Lightning Source UK Ltd.
Milton Keynes UK
UKHW030058250920
370471UK00003B/83